Ruthie's Daughter

Amy Denson

For my Mama and my Nunnie. Thank you.

Marchio Family Tree

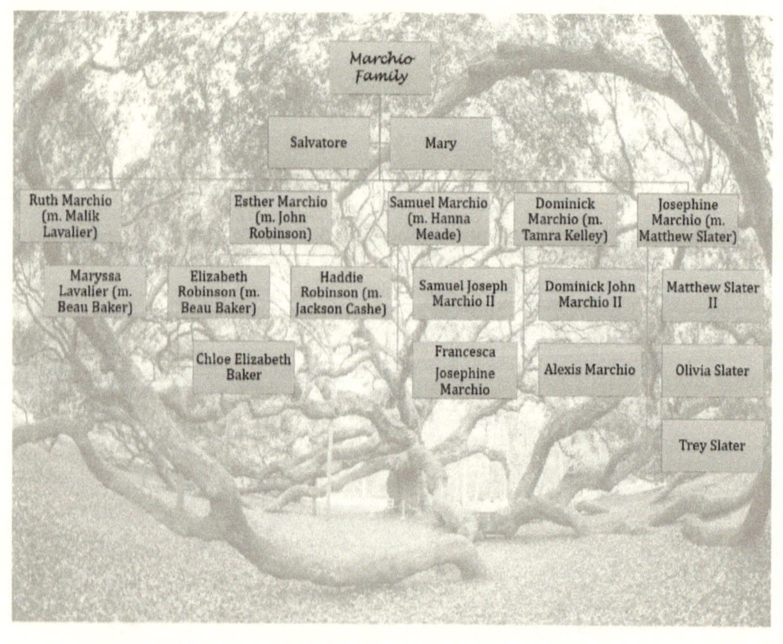

Prologue

The cold air burns as it enters Maryssa's throat. A puff of smoke, full and white, is visible with every exhale. The sun rises over the Washington Monument to her back. The Reflecting Pool is calm and peaceful. The city should warm up to seventy-five degrees today, but the early morning wind is frigid.

Maryssa shifts her hand warmers, grateful she chose her compression pullover with thumbholes instead of her typical t-shirt. The weather forecast was deceiving this morning. She would have turned into a popsicle without her last-minute wardrobe change. Her cousin Haddie gave her the navy and old gold pullover as a thirtieth birthday present. It matches the running shoes Maryssa designed online as a birthday gift to herself. Maryssa and Haddie keep pace as they jog along the National Mall. They turn before they hit Lincoln Memorial Circle and head toward Constitutional Gardens.

This is the new route they began running after Haddie got married and moved out of their apartment last summer. Their runs have become more crowded since then. The women are flanked by Secret Service agents and a small gaggle of paparazzi, no matter the hour. Maryssa never imagined photographs of herself would end up on the pages of magazines she used to buy for entertainment. Once a fun pastime now turns into worry for Haddie every time she passes a magazine stand or checkout line. Maryssa began appearing as a fuzzy blob in the background with the caption "First Lady's cousin."

Since Maryssa's internship under the hottest chef on the East Coast, "cousin" quickly turned into a full name with minor details. Last week she ended up in the *Scene and Heard* feature under a spread entitled *Thirty in their Thirties to Watch*. The article highlighted Maryssa's former ballet career before touting her chef cred. Maryssa was mortified when she walked into work the next day. Copies of the newspaper were posted all over the staff lockers. She can't complain. Maryssa is only on the fringe of celebrity. Her write-ups are still blurbs. Poor Haddie is media gold. Good, bad, lies, truth, it doesn't matter what is said. Haddie Robinson Cashe sells out anything with her picture on the cover.

As if on cue, Haddie turns to look Maryssa's way and smiles. As they head up Seventeenth, they begin to slow their pace to a jog, then into a brisk walk. Their panting steadies as they draw in the cold, barely-dawn air. Travis, in front of the women, takes their lead and slows as well.

Travis is the lead agent on the President's detail, but Jackson insists Travis run with Haddie. The man is tall and lean. Maryssa is convinced he must have played basketball in college. His athleticism is evident in his build, and Jackson ribs him about Army's basketball team. She should ask him sometime. Her mind wanders to the other agents and their backgrounds. She is shaken from her tangent thoughts as Travis slows his movements. He turns to face Haddie. His voice is deep and authoritative. Maryssa is not sure what he is about to say, but it's evident the man means business.

"Mrs. Cashe, we need to get you back to the White House as soon as possible." Travis and the other agents tighten their perimeter around Haddie and Maryssa. Maryssa bristles at the implication that something is wrong. Goosebumps prickle her arms as a shiver slices through her body.

It is so hard to wrap her head around the fact that her cousin is the First Lady of the United States. Haddie was furious with Maryssa for submitting her name for the reality dating show *Future FLOTUS?* last year. Haddie had every intention of getting herself vetoed off the show on the first day, but Jackson Cashe wormed his way into Haddie's heart. After one ill-fated assassination attempt and a deportation threat later, now Haddie was trying to get through physical therapy school from the East Wing of the White House. Maryssa shakes her head at the massive changes in their lives. Roommates since sixteen, the two currently live blocks away from each other, but worlds apart.

"Travis, what's wrong? Is it Jackson? Is he all right?" Haddie's quivering voice is etched with worry as she grabs hold of Maryssa's arm.

"President Cashe asked that we return as soon as possible, Ma'am. That is really all I know, but he insisted." Travis turns and picks up his pace as they all continue on the last leg of their running route.

Haddie moves her hand down Maryssa's arm to grab hold of her cousin's steady hand. The cluster briskly walks toward Haddie's new residence. By the time they reach the White House grounds, Jackson opens the door from the Oval Office. He walks toward them on the pathway. Haddie breaks into a sprint when she sees him. Sensing something seriously wrong, Maryssa keeps pace behind her cousin. They have been inseparable since birth, literally. Born one week apart, their houses were across the street from one another. They have been through so many ups and downs in their lifetime. Ominously, this feels like another down they need to traverse.

Maryssa stands back so that Jackson can have his time. His face is ashen and full of worry. Maryssa watches as he tells Haddie something quietly. Jackson's arms catch Haddie as she collapses into him. Her hands squeezing his navy suit for dear life. President Jackson Cashe turns his eyes to Maryssa. They are shrouded in sadness. He shakes his head as Maryssa slowly approaches the bad news.

American Post

World Enlightening News

Breaking News

The First Family is Planning a Funeral

By: Adam Herald

The father of First Lady Haddie Robinson Cashe passed away earlier this morning. John Edward Robinson III, 59, suffered a massive heart attack at his home and was rushed to the hospital where the doctors were not able to resuscitate him. Emergency services were called to the residence on Saint Clair Street at five o'clock this morning. An anonymous source who works at the hospital reported that Mr. Robinson was accompanied to the hospital by his wife, mother, and son-in-law. The President and First Lady arrived hours later once the floor had been evacuated.

Mr. Robinson, an only child, was born and raised in Charleston, South Carolina to John and Eloise Robinson. John began his career as the manager of Maria's Ristorante in downtown Charleston before buying the eatery from the previous owner, Malik Lavalier, his brother-in-law. John was an active member of the Chamber of Commerce and Small Business Alliance. He chaired the Charleston Memorial Marathon for the past five years. John was well known for his chili recipe and won the Charleston Chili Cook-Off three of the last four years.

In addition to being survived by the President and First Lady, John Robinson is survived by his wife Esther Marchio Robinson, mother Eloise Carmichael Robinson, granddaughter Chloe Baker, and son-in-law Beau Baker. He was preceded in death by his eldest daughter Elizabeth Marie Baker and his father John Edward Robinson II.

Arrangements for Mr. Robinson are incomplete at this time. Director of Communication Rich Miller read a statement from the first family this morning during his briefing, "Thank you for the outpouring of thoughts and prayers for our family. This is a great shock and time of sadness for us. We ask that you respect our privacy as we grieve and say goodbye to a wonderful husband, father, grandfather, son, and friend. Thank you."

Full coverage of the funeral will be announced as soon as details are released. Stay with The American Post for a close look into the First Lady's family.

Summer

Chapter 1

Maryssa

Italian funerals are events unto themselves. As integral to the culture as weddings, they last for days. The good ones last well over a week. Relatives converge to weep, laugh, and eat. A merging of people and food that can overwhelm the unconditioned. The immediate family for an Italian includes aunts, uncles, grandparents, all the way to third cousins twice removed. Along with family, they fill the house with food, lots and lots of food.

Today is no exception. The dining room table is abundant with bread, meats, cheeses, pasta, meatballs, sausage with peppers, and a sparsely touched vegetable tray. Desserts and coffee are unending on the large round table in the entranceway.

The Robinson's home is overflowing with funeral-goers paying their respects. Sadly, this is far from the first funeral they have survived recently. In the past four years, Esther Marchio Robinson has buried her daughter, her sister, and now her husband. The Marchio family arrived the day John passed and has been here supporting Haddie and Esther every minute since.

As Maryssa walks around the Charleston home of her aunt, she can't help but think about her own childhood. Maryssa remembers eating snacks after school in the kitchen and taking baths in the claw-footed tub. The girls constructed forts and pretend ballet studios all over this house and at Maryssa's home, right across the street. The thought of her mother's laughter makes Maryssa feel warm and empty all at once. This is the first time Maryssa and her father have been back to South Carolina since right before her mother's death. Between burying her Uncle John and reminiscing about her Mama, this week is taking a toll on Maryssa. Wounds may heal, but the scars of loss are never far from sight.

Nunnie Mary, the matriarch of the Marchio family, has been holding up Haddie and Esther all week. She appointed Maryssa as the media enforcer. In her wisdom, Nunnie Mary knew Maryssa needed a task to keep her busy. Maryssa chased off three reporters on the first day and practically tackled a photographer who stepped on the grass last night as they were coming home from the viewing. Thankfully, Maryssa's dad, Malik, caught her by the waist before any pictures were taken. They all knew the media would surround them like circling birds of prey, but the actuality of it is suffocating.

As she busies herself clearing plates and filling empty food trays, the sound of Haddie's voice catches Maryssa's attention. The two lived and worked together for thirteen years. Maryssa quickly recognizes Haddie's stressed out voice. She scans the room following the familiar sound. Maryssa spots Haddie near the front stairs talking with her grandmother Eloise. Sensing the need for backup, she heads over to Haddie just in time.

"Haddie, dear, how long will *these people* be staying?" Eloise Robinson is a genteel southern woman. She was born and raised in polite Charleston society.

"Grandmother, they are here to pay their respects to Daddy. This is normal."

"Maybe for your mother and her family, but not for me, and certainly not for most respected community members. We hosted mourners at the visitation and the funeral. Now is the time for us to mourn alone." Eloise straightens her back and lifts her chin. "Please ask these people to leave and have the house cleaned. The smell of the food is infusing into the fabrics. It is honestly making me nauseous."

"With all due respect, grandmother...."

Maryssa gently wraps an arm around Haddie's waist, preventing her from attacking her snot of a grandmother. "Mrs. Robinson, why don't you go upstairs and rest. I can bring up a cup of tea for you." Maryssa spins Haddie around and begins nudging her in the direction of the kitchen.

"Thank you, dear. That sounds lovely. Please use my rose tea service and don't forget the lemon." Eloise Robinson retreats up the stairway to her sitting room.

"Yes, Ma'am," Maryssa smiles. She turns before rolling her eyes. "How did I become the calm one in this relationship? You are wound too tight these days, Haddie."

Maryssa cuts off Haddie before she launches into another lecture about *Future FLOTUS?* and all the pressure she is under these days. "I know, I know. It's all my fault that you are the First Lady. I'm never sure if I'm supposed to say you're welcome or apologize, by the way." Maryssa offers an exaggerated eye roll before continuing, "I'm just saying that you becoming hot-wired makes me look like the sane one, and that is scary."

The two women head in the direction of the kitchen to hide from the crowd. "Thanks for saving me from insulting my grandmother. You always have my back."

"Insulting her or assaulting her?"

"Thanks to you, we don't have to find out which option I would have chosen." Haddie innocently smiles and winks.

As the two women reach the kitchen, Maryssa begins the mission of finding someone else to send upstairs with the tea service. She hopes she can find an aunt or a cousin who isn't sick of Haddie's Grandmother Eloise yet.

The house is a hub of activity. Stories of the dead are on everyone's lips. Laughter is inevitably followed by hushed whispers discussing the family of the dearly departed. In this case, the whispers are about what Aunt Esther and her son-in-law Beau will do now. Maryssa is careful not to stop and get dragged into answering questions about them today.

A continuous buzz of conversation floats into the kitchen. Maryssa surveys the room from the doorway before carefully planning her route. She finds a good-Samaritan neighbor to tend to Eloise, now she has other orders. Maryssa carries a cup of coffee and a small plate filled with food. The coffee radiates warmth to her hand. She squeezes behind cousins and friends as she snakes her way through the living room, careful not to be caught. Maryssa heads directly to her aunt and grandmother, both sitting on a floral couch in the formal living room.

Esther, or Aunt E to Maryssa, is clothed head to toe in black and sitting upright with perfect posture next to her mother, Nunnie Mary. Maryssa hands the woman coffee first then places the plate on the Victorian coffee table. Aunt E stares back with glistening eyes.

"I know you don't want to eat, but Daddy told me to force you." Maryssa genuinely smiles at her favorite aunt. "You haven't eaten since breakfast early this morning, and you need something on your stomach."

Aunt E sheepishly peeks into the coffee mug and back at her favorite niece, questioningly.

Maryssa softly laughs. "Yes, Ma'am. There is a little bit of coffee with your cream and sugar."

Aunt E scoots closer to her mother and pats the seat next to her. "Sit, sweet girl." She side hugs her beautiful niece tightly then takes her hand. "How are you and your father doing? This is the first time you've been back to South Carolina in a while. This must bring back such hard memories for you two." Esther rubs Maryssa's back soothingly.

Ruth Marchio Lavalier, Maryssa's mother, moved from West Virginia to South Carolina with her husband Malik to open a restaurant. Ruth's sister Esther followed her to Charleston. Esther was running to a new life while trying to forget an old love. She met and married John Robinson shortly after moving to the Palmetto State.

The families lived as a tribe until Malik was hired as the head chef for the White House. Even then, Ruth and E spoke multiple times a day. Five years ago, Maryssa's mother passed away from ovarian cancer one month after Esther's daughter Lizzie died from the same disease. Today they buried Esther's husband, John. Maryssa's heart broke for her aunt, who lost a sister, daughter, and husband in such a brief time.

Maryssa shakes her head and looks admiringly at the woman. "We're sitting in your living room at your husband's funeral, and you're asking how Daddy and I are doing?" Maryssa squeezes her aunt's hand.

"I'm tired of talking about me and all my losses. This entire room is doing enough talking about me. I don't need to add more narrative. I want to hear about you and Malik." Esther brings the coffee mug to her lips then turns back to the precious brunette sitting at her side. "You look so much like Ruthie. Sometimes it takes my breath away at the resemblance." Esther wipes a betraying tear that escapes.

Maryssa bows her head in humbleness at the compliment. Her mother was beautiful. She looks at her clasped hands before bringing herself back to the present. "You know Daddy; he's keeping himself busy in the kitchen. He washed every dish and has a rotation schedule for all of the casseroles people brought you in the freezer."

Esther conspiratorially leans in and speaks quietly but deliberately, "Tell him to dump Sarah Jean's beef stroganoff. That woman brings it to every single potluck at church. The first time I ate it, was the last. The smell alone will make your eyelashes fall right off your face." She shakes her head in unbelief.

"Is that what that was? Goodnight! I thought that was for the dog." Nunnie Mary scrunches her nose in disgust.

Maryssa laughs. "I will surely tell him. When I left the room, he and Jackson were discussing the influence of Cajun cuisine in the Louisiana Purchase. The discussion veered toward frog legs. That was my cue to hop out of there," Maryssa laughs at her own joke. "I don't know how your daughter puts up with

Jackson and his extensive trivia knowledge. He could win Jeopardy." Maryssa shakes her head.

"Haddie Marie finds Jackson fascinating. Maybe he can teach college when he's finished with this president thing. He has a sexy professor quality to him." Nunnie Mary winks at Maryssa. "He needs to use that charm of his to give me some great-grand-babies."

"Mother! That is my son-in-law you are talking about. Not to mention that my daughter is in physical therapy school and doesn't have time for babies right now." Esther swats her mother's knee.

"Gross, Nunnie." Maryssa laughs at her mischievous grandmother. "Only you would reference the President of the United States as a 'sexy professor.'"

"What? I'm old, not dead. He's a good-looking fellow. Those agents with him aren't too hard to look at either Maryssa Marie. Maybe you should offer them some coffee. That Travis keeps a close eye on you. He either thinks you're attractive or he's concerned that you're a terrorist." The spry woman winks again at her granddaughter.

"Nunnie, you are terrible." Maryssa rolls her eyes and laughs. "I'll be sure to tell Travis's wife that you find him attractive. She is a lovely woman. Works at a library, I think. Besides, I'm too busy for a man right now. I have to finish packing up my apartment and getting everything ready to move. I'm glad Haddie moved into the White House, and we didn't have to divide our furniture. Rock, paper, scissors over our amazingly comfy purple couch would have turned ugly, fast."

Esther takes a long sip of her coffee and relaxes into the sofa. "That is a good couch. I remember you two texting me pictures from the store. You must have tried out every possible way of sitting and laying on that thing. The store probably made you buy it after you two spent all afternoon trying it out."

Maryssa laughs hard at the memory. "We couldn't do that today. Haddie would be plastered all over the Internet and tabloids. We couldn't even get coffee after *Future FLOTUS?* aired without being followed by stalkerazzi. Of course, it's likely the store would have given us the couch for free knowing it would sell out instantly. The dress that Haddie wore to her college graduation sold out online in less than twenty-four hours. As much as I will miss Haddie, I will definitely not miss the constant gaggle of photogs."

"I still can't believe you're moving to West Virginia. Haddie will miss you terribly, but I know your mom would love that you are carrying on the family tradition." Esther pats her niece's hand.

Nunnie Mary settles in beside her daughter and wraps her arm through Esther's. "I'm so excited about Maryssa moving in with me. You and I can go dancing every night. I'm a terrific dancer."

"I hope you two will survive being roommates." Esther shakes her head. "I'll be honest, I'm a little worried about you Maryssa. I don't think she's joking about the dancing."

"I'm not." Nunnie Mary offers a deep chuckle and broad smile.

"I'm sure I'll be fine living with Nunnie. Who better to teach me the family business than the matriarch herself? Besides, she'll be too busy eating to go dancing. I plan on testing all of my recipes on her while the restaurant is being built. Uncle Sam wants me to help interview contractors the week I move. We have been emailing each other pictures for inspiration and planning. He wants to make sure the restaurant blends in with the rest of the vineyard. We both envision a rustic barnlike design for the restaurant that compliments the tasting rooms adjacent to the road. We're also thinking about building a fountain and large courtyard to bring the two buildings together for outside dining and entertainment." Maryssa looks at the two women staring at her. "I'm sorry. I'm rambling, aren't I?"

Aunt E and Nunnie both smile, which reminds her of Mama. She loves their smiles. "Absolutely not. In fact, I want to know more. Every single detail. I'm amazed and excited for you. Your mother would be so proud of you. Have you decided on a name?" Esther picks up some cheese from her plate and takes a small bite.

"I have." She pauses, this will be the first time she speaks the name out loud. She takes a breath before the unveiling. "In the spirit of Daddy's first restaurant which he named after Nunnie, and the person who planted the first vines, I'm naming it *Poppy's.* That's not all though. The inside will spill out onto a large patio. I was thinking about having a large fireplace and some firepits with a plaque that says 'Ruthie's Terrazza' so I'm honoring my Mama too. I think she'd like that." Maryssa waits for approval.

Esther smiles warmly at Maryssa while Nunnie slaps her knee. "Your Poppy would be tickled pink. You have made my heart smile Dear One." Nunnie Mary beams. "I can't wait for you to start this adventure. We definitely need to go out dancing now, to celebrate, of course."

"I don't think I can keep up with you Nunnie. You wore me out at Haddie's wedding last year."

Nunnie smiles. "What can I say? I hear music, and my body starts moving." The women all laugh as Mary shimmies and shakes in her seat while humming a sassy melody.

"Your Uncle Sam can't stop talking about your ideas. He already has five contractors lined up for interviews. Tells them all that his niece is coming home to complete the dream. He's training the boys to take over the vineyard. Once you three take the reins, he's ready to retire. You know, you'll be the oldest grandchild working in the business, that will make you the head of the family. Your mother and Poppy are smiling down from Heaven. We're so excited to have you home." Mary reaches across Esther and squeezes Maryssa's hand.

As the women sit talking about the restaurant and Maryssa's moving plans, the door opens, and a ball of fire comes running in toward Esther. The little girl with bouncy, brown, ringlet curls and big blue eyes, crawls over Nunnie Mary and jumps onto Esther's lap. "Nona! I've missed you!"

Esther laughs as she places a kiss on her granddaughter's head. "Chloe, you've only been gone for an hour. You didn't even have time to miss me." She turns the girl so she can look right into her eyes.

"Yes, but my heart is big enough to have fun aaannnddd miss you at the same time." She smiles proudly. "Daddy says that my heart is doubly big because I have my heart and my Mama's heart inside me. She couldn't leave me without leaving her heart, so I have hers too."

Esther's eyes begin to glisten with tears she's trying hard to hold inside her. "Your Daddy is absolutely correct. Your Mama loved you so much." She squeezes Chloe tight. "Where is your Daddy?"

Just then, Beau Baker closes the front door and heads directly to his mother-in-law. He is tall and broad. Beau always reminded Maryssa of a lumberjack. Haddie and Maryssa called him Paul Bunyan when he first started dating Lizzie. Maryssa laughs to herself at her memories of growing up with Haddie and Lizzie. Those days seem so far away, today especially.

Beau moved into the garage apartment behind Esther's house when Lizzie got sick so she and John could help with Chloe and get Lizzie back and forth to chemo treatments. After Lizzie's death, Esther cared for Chloe while Beau went to work. Beau has lost just as much as Esther. Maryssa watches as he walks across the room through all the mourners staring at him in pity.

"Beau, that was so sweet of your family to help with the arrangements for the memorial service and for all of the food." Nunnie Mary waits for him to nod. "Especially your sister. That baby boy of hers will be born soon. I'm sure she'll be happy to get off of her feet. She'll sleep soundly tonight."

"She comes from a long line of tough ladies. She's raising three strong girls, just like Chloe. This poor boy doesn't stand a chance with all of those sisters." Beau laughs. "My parents want us all to go to the beach after he's born so they can spend extra time with Chloe and the other grandkids. My brothers are already planning a deep-sea fishing trip."

"That sounds like fun," Maryssa observes.

"I just picture us getting lost at sea. Sunburnt, smelly, and wet while my parents have endless tea parties with warm cookies. I'd rather stay ashore." Beau rubs his strong jaw. "Speaking of cookies, I'm going to get something to eat. Mom, do you need anything?"

Esther shakes her head no as Chloe grabs cheese off of the plate and asks her dad to bring her some cookies. He beams at her as she snuggles closer into her grandmother's chest. As Beau walks off and Chloe eats, Maryssa can't help but think about how proud Lizzie would be of him. A devoted father and son-in-law. She starts to wonder herself what Aunt E and Beau will do now.

Chapter 2

Jackson

Chief of Staff, Madison Lyn, walks at a brisk pace down the historic corridor toward the Oval Office, newspapers in hand. Since becoming Chief of Staff for her longtime friend Jackson Cashe, she has been baptized by fire on a daily basis. While filming *Future FLOTUS?* last year, she dealt with Jackson's firing of the former Chief of Staff, her boss, and a botched education reform bill on her first few hours on the job. Her main goal is to support Jackson as he attempts to reunify the United States of America and the Allied States of America after the Great Separation. Each morning begins with good intentions but is usually sidetracked with unnecessary political drama instead of actual work.

This week has been relatively quiet since Haddie's father passed. While the media was a nuisance and shockingly intrusive, even for them, the coverage was positive as opposed to combative. Jackson and Madison returned last night to DC with their other college roommate and Director of Communication, Rich Miller. Haddie is staying in South Carolina for a couple of weeks with her mother. It seems the invisible truce with the media has ceased since their landing.

Jackson is very protective of Haddie. Although they met on a reality dating TV show, Haddie is exceptionally private and avoids the press at all cost. Her hesitancy to pose or do interviews only intensifies the media's desire to capture her. She has become paparazzi prey, which makes Rich's job that much more difficult. Today, however, Jackson's reaction to this will impact her as well.

Today's headlines will fire up Jackson and make Haddie even more camera shy. She'll either go into hiding or worse, this could be the breaking point when she returns fire on the media. That would be a disaster. Madison walks through her office on the way to Jackson's. She puts down her tablet and takes a deep breath before knocking. She hears Jackson through the heavy door, "Come in, Madsi."

She enters to find Rich and Jackson sitting across from one another on the champagne-colored silk settees. Jackson is still smiling and hasn't called out the armed forces yet, so obviously, Rich is a coward. She offers him a scowl as he shrugs in defeat.

"Come on, Mads, it can't be that bad. What is on the radar that has you glowering at Rich?" Jackson gets up and holds out his hand for the pile of newspapers Madison carries into the room.

She reluctantly hands them over one at a time as President Jackson Cashe reads each headline before taking the next paper from his friend. His demeanor becoming stiffer with each headline. His face is redder and his grip tighter. He turns to Rich, "Did you know this was coming?"

Rich begins his defense argument. "I wondered why they were asking so many questions about her wardrobe, but it was the entertainment channel, it didn't seem odd to me. I had no idea the others were covering it from this angle." He looks down at his feet before facing his friend. "Jackson, I'm sorry, I missed this one. My team is doing some research now. We will have a strategy before the next briefing to handle the allegations."

"Does Haddie know?" Jackson scans his two advisors.

"According to her detail, the paper is still on the front porch, but this is being covered on all the news channels, so there is a good chance she knows." Madison dismally answers.

Jackson looks directly at Rich. "Fix this. Now."

***

Haddie

The atmosphere in the Robinson drawing-room is electrically charged with emotion. The traditional southern home, donning double crown molding and marble fireplaces, hasn't seen this much excitement in years. While Esther and John Robinson moved into the family home with his parents, there is no mistaking the updating of décor was not part of the deal, especially with Eloise Robinson still living on the second floor. Floorboards creak beneath the hand-woven wool rug. Eloise's tea kettle whistles in the background. Voices stilled, until the commercial break.

"Seriously? You have got to be kidding me!" Haddie paces in the living room back and forth in the large room. Surrounded by her mother, her Nunnie, and Maryssa, she glares at the television then looks away again in disgust. "Don't they have anything better to report on than what style of shoe I wore to my father's funeral? Really? Jackson is planning a groundbreaking reunification summit, and all they care about is who designed the dress I wore to a funeral?" The pacing intensifies. "I don't even know who designed the dang dress. I went into a store. I bought the first black dress I saw. I left the store. That's it. According to them, I purposefully tried to take down the United States of America, with one dress. Who knew it was that easy to take down a country?"

Haddie continues talking to herself and pacing as the television personality returns from the commercial break. The effervescent, dirty blond attempts seriousness as she explains how Haddie is the personification of evil. "Welcome back. We are continuing our coverage of First Lady Haddie Cashe's choice of outfits for her father's funeral. In a shocking choice, Mrs. Cashe wore a black A-line dress with a lace overlay and black flats. While fashionistas everywhere are critiquing the woman's choice of wearing a cocktail dress to a day funeral along with ballet flats, reports about the designer are more disturbing."

Pictures of Haddie from the funeral begin to flash across the screen. "Mrs. Cashe chose a designer who was very vocal during the Separation of States. Mira Thompson, the daughter of conservative lobbyist, Michael Thompson, is a frequent contributor to Fox News. Remember that Mrs. Cashe is originally from South Carolina and has family in West Virginia. The American people are wondering if this was a statement by Mrs. Cashe in support of the Allied States of America. Coming into an election year, this type of statement could be a nail in the coffin for President Cashe's reelection bid. After we check the weather, we will bring in our political analysts as well as our fashion contributors to discuss the ramifications of Mrs. Cashe's clothing statement."

Haddie begins talking over the television again as the pacing resumes. Esther reaches for the remote to silence the TV and subsequent attacks on her daughter.

"They don't like my ballet flats? That's truly funny. You know what's really ironic? Two weeks ago, they finished a story about a teenage girl fighting back against body shaming and bullying and launched directly into a story about me. The segment began with questions over whether I am pregnant because I had a tummy pooch then criticized me for wearing high heels to a gymnasium where I read to children. They accused me of purposefully scratching the school's new gym floor." She stares at the women on the couch. They sit in silence in response to the rhetoric questioning.

"Apparently the anti-bullying message didn't resonate with them, or maybe I'm just fair game." More pacing. "Why would I intentionally scratch a floor? I can't wear flats, and I can't wear heels. Should I go barefoot? I better throw out all of my flip flops or I could start a nuclear war." Haddie huffily sits in her father's recliner.

Nunnie Mary is the only woman brave enough to interject into Haddie's speech. "I know this doesn't change anything, but King David had to hide in caves from the people he was to lead. I don't think they cared about his shoes, but the Bible mentions his robes frequently. Maybe you should wear sandals and robes everywhere, that will give the media something to cover."

The corner of Haddie's lip starts to curl up a little. Amused but still infuriated.

"Nunnie has a point, Had. You should design your own robe and slipper line." Maryssa laughs so hard she can barely get out the words. "You can call the line, Cave Clothes. The slogan can be 'Loungewear for leaders on the go, or on the lam.' You can design flats with an attachable heel, that way you are always prepared for gymnasiums or red carpets." The women burst into laughter.

"Maryssa may be on to something, sweetheart. What about skirts with built-in sweatpants in case you need to be more casual? Oooh, and reversible hoodies, one side can be sequined." Esther adds. "Your logo can be a dove with an olive branch in its mouth."

Maryssa holds her side from laughter pains. "No. No, she can't do that, then she will offend those who protect the rights of olives."

"Stop it. I'm angry." Haddie wipes tears of laughter from her cheeks.

The laughter continues as Haddie begins to calm down from the barrage of insults hurled at her. Nunnie Mary sits up quickly and grabs the remote. She increases the volume as Rich Miller walks on stage behind a podium in the press room. Silence follows as a room full of cameras, phones, and pencils are aimed at him.

"Good morning Ladies and Gentlemen of the press. Peter will be out for your regularly scheduled briefing momentarily, but first, I wanted to address a matter of national security." Everyone in the room sits up straighter and locks on to the man behind the podium. "It has come to our attention that First Lady

Haddie Robinson Cashe," he dramatically pauses. "Is an international spy." Another exaggerated pause. "Every wardrobe choice she makes is an attempt to overthrow the government of her beloved husband. It is shocking, I know. To remedy this, we now require her to wear only preapproved clothing from a drab uniform supply store. In a show of goodwill, we are asking that every member of the press with White House credentials wear matching uniforms as well." He pauses as the satirical report settles in across the room. Low chuckles slowly churn into uncomfortable laughter.

Rich gives it a minute longer to marinate before continuing. "In all seriousness folks, Mrs. Robinson Cashe was not making a political statement one way or another when choosing a black dress. Nor was she making a fashion statement on a red carpet or at an official event. She merely ran to the closest clothing store to quickly find a dark dress so she could mourn her father. She didn't spend an extended time shopping because she didn't want to cause her security detail extra work. She also wanted to spend every moment with her family as they made arrangements." Rich holds up a hand to refute the hands popping up with questions.

"I will not be coming out here to make a statement every time the First Lady is criticized in the press for her clothing. However, this is becoming increasingly commonplace during a time in which the world is addressing online bullying and body shaming. President Cashe would like the White House press members to serve as leaders for change in this area. With that said, he would like to form a committee to tackle this important platform facing our nation. If you are interested in serving, send an email to a member of the communication staff. We will sort through the applications and let everyone know the final list. In the meantime, please allow First Lady Cashe time to mourn the loss of her father without the added burden of shoe selection. Thank you for your time." Rich turns to the press secretary. "Peter, it's all yours." Rich walks off the stage as reporters shout questions at Peter.

Haddie's phone rings while a smile spreads across her entire face. "Hey, Babe. International Spy? That was classic Rich." She laughs as she walks across the room toward the traditional curved stairwell.

Esther looks at her mother and niece as they all breathe a sigh of relief. She says, "On that note, I think I'll start breakfast."

Chapter 3

Beau

Bright light creeps in through the crack in the blue flannel curtains. A ray of sunlight hits Beau directly in the face. He rubs his eyes with both hands and rolls onto his side. The empty pillow beside him never gets easier to see. It's been five years since ovarian cancer took Lizzie from him. They were college sweethearts.

He saw her on the first day of classes. He knew her name was Robinson comma Elizabeth from freshman English. A dark-haired angel with big curls surrounding her face. He tried to catch her after class, but she was sprite-like fast. He was so relieved to see her sitting under a tree outside of the building later that week. He thought he would have to wait until the next class to talk to her.

Lizzie sat on a blanket with books already scattered around her. Cocky, he walked right up to her and asked if he could share her blanket. She rolled her eyes at him and responded, "No." She looked back to the book on her lap. He was hooked. He spent the next two weeks bringing his own blanket to that same tree. His persistence and a fluke toilet paper incident broke down her defenses. He finally wore her down, and she relented to one date only. They were Facebook official four weeks later.

They married right after graduation. Bought a fixer-upper on the edge of town that they renovated together. Lizzie with paint in her hair was adorable. She wrapped the pregnancy test in a bag and gave it to him for his birthday. He had never seen her happier. Five months into her pregnancy, the doctor sat them down after an ultrasound. The diagnosis came next. Lizzie began evasive surgery and treatments as soon as she delivered Chloe. It all happened so fast. He went from becoming a new father to cancer expert, to a widower in less than two years. The first twelve months of Chloe's life were still a blur to him. Unbelievably, the second year was worse.

Shortly after Lizzie's diagnosis, she and Beau moved into the garage apartment behind Esther and John's house. John used it as an office but insisted that he'd much rather have his granddaughter there than a bunch of filing cabinets and old boxes.

Esther and John took care of Lizzie and Chloe during the day while Beau worked. He was a carpenter rising in reputation when Lizzie was diagnosed. He was an apprentice to a local contractor focusing on intricate woodworking. Beau's dream was to design built-in furniture and elaborate woodworking for homes. He was an artist.

After Lizzie died, his passion and vision died with her. He would get home in time to eat dinner with his in-laws and Chloe at the main house, then put Chloe to bed in their apartment. He went through the first six months in a zombie-like state of mind. Get up, get dressed, drop off Chloe, grab a travel mug of coffee, work, home, repeat.

One Friday night, another guy on the crew invited him out for a beer after work. John encouraged him to get out, and they would keep Chloe overnight. That beer tasted so good. The glass of whiskey tasted even better. The numbness that followed was insatiable. Beau craved that feeling of thoughtlessness throughout the day. He was going out after work more and more. The nights were getting later and later. When he didn't go out, he'd drown himself in whiskey after Chloe was asleep. Drinking kept him from thinking about Lizzie all night long, but every morning, he would see the empty pillow, and the longing would punch the air right out of him.

Beau started showing up late to work and making mistakes. He was getting sloppy. Around the time of Chloe's second birthday, he missed his mark with the hammer. A slip of the chisel landed him in the ER. After the cast was set and release papers signed, Esther drove him home in silence.

Esther told him she would get Chloe in bed and be over with something for him to eat. He walked into the sparse apartment and began searching for something to drink. Beau texted Esther to bring over his pain meds she slipped into her purse earlier. He continued rummaging through the cabinets but found nothing. He began getting agitated and fidgety when he heard a knock. The door opened, and Esther strolled in with a crock of soup and a plate of home-made bread. Beau continued looking in cabinets.

"You won't find any." Esther calmly said as she set up the food on the table. "John searched the entire apartment and poured out every last bottle. I just flushed the pain pills down the toilet too so you can stop texting about them." She continued moving around the room, picking up clothes and throwing them in a pile.

Beau remembers the feelings as if it had just happened. Rage. Anger boiled inside of him. He slammed the bathroom door behind him and stomped to-wards her. "You had no right to do that!" He practically yelled but attempted to control his voice somewhat. Snarling, "You don't know anything. Just because you help with my daughter doesn't give you the right to run my life. Chloe and I are just fine." He slammed his fist down on the table, spilling some of the soup over the rim.

Esther, not backing down, walked right over to her burly son-in-law and pointed her dainty finger right into his hard chest. "Enough is enough. Do you think you are the only one who misses her? Do you think you are the only person who wants to dull the pain? I see her every time I look at *your* daughter. I hear her laugh in Chloe's. I still smell her on her favorite blanket in her old bedroom. I also know that she would kick your rear end from here to next Sunday if she knew how you were behaving!"

Esther took a deep, calming breath and began talking softer. "Beau, Lizzie loved you with her whole heart. She saw great things in you. She was honored to be your wife and ecstatic to be Chloe's mother. You are not honoring her by drowning yourself in sorrow. You are making a mockery of her judgment and her faith in you."

The tiny woman slammed a hammer right into his chest that hurt much worse than the pain in his hand. She didn't back down as he stared right through her.

Beau pulled out a chair and sat. Head in his hands, he began crying. The emptiness and devastation pouring out of him. There was no more hiding from it. No hope in stuffing it in any longer. All the pain rushed over him like a dam breaking. Esther came around the table and hugged him from behind. She held him until the shaking stopped. She rubbed his back and handed him a tissue from her pocket. It felt like hours to Beau. He had no idea how long he cried. He felt empty. The pain so raw and heavy, it felt as if someone scooped his heart right out of his chest. He couldn't breathe deep enough to stop the suffocating need for more air.

He looked over at the refrigerator and saw the picture from the day Chloe was born. Lizzie looked like an angel. Chloe was such a small bean. She barely fit in the car seat he frantically attempted to buckle. Beau sucked in a deep breath and rubbed his fists against his eyes and cheeks. His breathing finally steadied.

Esther pulled the soup in front of him and unwrapped the fresh bread. "You're coming to church with us on Sunday and every Sunday after that. No more running from God. Lizzie loved the Lord. She is celebrating with Him. I'm mad and sad too, but I trust Him. I know that He is good. We need to focus on the blessings. Chloe is a gift. Her birthday is a time of celebration and new beginnings for us. We need to honor Lizzie by raising Chloe right. You need your strength. Eat."

Esther walked around the table for a cloth to wipe the spilled soup. "I put ibuprofen and aspirin in the bathroom cabinet for pain. Take the weekend to rest and get yourself right with your demons. We'll watch Chloe. I have a pastor friend who lost his wife a few years ago. He has been a huge blessing to John and me. I left his name and number on the counter. He says to call him any time."

Beau called Pastor David the next day. They met for coffee and started meeting weekly after that. Beau and Chloe went to church every Sunday with Esther and John. Some days were easier than others, but each day he had to make a choice to live. Beau went back to work as soon as his hand healed with his boss happy to have his protégé back at work.

John helped Beau clean out the garage and set up a workshop for his woodworking. The first project was a large wooden tree of life carved by hand with Jeremiah 24:15 at the tree's root. Beau gave it to Esther for Christmas. Together, the four of them worked as a comfortable family unit for the past three years. Chloe was the center of everything. Now, when he looks into his daughter's eyes, he sees the future instead of the past.

Speaking of the future, his thoughts are pulled back to the present when he hears her bedroom door open, followed by the pitter-patter of her tiny feet running across the open living space of the apartment. His door burst open, and she jumps right on top of him with a high-pitched giggle that only comes from five-year-old little girls. "Daddy!" She squeals as he starts tickling her and kissing her sweet cheeks. They laugh until they can't laugh anymore. "Let's go see Nona and Auntie Haddie, Daddy!"

"Good idea. Go get dressed. I'll race you!" Beau climbs out of bed as he watches Chloe bounce around the apartment like a fairy. She comes back out of her room wearing a purple tutu skirt and pink cowboy boots. Beau smiles to his core. They race to the door, walk slowly down the stairs, then sprint to the main house. Chloe leaves her father in the dust as she turns back, gloating that she won the race.

Chloe bounds into the kitchen through the backdoor. Esther stands at the stove frying bacon. The smell fills the air with a heavenly scent. "Chloe, my sweet girl. I'm making fried eggs and bacon. Does that sound good?"

The curly-haired girl runs across the room and buries her head into her grandmother's leg for a big hug. "My favorite!"

Beau walks in behind his daughter and closes the door behind them. "You're just too fast for me, Chloe." He laughs along with her.

"Chloe, Aunt Haddie is in the family room with Maryssa and Nunnie Mary. Why don't you go in there and visit until breakfast is ready."

"Is Agent Travis with them? I thought of a new riddle for him. He'll never guess this one." Chloe skips off down the hall calling for her favorite Secret Service agent.

Beau walks over and kisses his mother-in-law on the cheek as he sneaks a piece of bacon from the plate beside the stove. "Can I help do anything?"

"No, just sit down and have some coffee. I'm finishing the last batch of bacon now. I actually want to talk to you about something. Pour me a fresh mug too while you're at it and don't forget the creamer." Esther turns off the gas and places more bacon on the plate. She walks to the table and sits next to Beau.

"You're making me nervous, Mom. You have that serious expression on your face."

Esther reaches out and pats Beau's hand. "Beau, I moved to South Carolina with my sister and brother-in-law decades ago. I was so young. I was running from teenage heartbreak, looking for a new life. I met John and had two beautiful daughters. I helped out at Malik's restaurant with my sister then helped John manage it after we bought it. I made a good life." Esther twists her mug in her hands, remembering.

"Now, my sister, my daughter, and my husband are all gone. Haddie is married and living in DC. I have no job, and I'm living in my mother-in-law's house. Really, I have nothing left here for me but you and Chloe. Your mother desperately wants you to move in with them. Your brothers have an opening in your family business. I think it's time I move back to West Virginia."

Esther pauses, letting her words sink into Beau. "My mother is getting older and needs help with the farmhouse. Maryssa will need help with the restaurant. From West Virginia, Haddie will only be a car ride away as opposed to a flight. Eloise told me yesterday that she is moving in with her sister. The house should sell quickly since we're on the historical registry. It's time, Beau. It's time I return home."

Beau shakes his head in disbelief. "No way. If you go to West Virginia, we're going with you."

Esther stands to add more creamer to her coffee. "Beau, you don't have to look out for me anymore. You are so young and talented. You need to live your life. Find a wife, follow your dream of woodworking. Let Chloe play with her cousins instead of an old lady every day." She offers a bitter laugh. "Beau, I'm tired. My life is over. I have nothing left. You have your life ahead of you. Stay here and start over, let me go home and die."

"Wow, and I thought Chloe cornered the market on dramatics. No. I'm not staying here, and I'm not working at Baker Construction. I'm coming with you. Chloe has already lost a mother, and a grandfather, we're not losing you too. Where you go, we go."

"Beau, I can't ask you to do that. You have a family that can take you in and offer you a job and can help with Chloe. It is killing me to uproot you two, but I just can't stay here anymore. The memories are too hard to relive day in and day out. I can't ask you to start over in a new state. I arrived with nothing, I'm leaving with nothing, and I have nothing. God has taken everything from me. At least here you have your family."

Beau walks over to Esther and stands beside her, leaning against the counter. "Mom, you are our family. We're a team, the three of us. We've been through a lot together, and we'll make this move together. Where you go, we go, and that's that. Now, start frying those eggs. I'll start on the toast." He kisses her cheek and walks over to the breadbasket.

Chapter 4

Maryssa

The streets of DC are hot and muggy. Maryssa walks to work so she can enjoy her last week in the city. Haddie still calls South Carolina home, but Maryssa has been in love with the Capital City since they moved here at the age of sixteen. This is where she graduated high school, began both of her careers, and became an expert at the Metro. This is where she purchased her first piece of furniture and her favorite couch. She grew up in this city.

The city also holds sad memories for Maryssa. She passes the hospital where her mother died every time she travels to the White House for lunch with her father. The theatre where she danced for almost a decade, reminds her that her knees and toes will never hold the same youthful agility. She loves being a chef, but her first love is ballet. Her Mama came to every performance. Dance lost something without Ruth Lavalier in the audience. Remembering her life after the ballet and after Mama made her tired. Maryssa loves DC, but she is ready to leave and start her next adventure.

Ruth was resilient throughout her fight with cancer. Maryssa hated that analogy; fighting cancer. As if cancer was an entity one could fight and win against, or worse, lose to. Ruth didn't lose any battle. Maryssa misses her mother so much. Maybe that is why she is moving to West Virginia. Maryssa wants more of her Mama. Memories and stories from those who loved her most will surround her as she starts act two of her life.

Today is her last day at Savourer, the hottest dining experience in town. Since the Separation of States, Washington has practically turned into a suburb of New York City. Only a three-hour train ride or four-hour drive, celebrities who penetrated politics are now living in both cities. Little by little Washington, DC blossomed into a trendy offshoot of the Big Apple. That is how Maryssa's boss, the most renowned chef in the country, ended up one mile away from the White House. Jacques Boucher is a presence to behold in the culinary world. He is a gifted genius. With five restaurants worldwide, Savourer will become the flagship in his harbor.

This year has been the most significant learning experience in her life. At twenty-three, she was offered the opportunity to dance in Paris as part of a touring troupe. She fell in love with Paris and learned much about herself and her craft, but this internship is different. Jacques is intense, all the time. He frequently wakes in the middle of the night and calls Maryssa to share an inspiration derived from a dream or to share his latest and most fabulous idea. She was transported into his world. It has been equally exhilarating as it has been exhausting.

The streets of Logan Circle are bustling this morning. Maryssa reaches the converted historic building that is Savourer. The heavy glass doors open to another world. The exposed brick walls contrast the warm wooden beams criss-crossing the ceiling. Sturdy leather and wood chairs line the walls and modern square tabletops. Bright, crystal globes of varying sizes are suspended along the ceiling, offering just the right ambiance and lighting for fine dining and socializing. The atmosphere is intimate and sophisticated, just like Jacques.

The sounds of the London Symphony Orchestra waft through the air as Maryssa enters the kitchen. Sure enough, Jacques is standing over the range, adding a dash of something into his saucepan. He hums along as he stirs meticulously. Maryssa clears her throat to let him know she is here without disturbing the man.

"Ah, ma plus chère, you are here!" He exclaims. "Come. Taste. My mother loved gumbo as a child, but I've never mastered it. I think the key is adding mussels." His mother moved to America when Jacques was fifteen. His accent is a charming mixture of French and southern dialects.

Maryssa approaches and sips broth from the spoon and shakes her head. "It's amazing. My favorite gumbo starts with a roux and has sausage and shrimp, so I'm partial to those." She shrugs.

He leans down and kisses her platonically yet intimately on the cheek. "You have a gift with Cajun food. I think you are choosing the wrong ancestry to base your restaurant." Maryssa's father was born and raised in New Orleans, but he jokes that he is Italian by marriage.

She turns and heads toward the staff closet, where she places her things inside her locker for the last time. She dons her chef jacket and checks the mirror to ensure her long brown tendrils are still neatly secured in a tight bun. A girl can leave the ballet, but the ballerina never leaves the girl. As she closes her locker, she takes in the room. When she started working, there were speculations that she earned the coveted role because of her father's connections in the culinary world or because she was an attractive woman. Why else would the infamous Jacques Boucher invite a woman as his intern? Maryssa is sure there are still doubters, but she has earned the respect of the staff she has come to love. It will be difficult leaving them today.

As she enters the kitchen again, Jacques has two place settings ready. Two bowls filled with gumbo, freshly baked bread, and two glasses of a new chenin blanc. He pulls out a chef's stool for her as he takes the one next to her. He guiltily shrugs, "A last meal of sorts."

"I remember my first week. You made a batch of gumbo for your mother's visit. It was delicious, but you said it was rubbish then threw the pot against the wall and took her to dinner instead." Maryssa chortles. "I was still terrified of you and that day scared the snot out of me." She breaks off a piece of bread to dip as she breathes in the spiciness before her.

"And now? Are you still 'terrified' of me?" He searches her eyes.

She chews as she ponders his answer. "Sometimes. You are brilliant, and I think your brilliance comes with great passion and gusto."

"I have never heard passion used in a derogatory tone before, so I will accept that as good." He winks then lifts his spoon to his lips but not before taking a jab at her. "And your passion will be hidden in the hills of West Virginia."

Maryssa slowly sips the dry white wine. "Yes." Attempting to avoid the same discussion they have been having for weeks.

"I have only had four other interns, you know. They have restaurants in New York, Los Angeles, Houston, and Tuscany. You, you take my wisdom to the hills to die."

Maryssa knows all about Jacques and his interns. As with his previous restaurants, Jacques reached out to area culinary schools to find a protege. Maryssa surmised quickly that the gesture is more about ego and legacy than benevolence. His previous four interns had their choice of backers for restaurants. They also have their share of notoriety. Intern number two wrote a tell-all book entitled *Fire in the Kitchen,* which is still on the bestseller list.

Maryssa won the coveted role of his intern out of hundreds of applicants. Peter, Jacques' trusted personal assistant, narrowed the field down to ten. Each finalist was invited to spend one day in Jacques' New York restaurant. The final three shadowed Jacques for the day, working with him and his staff in the evening. Maryssa was the only candidate not thrown out of Jacque's' kitchen. She is also the only female intern he has ever chosen.

"Ah, I have hit a sour note in our meal. La femme se tait." Jacques continues eating.

She places her glass gently beside her bowl and turns toward her mentor. "The woman is silent because the woman is exhausted from having the same discussion. Yes, my passion is in West Virginia because that is where I am inspired. I want to be immersed in the culture in which I was raised. I want to simmer the tomato sauce recipe that my great-grandmother carried in her bag across the ocean, not once, not twice, but three times before being granted entrance. I want to learn how to encase my own sweet Italian sausage for a fusion gumbo."

Feeling herself losing some of her composure, she ends with her final blow. "I also want to pair my creations with wine that takes your breath away with its uniqueness instead of drinking only wine you have flown over from France." She huffs as she dips another piece of crusty bread.

He laughs at her. "There is that passion I love. All right, all right." He holds up his hands in surrender. "I will support your decision to leave me if I must. Just know that you always have a place in my kitchen. Now, finish eating and tell me what you think of the mussels."

The next few minutes remind Maryssa of what she'll miss most about her time at Savourer. Jacques taught her to become entranced with the smells and the texture of food. His eyes close. His head falls backward in awe. The kitchen is his studio. She has learned more from Jacques in one year than most chefs learn in a lifetime. Forgotten is the divide, the two converse like old friends, enjoying the moment before them.

He drinks his wine while watching her experience his creation. Her spoon rests in the empty bowl as he fills her glass. After a moment, he reaches over and places his hand over her delicate fingers. Maryssa, already sitting with perfect dancer posture, straightens even more as if a string is pulling up at the crown of her head.

"My inquisitive Maryssa, you have learned much from me, no?" She nods. He reaches out for her other hand, effectively turning her to face him.

"I have also learned from you. You have brought something out in me that I have been missing for years. You lit a new fire of excitement in my cooking and in my life. You have also taught me patience." He wryly grins. "You are leaving me, no?" She nods.

"This past year, I have tried to seduce you day in and day out, no?" She nods again, but this time adds a classic Maryssa eye roll. "And every advance, you answered stoically that you want to make a name for yourself based on your work and not rumors."

Maryssa takes a deep, steadying breath. She knew this conversation would also come today. Jacques, twenty years her senior, is ruggedly handsome. His romantic endeavors are as infamous as his food is extraordinary. Maryssa would be lying if she said she didn't have a mentor-inspired crush on the man, but her gut always told her to run.

"But today, today you are leaving me. I have no authority over you. I will no longer be your boss. You will no longer be my intern. We will both be chefs with our own separate restaurants. I ask you once again, reconsider. Stay here with me. You can open your own little Italian restaurant in Washington. If you won't accept my help, accept your father's. Stay and see where this takes us. We could be a great love story, you and me. We can travel the world eating and drinking and loving." Jacques squeezes her hands in anticipation as he stares deeply into her eyes.

Surprising even herself, Maryssa places a hand on the side of his face. "No." She shakes her head in kindness but still resolved. "This is a different variation of the same conversation we have been having for a year. You are a force, Jacques. Your brilliance overwhelms me. I will forever be indebted to you for all that you have taught me, but it is time. I am ready. I am leaving. Please let me go without any bad feelings or weirdness between us."

He leans in and kisses the inside of her palm. "L'amour perdu. The one who got away."

"You can always come and visit me. You can tour the vineyard and maybe find a better pairing for your new gumbo recipe." She offers a soft laugh.

"This was too dry." He agrees with a shrug. "But the mussels, no?" She nods before collecting the empty bowls.

"Your mother will love it."

They both turn as they hear laughter coming in through the front door and into the kitchen. Jacques' assistant, Peter, and Simone, the head bartender, are mid-conversation as they enter the chef's domain. Simone immediately heads toward Maryssa and plants a kiss on both cheeks. "Are you finally gonna let that hair down tonight, ballerina? We are throwing you one heck of a good luck party! Hashtag Bosslady!"

"I'm not going to lie, Simone, I'm a little scared, but very excited." Maryssa offers in response. "I can't stay out too late. I have a day full of packing tomorrow and dinner with my family."

"Don't give me that excuse. You have a two-bedroom apartment, and one bedroom is already empty. I'll help you pack. Tonight, we're starting here with 'Marysheeno Shooters' that will knock off your ballet slippers. Do you see what I did there? I've been working on the name for weeks." Simone hip-bumps Maryssa.

Jacques clears his throat. "Peter, I need a word in my office. Simone, please make sure the staff holds off tasting your concoction until service is finished tonight. I'd hate to lose an intern and bartender on the same day." Jacques is back to all business.

The women laugh as they walk in the direction of the staff locker room.

Chapter 5

Beau

Beau drives down the two-lane country road. He passes the sign for Raffaluzza Vineyard and turns onto the private driveway off the main road, Esther is trailing fifty yards behind him. He watches as his mother-in-law slows down to watch a horse on the fence line. According to his side mirrors, either Chloe wasn't impressed, or the horse moved at the sight of city slickers. He guesses the latter is the case.

This is Beau's first trip to West Virginia. He always assumed he would visit with Lizzie one day. She loved spending summers here with her Nunnie and her cousins. The way she talked about the vineyard made this place seem magical. They were young and poor after they were married. Vacations weren't on their priority list. Then came the diagnosis. As hard as he tries, Beau still classifies everything in his life as before or after the diagnosis. Chloe visited a few times with Esther and John, but Beau usually stayed in South Carolina. He wanted to experience this moment with Lizzie. Now, it seems bittersweet.

The wheels come to a stop as they crunch some gravel. The gears sound as tired and as stiff as Beau feels. He climbs out of the rental truck and stretches between the seat and the open door. The white farmhouse is a welcome relief from the endless miles of asphalt. He is positive the stiffness will last an eternity. They got on the road this morning by six, but with a five-year-old, the stops were frequent and lengthy. Beau pulls his right arm across his chest then his left. A twist of his trunk and a roll of his neck help ease the tension little.

The silver sedan parks beside him. The engine goes silent. He watches as Esther and Chloe make small movements inside the car. The doors open as Esther stands outside of the car staring at her teenage home. Chloe bounds around the car to hug her daddy. "I'm so glad we're here, Nona! Daddy, I hope you love it!" She squeals as only a little girl can.

Beau watches Esther's face. She warmly smiles at her granddaughter, but she isn't her old self. Beau has seen Esther grieve before, but this seems different. It's almost as if the weight is too heavy this time. She became more despondent with each box packed. He knew Esther wanted to move home to be near family, but he could tell she was nervous. Beau couldn't figure it out yet. Something just didn't feel right.

Just as Esther turns to look at Beau, the front door opens, and people come out in droves. Kids are running down the stairs straight to Chloe. A gaggle of siblings, nieces, and nephews surround Esther at the car offering hugs and handshakes.

"Why do you look so surprised, E? This is a homecoming celebration. The prodigal has returned." Her brother Dom laughs and hugs his sister tightly. "We've been here waiting for hours, did you get lost? Couldn't remember how to get home?"

Aunt Jo pushes him away from Esther. "Stop it, Dom. We all just pulled in a few minutes ago, Sissy. In fact, he was the last one to arrive." Jo envelopes Esther in a long embrace. "We're so happy you're home."

"Move over, Jo, it's my turn." Sam is tall and sturdy, just like their father. His greying hair, the only betrayer of his age. "Mini E, home hasn't felt the same without you. Now all is right with the world." He holds his sister tightly as the family encircles them.

"I can't believe you all came." Esther wipes tears as she is wrapped into the cocoon of her brother's arms. "It's nice to finally get out of the car."

Sam's wife, Hannah, walks around the group to hug Beau. "We're happy to see you too, Beau. I hope you know what you've gotten yourself into with this clan." She laughs as the group takes turns giving Beau welcome hugs and pats on the back.

Chloe is bouncing from cousin to cousin. Kids everywhere are running around the car and the truck. Giggles and laughter fill the late afternoon air. Crickets are playing a symphony in the background. The leftover humidity from a stubborn summer is cut by a small breeze coming from the tall oak trees surrounding the property.

Everyone turns as Nunnie Mary whistles from the front porch. "Let's eat before the food gets cold. Those boxes won't move on their own. They can wait. My lasagna won't." She turns. Like ducks, everyone follows their matriarch into the farmhouse, talking and laughing.

Beau walks inside the house behind everyone. He tries to see this through Lizzie's eyes. He has heard so many stories, now he sees it with his own eyes, through her memories. The front porch swing was her favorite part of the house. She talked Nunnie into letting her sleep on the porch one night. He remembers Lizzie's telling of the story more than the story itself. Her dimples, so deep from smiling and laughing, she almost couldn't get out that she ran inside after hearing her first coyote howl. He sees the long banister where Lizzie would have sliding races with Haddie and Maryssa. That particular favored activity ended with Maryssa getting a split lip and stitches if he remembers the story correctly. Lizzie loved this place.

He has pictured this house through Lizzie's memories a million times. The smells and rooms of the farmhouse feel odd, almost like coming home to him. Beau relishes the memories Lizzie shared with him about this house. As he walks through the Marchio family home, he's grateful their daughter will make her own memories in this place, in the footprints of her mother.

***

Esther

After a delicious and loud dinner of lasagna and insalata with lettuce and tomatoes from Nunnie's garden, the family gets to work. Some begin unloading the truck while others help Esther unpack suitcases and make beds upstairs. The younger cousins play games on the spacious front porch. As the boxes are distributed upstairs and down, Esther sees a full life that ended tragically. She sees loss and solitude, even when surrounded by family.

The only furniture is Beau's for when he and Chloe eventually find an apartment. Esther's *sweetheart* of a mother-in-law, Eloise, allowed her sisters' children to raid the family home while Esther was out running errands for a day. Esther came home to a decimated shell of a home. Another blow she trudged through over the past two months. Eloise felt the family heirlooms should stay in South Carolina, not *up north* where they would not be appreciated.

Eloise donated what remained of the antique furniture to a historical society in town. Esther had no need for antiques. She had no need for any furniture at all. She donated John's clothing and everything else that impeded her desire to downsize and get home. As expected, the house sold the same week it was listed on the market. Esther received nothing from the sale. She left with only her clothes and memories packed in boxes.

Jo, the baby of the family, brings in the missing sheets for Esther's bed. "Found them. They were in the box with towels and random bathroom items." Jo begins unfolding the bedding. She finds the fitted sheet and tucks one corner around the mattress. Esther helps with the other side.

"I know they say you're not supposed to do anything drastic, like move after the death of a spouse, but I'm really happy you are home. How are you holding up?" She sheepishly looks at her older sister.

"I just couldn't bear to live there anymore. That town reminded me of loss. I lost everyone I loved there. I saw them everywhere I looked. I had to leave. It's almost as if I was punished for leaving for greener pastures when I was nineteen." Esther stares out the window. Her face etched with melancholy.

Jo blanches at Esther's words. "Wow, and Sam and Dom call me the dramatic one. You seriously don't believe that, do you?"

"Honestly, Jo, I don't know what I believe anymore. I see everyone here doing well and prospering from the vineyard. I have lost more than I have these days. I wanted to be home before the harvesting. I just want a piece of the scraps."

Jo rolls her eyes at her sister's proclamation of misery. "No one has a perfect life, E. We all have journeys to walk. Some are walked on busy streets for all to see and others are on secluded country paths, but we're all walking." Jo thinks of her own journey.

Esther pulls out the comforter that used to cover her marriage bed. She hasn't laundered it. It was wrapped in plastic for the move. She breathes in the smells as she unfolds the fabric. Familiarity and longing fill her senses. The sisters continue to work in silence to get Esther's bed made.

They fill the cases with pillows before pulling up the comforter. "I'm truly sorry for the reasons that brought you home, but I am glad you're here. I'd love to spend more time with you. Growing up, I was so envious of you and Ruthie. The boys had each other, and then you two flew south before I was old enough to enjoy the girl time. It will be nice to have a sister."

Jo sits on the edge of Esther's bed as her sister bends down to open another box. "I'd keep your distance from me, you'll probably get cancer and die, or maybe have a heart attack, or develop a life-altering disease. I'm an omen of bad things." Esther laughs, bitterly.

Jo watches Esther move around the room. Growing up, Esther had vibrant chestnut brown eyes and hair. She had a glow about her; rosy cheeks and olive-toned skin. Her laugh used to be buoyant and contagious. Boys were continually coming around the house to see her and Ruthie. Jo would follow them around and idolize their teenage lives. Watching her now, Jo sees sadness. Esther's eyes are dull and dead inside. Her coloring, ashen. The chestnut locks highlighted with streaks of gray. Esther is home, but she is not the same woman.

Chloe bounces into Esther's room with Maryssa in tow. Her curls bouncing, and her eyes shining. "Nona! You have to come and see my room. Maryssa helped me make the bed. It's a daybed, so it can be a couch at daytime and a bed at nighttime. Maryssa said it was Nunnie's knitting room. It is filled with so many pretty colors. Come on!"

Esther accepts Chloe's offered hand as they head off down the hallway. Esther's placated smile firmly fixed in place.

Yes, Esther is home, but she is not the same Esther.

Chapter 6

Maryssa

"You are a lousy jerk." Maryssa scowls as she crosses the kitchen and peers out the window encased in the back door.

The sight of the rooster beyond the back porch railing elicits a loud groan and snarl from Maryssa. The rooster's dark brown feathers and bright red comb along with his perch overlooking the hillside give him a regal look. Maryssa only sees him as the evil monster who awakens her every morning at six-fifteen. Without fail.

Contrary to popular belief, not all roosters offer a loud cock-a-doodle-doo at the crack of dawn. Mr. Bubbles, not as bubbly as his name conveys, is more reliable than an alarm clock. He moves a little to the right to bathe himself in sunlight, effectively blocking Maryssa's view of the vineyard. Maryssa glares once more as she turns to fill her travel mug with hot coffee.

"Will you two ever be friends?" Nunnie chuckles as she enters the kitchen behind Maryssa. The older woman is dressed in jeans, a long-sleeved red shirt, and a black vest. Her light brown hair curled and pinned back at her temples. Instead of going grey, which she still denies, her natural dark brown became lighter and lighter with the help of her hairdresser. At eighty, her face is remarkably smooth and vivacious. The only lines, slight at the corners of her eyes and mouth, are solely from a lifetime of laughter.

Maryssa stares at her grandmother for a moment taking in the strength and compassion that flow from the woman. "What on earth are you staring at? Did I leave my curlers in too long? Is there lipstick on my teeth?"

Maryssa crosses the room and embraces her grandmother tightly. "No, Ma'am. I'm just so grateful to be here with you." The women part slightly and look at each other. "I could live without the rooster wake-up call every morning, but you? You, I look forward to seeing every morning."

"Now, now. Mr. Bubbles just wants to make sure we're up and at 'em every day. The early bird gets the worm, and the spry chicken gets the feed first." Nunnie refills her mug of coffee and heads to the kitchen table. She picks up the newspaper and folds the front page in half, making it easier to read. "What time is Sam coming to fetch you this morning?"

Maryssa sits beside Nunnie at the table. Her hair pulled back into a low ponytail. Curls cascading down her back. "Uncle Sam scheduled the first interview at nine. He's on his way now to pick me up so we can do another walkthrough before the contractors come. Our tight timeline will be the biggest factor. Since the family barn is already piped, plumbed, and wired; other than updating to an industrial kitchen, the overhaul will be mostly aesthetic."

"I think your Poppy always had this in mind. We fought for weeks over that barn." Nunnie shakes her head. "I loved the idea of a barn to host family events, but I wanted him to build it on this side of the property near the house. He insisted we build by the main road. That man was always thinking of what would come next." She pushed up her reading glasses while flipping the paper. "Testardo come un asino," Nunnie mutters.

"Hey! I know the bad words." Maryssa scolds her grandmother. "That stubborn *mule* is saving me time and money." She laughs then takes a long, warming drink of coffee. "I'm so nervous and excited at the same time. We're going to ask that the kitchen be finished early so I can finalize the menu and planning while they work on the dining areas and patio. I still need to hire and train staff, plus, order all of the furnishings."

Maryssa collects scattered plans and lists from the table. She organizes them into her rose-colored binder. "There is so much to do before spring. I really hope we'll be open by Valentine's Day, but I know that April is more realistic."

Nunnie places a hand over Maryssa's. "Sweet girl, the color of fret doesn't flatter you. Are you not more important than a sparrow or flowers in a field? Do not worry, for this is a fertile season for faith growing. It will all happen in God's timing. You know this."

Maryssa leans over and places a sweet kiss on Nunnie's cheek. "You are so wise."

"Ah, wisdom comes from a life of being planted well so that we are watered and pruned by the Master Gardener." Nunnie goes back to reading her paper. After a quick beat, she points down at the article, "It looks like the Davisson Brothers Band is playing tonight at Joe's, shine up those dancing shoes."

Maryssa shakes her head, knowing today's lesson is finished, for now. "You are wisdom mixed with ornery."

The back door opens with a melodic creak into the kitchen. "Ah, my favorite oldest son. Would you like some coffee, Sam?" The tall man with salt and pepper hair walks through the door followed by an equally tall and much younger man in tow.

He bends down to kiss his mother's cheek. "Good morning, Mama."

"Your favorite grandchild is here too, Nunnie. And I would love some coffee."

"Hey! You are not the favorite, Sammy. You are just the most annoying." Maryssa bellows as she stands to hug her uncle. "I'm ready to go Uncle Sam. I have my coffee and my idea portfolio." She punches Sammy in the arm then shakes her hand in mock pain. "Why is *he* with you?"

Sammy laughs.

"You two knuckleheads need to get along, so I can retire. As the two oldest grandchildren, it's your responsibility to take care of the family and run the business." He holds up his hand to thwart Maryssa's protest. "I will clarify, the two oldest living in *this* country. Haddie doesn't count since she went off and married a foreigner." He chortles at his own joke before continuing. "I am serious about retirement. It is time for the next generation to cultivate and flourish the Marchio name. We have trained you well, young Padawans. 'Go forth and prosper' or is it 'live long and prosper?'."

"Someone has been binging on sci-fi shows." Sammy slaps his father on the back. "Thank you for your words of wisdom, Father Spock."

Sammy crosses the farmhouse kitchen to fill his battered travel mug. "I'm just dropping you two off at the barn while I make my rounds. I need to check on a few slopes that are showing signs of erosion. I'll pick you up in time for a late lunch in town with some restaurant food supplier dude." Sammy kisses Nunnie on the cheek before heading to the door where he stops and holds out his hand in a gesture, "After you, Princess."

Maryssa slides into her pink and gray puffy jacket as she grabs her pink floral tote. Intentionally bumping into her cousin's shoulder as she passes by on her way through the door. "Oh, I am terribly sorry. I didn't see you standing there, Sammy."

They hear Nunnie chuckle as the door closes behind them.

The three of them drive the vast acreage of the property. Sunbeams penetrate the clouds allowing shining rays of light to cover the lush green vineyard. Maryssa's Mama used to call them prayer-beams. Orange, yellow, and red leaves peek out among the dense green foliage in the background of mountains. Maryssa takes a deep breath. She loves this place. She spent summers here with Haddie and Lizzie when they were younger, but fall visits were her favorite.

The entire extended family helped with the harvesting every year. Since the beginning, the vineyard was a family affair. All the cousins and aunts and uncles came for a huge family reunion during harvest season. Everyone would sleep in tents or campers near the barn. Each day culminated in a massive bonfire and feast fit for a king. She missed those days.

Maryssa's favorite part of harvest week was the family talent show. They would sing, dance, tell jokes, put on skits, and even some juggling would be attempted. The crowd favorite every year was Aunt Lena, Aunt Ethel, and Aunt Roxie hula dancing. You haven't lived until you've seen three-round Italian ladies in grass skirts pretending to be hula dancers. Her cheeks pull back into the sincerest of smiles as Sammy's truck begins to slow.

They park outside of the rustic structure that is the family barn. "Here's your stop. I hope you find a contracting team that fits your time frame. Remember, my roommate Tony is coming out with a bid today. Not that I'm pushing for him, but, I might not pick you up if you don't hire him." Sammy offers a cockeyed grin and winks.

"Tony will be given the same consideration as every other contractor, even if he is your friend. We won't hold that against him." Maryssa messes up her cousin's hair from behind as she climbs down the runner on the truck. She turns to take in the barn.

Over the years, the large wooden structure has been used as a family gathering place for holidays and parties. Haddie and Jackson had a very intimate wedding ceremony here last year. A large reception was held at the White House for the public to celebrate, but this was their secret spot away from the press. The country thought they were at Camp David, which made it easier to pull off the secret nuptials.

The inside of the barn is completely open and can host around two hundred people comfortably. Maryssa wants an addition off the side to house an intimate bar area and waiting space that spills over onto the terrace. She twirls, taking in the scope of what is before her. The kitchen is large but needs work to transform it into an industrial restaurant space. All the bones are here, but the contractor's team will have their work cut out for them, especially to get it ready by April when the tasting rooms open for summer hours to customers.

Uncle Sam walks over to a picnic table and places his notepad and pen next to a chair at the end. Maryssa follows and begins spreading out her papers. They talk over the plans and make some notes.

The sound of truck tires on gravel approaching the barn draws their attention. Uncle Sam walks back to the door and calls, "Here we go. I hope you're ready."

Three hours later, and Maryssa's head is spinning. There are so many bids and ideas to consider. They have one final appointment before lunch. Every contractor scoffed at a timeline ending in mid-February. Upscaling the dining area shouldn't be difficult as long as Maryssa has her design elements ordered and delivered within the month. Upgrading the bathrooms and kitchen would prove more time consuming, but doable. Their main concern is adding to the structure to provide a bar area with additional seating near the front doors. The patio would need to be subcontracted out which would push the opening date back, even beyond April.

Everyone insists they need to break ground before winter hits hard, but schedules were already tight. Uncle Sam keeps reminding her not to worry, but Maryssa is feeling a bit overwhelmed.

"Are you ready?" He asks as the sound of tires again approach the structure.

Maryssa nods and rubs the back of her shoulder as she rolls her neck around in circles. Her hand slips beneath the collar of her cashmere cable sweater she chose to wear today. It barely kept her warm in this spacious room.

"I suppose so. I just hope we've saved the best for last."

"The last contractor is Tony. At the very least, we will be entertained." Uncle Sam laughs as they watch the door push inside the space. She is surprised to see Beau enter behind Tony. The two men walk across the vast expanse, looking like twins. Both wearing well-worn jeans, flannel shirts, steel-toed boots, and light brown utility jackets. The only difference is the color of their hair. Tony's hair a wavy, jet black. Beau's sandy blond is scruffy and in need of a trim. Tony carries a notebook and a measuring tape. He extends his hand to Uncle Sam first.

"Well, if it isn't the person who eats me out of house and home on the weekends. When are you and my son going to learn to cook, so you stop eating at your parent's houses all the time?"

"Our stove is broken." Tony laughs.

"You want us to hire you to remodel a kitchen, but you can't fix your own stove?" Sam pats Tony on the back.

"That's why I brought a secret weapon. Beau is my newest hire. He has an impeccable resume and carpentry portfolio. Bonus, Nunnie Mary is his reference." Tony's smile oozes with confidence at his cleverness. "I figure hiring him provides me some leverage. If you hire me, you provide work for Beau. I don't even feel bad for preying on your family loyalty." Tony reaches out to hug Maryssa, Beau follows.

"Hey, Maryssa. Sam." Beau and Uncle Sam man hug, complete with a thump on the back. "Tony wanted me to bring Chloe too, but I thought that might be overkill." A small wave of laughter flows between the four. They all sit and begin talking business.

Fall

Chapter 7

Beau

The front door opens to smells of garlic and tomato sauce coming from the kitchen. Voices and laughter float down the hallway. The cozy country farmhouse is alive with family. Beau walks through the living room and into the kitchen. Mary, Maryssa, Esther, and Chloe are dancing to the music playing in the background while setting the table and fixing dinner. Chloe runs and jumps into Beau's arms as soon as she turns and sees him. The women all turn and smile.

"Daddy!" The small girl buries her head into the neck of her father. She looks back up at him with wonder in her eyes. "Nona and I went to pick apples from the tree out back after school today. Then Maryssa showed me how to make apple pie. We sliced the apples and rolled the crust. We used a special silver thing to make cinnamon sprinkles on the top, and we made our own ice cream. And it's vanilla, my favorite. Maryssa says next time we can make banana ice cream. She said that was Mama's favorite when they were my age. It smells so good. I can't wait to eat it. Nona says I have to wait until after dinner, but it's sketti, and I love sketti, so I'll definitely get ice cream tonight."

She hugs her father tightly one more time. "I missed you! How was your day, Daddy?"

Beau beams as Chloe finally takes a breath. He places a kiss on the top of her brown, curly hair. She smells of cinnamon and vanilla. "It seems my day was not as fun as yours, sweetheart. I'm very excited to try your pie and the ice cream. Did you thank Maryssa for letting you help?"

"Of course, Daddy. 'Please and thank you go together.' I asked her to please make it then I said thank you when she said yes." She beams back up at him.

Chloe jumps down and goes back to her work in the kitchen. She picks up the napkins and forks to continue placing them around the table.

"Well, Beau, we hear you will be working at the barn with Maryssa and Tony. I hope Maryssa doesn't drive you crazy with her diva chef behavior."

"Nunnie! You know I'm not a diva. If anything, Tony is the diva. His list of concerns almost made me forget who was being interviewed." Maryssa laughs as she strains the pasta in the sink. Steam rising and heating her face. "Between Tony and Uncle Sam, I don't think Beau or I got a word in edgewise."

Beau muffles a chuckle as he watches the activity in the room.

"I've seen my brother in action. I'm sure the room got an earful today." Esther offers a rare half-smile as she cuts tomatoes.

"Maryssa is correct. Sam has nothing on Tony. Tony is a trip. He's a great guy and really knows the contracting business, but he likes to talk, a lot." Tony reminds Beau of his brother Matt. Matt is the business brains in their family. He runs the office while Beau's dad and other brothers do all the building.

Beau takes off his well-worn baseball hat and runs his hand through his wavy hair. "His crew is great too. They must all be friends with Sammy and Tony, so I'm sure it can get really intense sometimes."

"I remember one time. I think it was the summer after middle school. We were suntanning on the shore at Tygart Lake when Sammy and Tony came. They wouldn't stop talking about the girls they just met. Bragging about their coolness. Frankie Jo jumped up off of her towel, walked right over to Tony, and placed a big fat kiss on his lips." Maryssa laughs so hard she's almost doubled over in pain.

"Oh my, Francesca has always been brazened. Sam has his hands full with that one. What did Tony do?" Esther asks.

Maryssa continues her story, trying to contain her laughter. "He stood there like a deer caught in headlights. Not one word."

"That was surely a first for Tony." Nunnie laughs.

"Oh, it was. Tony stared at Frankie like she was an alien who just sucked out his brains. Sammy fell to the sand laughing. Frankie deadpanned, 'That's what I thought,' and went back to her towel."

"No way. A speechless Tony? That's great. Thanks, Maryssa. Now I have to control my laughter tomorrow at work. But, I will definitely tuck that bit of information in my back pocket." An ornery smile crosses Beau's face.

"It was killing me today not to tell the story, but I didn't think Uncle Sam wanted the image of his precious Frankie Jo kissing Tony, stuck in his head."

"Trust me, Sam is not shocked by anything Frankie does. Now, Tony being shocked into silence, that would have done it." Nunnie replies while shaking her head.

"Well, Tony is fortunate to have someone of your caliber on his team now." Esther finishes tossing the salad with dressing. She places the large wooden bowl on the round table. "Did you tell him about all the work you did for our restaurant in Charleston?"

"I showed him my portfolio when he interviewed me. Right now, he wants me to work on detailing and finishing work, but he has some plans for custom-built cabinetry too. After talking with Sam and Maryssa, I'm hoping to do some special projects at the barn and the tasting room. They want some custom-built wine racks and carving art for the foyers."

Maryssa brings the spaghetti bowl to the table and pulls out her chair. "I remember that hand-carved gazebo you built for Lizzie at your first house. That was so gorgeous. I would love something similar off the terrace. That would be a perfect spot for outside weddings."

Beau lowers his gaze to Chloe.

"You built Mama a-zebo?" Chloe looks up at him. "What's a zebo?"

A wave of soft laughter surrounds her. "A Ga-zebo is something for outside that has a roof but no walls. I built one for your Mama because she loved sitting in the backyard but didn't like the hot afternoon sun hitting her. So I built her a gazebo with benches all the way around it." Beau taps his finger on the tip of her nose.

"It was much more than just a simple gazebo, Chloe. Your Daddy carved your Mama's favorite flowers into the posts that held up the roof and stained it to match the wood from the nearby trees. Your Mama used to say she felt like she was sitting in a tree." Esther turns her head away quickly to prevent the little girl from seeing her red, watery eyes.

Nunnie Mary squeezes Esther's arm as she passes for the table and attempts to shift the focus of the conversation. "Beau, I can't wait to see your new artwork at the barn. Now let's eat before the food gets cold."

They all gather around the table to sit and eat. Nunnie Mary offers a blessing over the food and the hands who prepared it. After the "Amens," food is passed back and forth in a seamless manner. Warm bread is spread with butter. Hot spaghetti is twirled on forks. Baked zucchini straws are dipped in marinara. Silence envelops the table while they all enjoy the bounty before them.

Nunnie Mary studies the sadness on her daughter's face. The deep circles under hollow eyes, seem almost bruised in color. Her breath is shallow, as seen by the rise and fall of her chest. Her plate remains full even as Esther pretends to eat by nibbling. Mary's precious daughter is in a profound pit and has set up camp there in the darkness. Mary offers a silent prayer.

"Beau, I've been doing some thinking."

Maryssa almost chokes on the food she is chewing. "Uh oh. Run while you still can, Beau."

"Oh, hush now." Mary chides her laughing granddaughter. "Beau, the upper floor of the barn is already sectioned off into a guest loft. I know you talked about getting an apartment for you and Chloe, but I would hate to lose you two after having this big old house filled again. It is so wonderful having you all here and filling it with people. If you move into the barn, you and Chloe will have your own space, but you'll be close enough for all of us to pitch in and help with her." Nunnie smiles as she reaches for another piece of bread, knowingly overstepping her bounds, but not caring one bit.

"Daddy, please? I would love to live in the barn! Please, please, please?" Chloe squeals with delight.

"I don't know, Chloe. I didn't realize that was an option." Beau's internal wheels are turning at full speed. Processing. "Are you sure?" Mary smiles and nods. "Maryssa, don't you want that space? For an office or apartment for you? It's a big space. Great bones."

Maryssa takes a sip of her iced tea to wash down her bread before responding. "Nope, it's all yours. I'll have plenty of office space off of the kitchen. Besides, I think it would be better if I lived here with Nunnie. Living and working in the same place would drive me nuts. I need to get away from the restaurant at night."

Esther sits enraptured with the hope of keeping Chloe and Beau close without smothering them. She has tried to balance using him as a crutch and setting him free since Lizzie died. Her head looks back and forth as everyone talks through the logistics. Hope begins to creep into her bones, even if it's just for a second.

"Then it's settled. Beau and Chloe will stay right here on the farm. Here is to new beginnings." Nunnie raises her glass. "Salute!"

Glasses clink, and food is eaten. Near the end of the meal, Nunnie reminisces. "I love this farm, but the family is what makes it work. This is precisely why our parents sailed here from Italy. You know, Poppy's father made wine for the neighborhood in barrels behind his house from blackberry bushes in the hills. The Italians lived in North View and Montpelier. Communities are what helped us all to survive back then. Everyone pitched in and helped. I remember holidays where entire streets would come together to piecemeal a feast. Salvatore's wine was exceptional."

"Poppy and I moved in with him after we were married and Poppy learned all the techniques from the old country. The entire cellar was filled with bottles and tools. The original barrels are on display in the storehouse." Nunnie Mary's eyes are far away, remembering.

"Did you know that Poppy won this land outside of town in a poker game? I thought he was teasing me or had been drinking when he came home that night. Salvo bought the first few vines with money made working in the glass factory. He never could go into the mines, so he worked in the factories. He saved one dollar from every paycheck. Five vines turned into ten, and now his granddaughter will be building a restaurant on the land where his oldest son and grandsons run his vineyard."

Mary looks around the table as all eyes are on her. She shakes the cobwebs of memories from her head and stands as she gathers plates. "Well, all I'm saying is that he left a mighty fine legacy. He would be tickled."

Chapter 8

Malik

Malik Lavalier pulls his silver SUV onto the one-lane, paved road. The curvy driveway is treelined and leads to the Marchio family farmhouse. The family farm is located on the back three acres of the vineyard. A large pond separates the backfield of the vineyard from the house. Malik passes the pond and family pavilion on the right as he drives slowly down memory lane.

The air is chilly, but he rolls down his windows so he can smell the fresh, sweet smell of the land. The grass is a deep green. He regrets not coming sooner to visit. He almost missed the gorgeous tapestry of greens, yellows, reds, oranges, and purples. The mountains of West Virginia in the fall are breathtaking.

Malik breathes deeply as he pulls in front of the white, colonial farmhouse. The bright red door welcomes him home. He cuts off the engine and climbs out of his car. Stretching his legs and assessing the property.

"Daddy!" Maryssa throws open the front door and runs down the stairs, right into her father's arms. Malik picks her up off her feet and swings her around before placing her back on the ground. He pulls her back to stare at her face, longingly.

"How is it possible that you get more beautiful every day? You look so much like your mother." Malik beams with pride.

"You are biased and wonderful." Maryssa studies the man she adores most in this world. "Daddy? Have you lost weight? There is something different about you." She steps back to take him in and solve the puzzle.

"I'm just excited to see my only daughter." He earns a smirk, letting him know that she doesn't buy his answer. He pats his stomach. "Haddie had me overhaul Jackson's diet. She is worried about his latest cholesterol numbers. It seems the White House kitchen staff has slimmed down as well. You should see Marcus. He lost the weight of an entire person."

Skeptically, she continues her intense visual investigation. "Maybe. Something just seems, I don't know, different about you."

He pulls her close for another hug and kisses the top of her head. "It's so good to see you, sweetie."

"Come inside and see everyone. We just made pumpkin chocolate chip bread. It's delish." Maryssa wraps her arm into the crook of her father's and turns to walk inside the house. "How was your trip? You know our airport has a direct flight to Dulles, right?"

"What? Fly and miss all this? The drive was absolutely amazing. I felt like I was traveling through a Bob Ross painting. A five-hour drive through the mountains is exactly what I needed. Plus, I stopped and met a friend from culinary school. He owns a German restaurant in Martinsburg. His beer-braised brisket is out of this world." Malik squeezes Maryssa's hand.

"That's a mouth full. Try saying that three times fast. Beer-braised brisket. Breer-braised biscuit. See, I can't even do it twice in a row." They shake with laughter.

The aroma of pumpkin mixed with apples and cinnamon springs forth as soon as he enters the house. Esther, Mary, and Chloe all greet him by the front door with hugs.

Malik feels at home in this house. He married Ruth under a grand old oak tree beside the pond. They spent every spring and fall here, helping with planting and harvest. Malik's heart overflows with happiness that Maryssa gets to start a life on this farm.

"Malik!" Nunnie brings the man in for a hug. "It has been too long."

"Mary, I was just here helping Maryssa move." He laughs.

"With family, even one day is too long." She wraps her arm in his as she leads him toward the kitchen. "You've lost weight. It's good that you are here so we can fatten you up."

He laughs. "Your cooking is the best part of the trip."

"Always the charmer," she swats his arm.

"The whole family will be here later for dinner. We're making homemade ravioli. We'll eat some and freeze some. Plus, Sam is bringing a special new wine that has been fermenting since last fall in a toasted barrel. He only got about two hundred bottles from the batch. He's been saving it for his 'fancy chef' brother-in-law." Nunnie smiles at Malik.

"That sounds intriguing. I can't wait to try it. That reminds me, I need to stop at the warehouse before I leave next week. I promised a chef friend of mine a few cases from my favorite vineyard for her restaurant in the city." Malik looks at Esther, "And Haddie specifically asked for a case of the Bella Luna dessert wine for the residence."

"I'm sure she did. I think the election process is really starting to wear on her and it hasn't even picked up steam yet. Jackson is starting to travel more frequently. She is obviously very busy with classes, and now they want her to make speeches. They're coming here for Christmas, so I plan on spoiling her." Esther offers a worried smile.

Maryssa passes out plates with pumpkin bread. Everyone gets quiet as they eat the moist, flavorful concoction. "I plan on spending her entire break baking with her. Any time we were stressed in the apartment, we baked. Whenever one of us pulled out the tiramisu recipe, we knew there would be a lot of talking and measuring."

They fall into a relaxed rhythm of conversation. After everyone finishes eating, Malik joins Esther on the front porch swing as he waits for Maryssa to grab her keys and design plans for the restaurant. He places his arm around her shoulder as she wipes away a stray tear. The front porch wraps around the sides and front of the house. In the summer, ceiling fans cool off the heat of the day. Today, there is a chill in the air. Fall in West Virginia is breathtaking with leaves of brilliant colors, but the night chills quicker when October hits. Esther is wrapped in her warm wool coat. Her knees curled up to her chest.

"How are you holding up since the move?" Malik squeezes her shoulder tighter.

"We sure have seen a lot of loss between us, haven't we?" Esther offers a soft, ironic laugh. She leans her head on his shoulder. "How long does the emptiness last?"

He doesn't answer. Knowing that more questions are coming.

"I was obviously utterly destroyed after Lizzie died. I couldn't breathe. I could barely function. Then Ruth left us. Now John. I can't seem to catch my breath. The pain in my chest is so deep. So oppressive. I try to be strong for Chloe, but I feel like the walking dead. I feel like I should change my name to Bitter Betty." She offers a broken laugh. "I'm always waiting for the next death. How can life get any worse? It takes all my energy to get dressed. I'm forgetful. I can't focus. It takes effort to keep breathing."

"E, I wish I had answers for you. It took me six years to go back to South Carolina after Ruth passed, so I'm probably not the best person to ask. I know that it gets easier to breathe. I woke up every day and kept breathing. Each day wasn't as hard as the last. One day, I woke up and realized I didn't have to fake my way through the day."

She wipes tears as the swing sways back and forth beneath them.

"It's probably good that you moved back to the farm. Having Maryssa and Haddie with me every day helped me after Ruth. Seeing their hope and watching their lives, kept my eyes focused on the future. Staying in Charleston would have been hard for you, and Beau, and Chloe. You all needed a fresh start. A new hope for the future."

They sat in silence for a moment. The large, white porch swing rocking. The soft squeaking of the chain makes a melodic song. "What about you, Malik? Do you have hope? Maryssa is here, and Haddie is so busy with school and Jackson's presidency. How are you doing?"

Malik rubs his chin before answering. "Haddie and I have lunch once a week. She comes down to the kitchen every day to see me. I think Maryssa told her to check in on me." They both chuckle at the thought of the girls checking on their parents.

"There is something. Well, someone who has made me think of more than just surviving the day." Malik stares out over the horizon. "The chef I mentioned inside earlier? The one I'm bringing wine back to in the city. We both started guest lecturing at the culinary school where Maryssa graduated. We sat on a few panels together. One day, she asked me out for coffee." He snorts, "Apparently, she got tired of waiting for me to ask her."

"It's still hard though, dating, I mean. Victoria asks questions about Ruth. Says she wants to get to know her since Ruth is a part of me. Turns out, we attend the same church only during different services. We joined a small group together. We spent a lot of time talking about food, life, travel. The friendship grew into a special relationship and, well, I'd like to ask her to marry me." He shakes his head. "How ironic. You are the only person who knew I was going to propose to Ruth and now you are the first person to hear about Victoria."

Esther sits up in the swing and turns to her brother-in-law. Her warm smile is genuine and sincere. "Malik, I think this is wonderful news. I'm truly happy for you, and I can't wait to meet her. Victoria? Is that her name?" He nods. "So, I take it by your nervousness that Maryssa doesn't know yet?"

"No, I'm going to talk with her this week. I'd like to bring Victoria for Christmas. She doesn't have siblings. Her parents have both passed. Do you think Mary would be okay with me bringing her? Huh, this whole situation is wrought with irony. I asked your father's blessing for Ruth's hand on this farm, now I'm here asking Maryssa for her blessing." Malik stares off into the distance.

Esther settles back into Malik's side. "Mama will be thrilled, you know that, and so will Maryssa. She's been trying to fix you up on blind dates for years. She just wants you to be happy. Honestly, It's Victoria I feel bad for in this situation. Coming here for Christmas is baptism by fire. We are fiercely protective." They both laugh and continue swinging.

The front door creaks open, followed by Maryssa's excited voice, "Daddy, let's go see the barn!"

Chapter 9

Maryssa

Maryssa and Malik pull up to the barn. Construction trucks surround the structure. The place is swarming with workers. They walk through the plastic sheet covering the entrance. A country radio station belts out some classic songs. Someone sings loudly about fishing in the dark.

Maryssa turns to her father, "Ten bucks says that terrible country crooner is Tony singing." She laughs as they walk further into the construction zone. She grabs two hardhats from the table and hands one to Malik. They walk to the project board. Plans and work duty lists are tacked up for everyone to see. Maryssa proudly points to what has already been completed and shares her own ideas that were incorporated into the designs.

"Do you see how we divided the structure into two separate dining areas? Over here, the bar is more casual and is opened to the kitchen so patrons can relax and watch the action. The main focus is the brick oven and dough tossing for pizza. Over here is the traditional dining area where guests enjoy cozy yet sophisticated fine dining. The décor allows us to host high end as well as large casual events with little changes other than the linens and tabletops. When we have larger groups with high-end needs, the bar area can easily be transformed into a wine tasting room with the brick oven window closed to the kitchen and hidden with a wine rack that fits perfectly into the open window slot. Beau built it. He is a very talented woodworker."

Maryssa whispers, "Beau really should be doing more than working for Tony. Tony knows it, but I don't think Beau does." She straightens as she hears the singing coming closer. "Isn't it magnificent, Daddy?" She looks back at her father, who is beaming. "What?"

Malik leans down and kisses his daughter on the top of her head, which is covered by her curly brown hair. "I'm just so impressed with these designs. I'm not surprised one bit, but I am definitely blown away by your attention to detail. You see things like your mother. When we walked into potential restaurant properties, I would see the bones in a blank space, but your Mama, oh, she would see the entire layout as a finished project. She knew where everything should go and why. It is a gift, mia bella, and you seem to have it." He squeezes her shoulder and pulls her closer as he points back to the board. "Now, what is happening over here? Is that a patio dining area?"

Tony walks up behind them, his singing trails off as he gets closer. "That is Ruthie's Terrace, the outdoor area Mary Marie designed. It's amazing. With small seasonal changes like heaters and heavy plastic, she can use it year-round."

Maryssa draws circles with her fingers as she points. "I want this to have a backyard barbecue feel. Over here, can't you just see a cool fire pit for outside concerts? I can set up bands over here, and here, people can sit on blankets or chairs to watch."

Tony pats Malik on the back. "At first, I thought she was too ambitious, and a little crazy, but she backed it up with a detailed layout and suggested materials list. That's when I realized that little Mary Marie is legit."

Maryssa stretches forward to see Tony on the other side of her father and offers a dramatic eye roll.

"Mary Marie? Are you changing your name?" Malik looks back at his daughter.

"Apparently, Tony loves nicknames. First I was Mary Mary Quite Contrary, then I was Lady Boss Mary, but he couldn't handle that one." She smirks. "Mary Marie has stuck.....for now. Poor Beau, the personification of humility, has the ironic nickname of Thor."

"He hates it," Tony laughs as Maryssa smiles and shakes her head.

"Speaking of Thor. He is actually outside working on the terrace now. He has been walking the vineyard after work with Chloe picking up broken vines and branches for a project. It's going to be really cool when he's finished. Chloe even helps him place the sticks. Now, that Chloe has only one fitting nickname, Princess Angel. We all love when that kid comes to visit, but don't tell her that or we'll never get anything done."

"Tony, I have to say, I'm surprised at all the progress around here in such a short time."

Tony rubs the back of his neck as he turns and inspects the job site. "Nunnie Mary calls it Divine intervention. It all just seemed to work out perfectly. We finished the last two jobs ahead of schedule, which never happens, and the next project got pushed back because of zoning issues. The timing allowed us to start early and work a full crew on this project until after Christmas."

"I've been in the restaurant business my entire life, and have never seen such great fortune when it comes to construction. As usual, I agree with Mary."

Tony laughs, "I don't think anyone is brave enough to disagree with Mary Marchio. You should go out and see Beau, he is hand carving the legs for the outside bar area." Tony pats Malik on the back and walks away, singing about how he is working on his next broken heart.

"Hmm, it seems you have an admirer." Malik's eyes follow Tony as he leaves the room.

"HA! Daddy, you are crazy. Tony is a flirt and a player. I feel bad for him when he meets his match in a woman. He's going to fall hard and fast."

Malik rubs his chin. "That's what I'm afraid of, sweet girl." Malik reflects quietly for a second before redirecting Maryssa and himself. "Let's go check the kitchen then find Beau."

Maryssa walks Malik around the kitchen where they discuss every potential appliance, countertop, utensil, and prep station. He asks questions as Maryssa impresses him with the well thought out reasons for her answers. His approval and praise of her kitchen domain have her tearing up a little. They end the moment with a long, magic hug that only a good daddy can give.

They walk through the dining area. Maryssa opens boxes of linens and seat covers to show Malik. The crate filled with dinnerware is opened, and Malik moves the straw out of the way to reveal glossy white, sturdy plates. A vibrant, thick stripe crosses the plate. Each line crosses the other dishes at different angles and in various vibrant colors. The modern design mixed with the classic white is comforting and exciting at the same time.

"You designed these?" Malik asks, amazed.

Maryssa's smile is unstoppable. "Yes, I did. I used that friend of yours you told me to call. I told him what I wanted. He helped me design my own line. The plates remind me of Nunnie's dishes and bowls that were made from the plant where Poppy used to work. I chose the colors based on Rafaluzza's wine labels so it all ties together. The melting of old and new is my overall vision. A fine dining experience will be expected, but I want people to feel like they are at home when they come here to eat. Like they are in their grandmother's kitchen. If they didn't have that, then they'll at least have that feeling after eating at Poppy's."

Malik turns to Maryssa and looks deeply in her eyes. "There are no words to describe how proud I am of you. You've always exceeded my expectations, but this, this has blown me away. Your mother would be swinging from the chandeliers screaming her praises. You are a remarkable chef and businesswoman. Maybe I can get a job here after I retire."

"Ooohh, now that's a topic I would love to talk about with you. I know you want to stay at the White House for Haddie and Jackson, but I'm ready for you to come here any time you want." Maryssa walks over to her Dad and places her arm in his.

He pats her hand and starts walking towards the glass doors leading to the terrace. "Well, there is more to talk about than you think. After we visit with Beau, we should drive the property. I actually have some news to share with you, plus I'd love to see the oak tree where I married your Mama. That was her favorite spot on the farm." The two of them walk through the glass doors and out onto the stone patio to find Beau.

Chapter 10

Beau

The horizon is spectacularly painted in blues, purples, pinks, and oranges. Fall brings earlier sunsets in the east. Beau stares out his truck window at the beauty of the land. He pulls in front of the Marchio family homestead and is not surprised to find the driveway overflowing with cars. He chuckles as he thinks about where his life has taken him. Lizzie is probably eating popcorn in Heaven and laughing at him right now.

Beau grabs his lunch pail and water cooler. He climbs out of his truck, crosses the expansive driveway, and walks around to the back of the house. He takes the stairs two at a time and stands on the back porch that leads to the mudroom. The mudroom is one of the largest rooms in the house, a necessity for a farmhouse.

Laughter spills out from the door before he even opens it. A smile stretches across his face. The smell of garlic and roasted peppers hits him as the warmth from the roaring fire calls to his cold and tired bones. He takes off his steel-toed boots and heavy work coat, both covered in sawdust and debris. He walks into the kitchen to clean up his things from work.

"Daddy!" Chloe runs over to him as he quickly bends down to her level. She wraps her tiny arms around his broad shoulders and squeezes tightly. He kisses her head and breathes in her smell. "I've been working on my bear hugs. Can you tell?"

"I sure can! You almost crushed me with that one." He winks at her as he takes in her appearance. "Well, you're either helping to make the homemade pasta, or you walked through a flour mill today. Which is it, Snow White?"

Chloe's dimples deepen. She laughs while talking. "Silly Daddy! I'm making nokies. I mean nock-lees. I mean. Well, I can't say them, but they are fun to make." She pulls her father's hand over to the table. "See?"

Shouts of greeting welcome Beau. The kitchen is filled with Lizzie's family. Mary, Esther, Maryssa, and Uncle Malik. Sam and Hannah's family. Uncle Dom and his wife Abby along with their kids and grandkids. Aunt Jo is also there with her two youngest kids.

They all squeeze around the table working in stations. Some are measuring the ingredients. Uncle Sam and Sammy are kneading the dough. The kids are all rolling the dough into long snakes. The aunts are filling ravioli with some kind of mixture before folding the dough back over the tray and cutting it. Uncle Dom is teaching the kids how to feed their snakes into a machine that pops out the pasta as he cranks it. Teasing and laughter abound at every station.

The warmth of this family is overwhelming. Beau feels like an outsider watching a movie. Sometimes he is lucky enough to play the role of an extra.

Malik walks over and pats Beau on the back. "Go clean up and join the fun. When we're finished, we'll grab an apple cider and sit on the porch."

"Now, that sounds like a great plan." Beau heads upstairs. He quickly showers and changes into clean clothes and grabs the small wooden heart he finished carving for Chloe today. The aromas waft up the stairs as his stomach loudly rumbles and growls. He hits the first floor as large bowls of pasta are being placed on the extra-long dining table. He walks to the table as people begin to sit and fill their glasses with water or wine.

Uncle Dom pulls out a chair and motions for Beau to sit. "Well, it looks like our Lizzie married a smart man. He shows up just in time for dinner. Please, sit." He laughs.

Aunt Jo pushes her brother's shoulder. "He seems to have learned from you, dear Dominick. You have always shown up just in time for dinner." The whole room laughs.

After a blessing by Nunnie, the food passes back and forth on the table. Maryssa and Esther stand at the heavy glass bowls of pasta and scoop some onto everyone's plates as they pass. Multiple conversations are happening all around the table and are frequently interrupted by someone sharing a story loudly to someone at the other end of the table. The volume steadily increases throughout the meal while stories get funnier and more embarrassing.

Beau surveys the table, and the family members gathered tonight. He watches as Esther wipes a stray tear when Maryssa shares the story from his wedding day when John walked Lizzie down the aisle, and her train knocked over a tall flower stand. The crash startled the entire church. Lizzie didn't miss a beat with her comedic timing for all to hear. The whole church was in stitches as they walked down the aisle. Beau didn't think he could fall in love with her more, but he did at that moment.

"John and Lizzie looked like an Abbott and Costello act." Sam roars with laughter. "Poor Aunt Lena lost her dentures laughing so hard." He wipes his eyes as he recalls the memory.

"You mean her 'false teeth' that's what she called them." Nunnie Mary adds, laughing heartily.

The stories continue as the kids move into the other room to play as the adults sit around the table talking and tasting Sam's new wine creation. Beau hears Chloe laughing with her cousins and is grateful that he came here with Esther.

"Sam, I think this is the best creation yet," Jo says while swallowing the last drop in her glass and holding it out for a refill. "It has a taste of hops to it. It's so unique."

Sam looks at his baby sister, enthralled by her keen senses. "I'm impressed, Jo. You nailed it. I took a chance with this one. I worked with a brewmaster in Morgantown to help me with the balance. I got the idea from Sammy and Tony after they botched a homebrew last year."

"Hey! It wasn't that bad!" Sammy protests at the end of the table.

"Their apartment smelled like burnt toast for weeks," Hannah adds. More laughter erupts from the group.

Slowly, the conversations shift back to individual ones. Maryssa, Uncle Malik, and Esther are talking about Haddie's visit over the holidays. Sounds ebb and flow as plates are carried to the kitchen and the cleanup process kicks into gear. Beau watches the family work together like a machine. Everyone doing their part. Some washing, Some drying. Wiping tables and cleaning floors. Sam and Hannah steal a kiss as they pack up leftovers for everyone to take home. Beau remembers John quoting the old proverb about many hands making light work every night after dinner. The memory warms Beau's heart.

Beau feels a steady hand on his shoulder. He turns to see Malik with two bottles of apple cider held by their necks in the older man's right hand. Malik conspiratorially tilts his head in the direction of the porch. Beau nods in understanding and the two men sneak out the back door and find seats in the wicker rocking chairs.

The porch is lit by an almost full moon and light spilling out from the windows inside. The back porch, mirroring the front, spans the entire back of the house. It is screened in and decorated with a cozy country feel. Cushions and blankets on every chair. Two small porch swings on opposite ends of the expanse. The porch feels like an extension of the home. Beau and Malik settle in their chairs. Malik draws a long sip as he takes in the moonlit land and rolling hills. Beau follows with his own swig of tangy, homemade cider.

"I can't believe how big Chloe is getting. She is turning into an independent and strong young lady." Malik shakes his head in wonder. "She reminds me so much of the girls when they were younger. Boy, you can't get anything passed her." He chuckles. "I tried to ask her about her last visit with Haddie. I ended up getting a history lesson about the White House. You may want to limit her time with her Uncle Jackson. I think he's trying to turn her into a child history prodigy." The two men laugh.

Beau rubs his chin. "I told Jackson the same thing last week. He sent Chloe two White House photography books and wrote notes in the margins. Chloe is the only person who loves hearing his random factoids. Five-year-olds and their endless questions are his dream audience."

They sit in silence for a few minutes. The sounds of fall filling the space. Malik looks at the young widow. "You really are doing a great job with her. Lizzie would be very proud of you. She's a blessed little girl."

"Thank you. That really means a lot to me. I couldn't have done it with without John and E. It was rough at first. They helped me come out of the fog. It's still hard. I don't want Chloe to miss out on any mom things. I ask myself, countless times a day, what would Lizzie do." Beau takes a long drink from his bottle and holds back the lump in his throat.

"It's admirable that you came here with Esther. Most people would have stayed in their comfort zone with their family."

"She tried to convince me to stay, but that was never an option. She has already lost Lizzie and John. I know she was trying to be stoic, but I don't think she would have recovered from losing Chloe. We're a team, the three of us."

"There is a bond when people suffer profound loss. No words need to be spoken, but the knowledge and morbid comradery are present. Others can imagine, but they don't know the demons intimately. Maryssa and Haddie walked that journey with me. You're right about Esther. She's comforted having you both with her."

Beau nods in acknowledgment.

"Every year, on Ruth's birthday, I still make her favorite dessert. I have a sweater of hers that she used to wear all the time. I never had the heart to wash it after she passed. I keep it in a box in my closet. I'm not embarrassed to say that I pull it out to smell it every once in a while. One time, I actually caught Maryssa holding it to her face. We both joked about the other breathing too much and threatening the lingering scent. I don't think that missing part ever goes away, but having a replica helps fill the void. Maryssa and Chloe are the spitting images of their mothers. A big part of Lizzie will always live in Chloe, and you, no matter where life takes either of you." The pause did not go unnoticed by Beau.

The creaking of the rocking chairs fills the air. Beau and Malik slowly finish their cider. Beau talks about the apartment he's finishing above the restaurant and the work on Ruthie's Terrazza. The conversation is easy and comfortable. Both men head inside when Nunnie Mary peeks her head outside to let them know dessert is on the table.

"Here I thought we were successful sneaking out here unnoticed. That woman knows everything," Malik muses.

"I'm learning that first-hand. She is always one step ahead of everyone else. I'm beginning to think it's a byproduct of running this clan."

Malik grins and nods in agreement.

Chapter 11

Esther

"Chloe, over here," Esther waves to Chloe from the other side of the school crosswalk.

Chloe crosses the street. She looks up and gives the briefest of smiles.

"Hi, Nona."

They walk to Esther's car, parked in the crowded school lot.

"Someone is unusually quiet today. Everything okay? Did something happen at school?" Esther takes Chloe's tiny hand in hers as they maneuver around people, cars, and busses.

"I don't want to talk about it." Her head stares at her feet, scuffing the pavement.

Esther helps Chloe climb into the backseat and fastens her seatbelt. While climbing in the driver's side, she catches a glimpse of Peggy Anderson, an old friend from high school. Esther watches as Peggy picks up and twirls a beautiful little girl in a circle. They both look stunning with their shiny blond hair and designer winter boots. Esther looks around to see if Wes is with Peggy picking up their granddaughter. A wave of envy washes over her. Wes Anderson. She hasn't thought about that name in years.

"Nona, did you hear me?" Chloe breaks the silence.

Esther shakes the cobwebs and starts the car. "I'm sorry, sweetheart, I didn't. What did you say?"

"I had to move my apple today because Jen Z. told the teacher I stole her headband from her backpack. I told her that I didn't want her stupid headband and that she probably lost it because she's stupid like her headband. Mrs. Evans asked us both to tell our stories, and Jen Z. lied to her and said she saw me take it, but I didn't take it. Then, Mercy came over and told Mrs. Evans that she saw Jen Z. hide it under her desk. So, the teacher made Jen Z. move her apple for lying, and I had to move my apple for calling her stupid. I had to sit on the benches forever at recess all because of Jen Z. and her dumb headband." Chloe sits in a huff in the backseat.

"Chloe Elizabeth Baker! We don't use mean words. You are lucky you only had to move your apple. I hope you apologized to Jen Z. and to your teacher." Esther quickly glances at Chloe in the rearview mirror.

"Nona, it's not my fault that she is stupid." Her arms are crossed tightly as she stares out the window. Her eyes are red and beginning to tear. "No one at my old school was mean like Jen Z.." The last words quivering a bit.

"I'm sorry, Chloe. I know moving to a new place can be hard, but you'll make friends. In the meantime, we don't call anyone stupid, okay?" *Even if they deserve it.* Esther makes a mental note to have Beau speak with Mrs. Evans about Jen Z, the bully of kindergarten.

Chloe fills Esther in on the rest of her day as they drive back to the farmhouse. The school's pizza is the best pizza Chloe has ever eaten, but the milk was warm, so she got a cup of water from the fountain. Mercy, as it turns out, goes to the same church as Nunnie Mary and is very nice. Lastly, and most importantly, the big slide is super fast, so Chloe has to be careful not to fall on her bottom at the bottom of the slide.

As they turn on the driveway, Jo's car passes them. She waves but doesn't pull over or roll down her window. Her face looks blotchy and red.

By the time Esther and Chloe walk in the house, they smell the sweet smell of Snickerdoodle cookies. The sounds of Nunnie and Sam talking in the kitchen trail behind the aroma of cinnamon. Chloe runs upstairs to change and get her favorite stuffed animal. Esther heads toward the voices.

"Are you two solving all the world's problems over cookies?" Esther quips as she unzips Chloe's backpack.

"Ah, here is the person we were waiting for. Maryssa just pulled these cookies out of the oven. Grab one while they're still warm." Nunnie places a plate on the round kitchen table.

"I passed Jo on the driveway when we were coming home. It looked like she had been crying. Did I miss anything?" Esther begins emptying the pink and purple bag.

Mary pulls out a chair to sit at the table. "It's Jo's story to tell. You'll need to ask her, but she did come by because she needs some help. She has to take some time off of work. She will need to be home for a few weeks, maybe a couple of months. Jo was hoping you could help Sam and cover for her at the warehouse a couple of days a week. She wanted to ask you herself, but she needed to get home before the school bus got to her house."

Esther stares at her mother and brother in disbelief. They certainly can't expect her to cover for Jo right now.

"We're working with our distributor to increase our market reach. We have a big launch this summer. The paperwork is extensive and time-consuming. Jo has it all under control, but then this happened." Sam finishes his mug of coffee. Worry lines etched his face. "She can work on the product launch from home, so we'll need help with the day to day paperwork that gets processed at the warehouse." He must sense Esther's fear because he continues, "It's not that much work, mostly filing and organizing, basic business math."

"I don't know. I have no idea what the business end of a vineyard looks like. Toward the end, I barely did anything at the restaurant either. I would probably be more of a nuisance than a help." Esther argues her case.

"Jo can train you. She's a whiz at the paperwork. We just need some extra hands on deck right now," Sam reasons with his older sister.

Esther begins shaking her head in defeat. "Isn't there anyone else who can help? I just don't know if I can do it right now."

Mary, unsure of how hard to push her daughter, attempts to seal the deal. "Well, your sister needs your help, and it will be good for you to get out a little instead of sitting here with me all day."

Mary pushed too hard, Esther bristles. "I'm sorry, mother. I didn't realize I was cramping your style. Why does Jo need to take off work anyway? Something wrong in her perfect life with her healthy husband and children?" Esther zips the backpack with a little more force than she expects.

Sam makes a defensive sound as he begins to explain, but Mary gently pats his arm. "Honey, go-ahead home. Esther can call or text you later with her decision."

Sam reads his mother's expression as she lets him know with a look that she'll deal with this. "Okay, Ma. Love you. Sis." He nods to his sister, kisses his mother, grabs his coat, and heads out the back door.

Mary studies her daughter for a moment before responding. "Dear one, this has nothing to do with me. I merely thought getting you out of the house around other people would be good for you. You need to start living again."

Mary holds up a hand as Esther attempts to protest. "You are surviving, there is a difference. As for Jo, I told you already, it is your sister's story to tell, but she came here to ask for help. We are family, and that's what we do. That is how Daddy and I were raised, and that is how we raised our family. As for your sister's *perfect* life, you of all people know that nothing is perfect. Maybe if you spent more time living with those around you, you would see beyond the tunnel where you have set up camp."

Esther stares at her mother, not sure whether to run or cry or yell. She pulls out a chair and sits.

Chloe races into the kitchen with Maryssa close behind her. "Hi, Nunnie. Did you already get your eggs from the hens today? If not, I can help but after I eat Maryssa's cookies."

"Sorry, sugar. I picked up the eggs this morning. I do want to check on Henrietta though. She seemed a little spooked. Maybe we can peek in on her later. How was your day at school?"

Esther sits quietly as Chloe recants Jen Z.'s accusations and explains the entire apple moving fiasco while devouring cookies and milk.

Mary hands Esther a cookie and rubs her back while Chloe tells them everything that happened in kindergarten today.

When there is finally a break in the conversation, Esther asks, "Mom, if I help Jo at the warehouse, will you be able to help with Chloe after school a couple of days?"

"We'll have to figure out our schedules. I'm signed up to help at the food pantry until after Christmas, but we'll make it work."

"I can help." Maryssa chimes.

"You're busy with the restaurant, Maryssa, you don't have time." Esther quickly responds.

"Not really. I can't even get into the kitchen area at all right now. Plus, Tony said the main dining area is off-limits for the next couple of weeks. Even then, I'm mostly in planning mode until more construction is completed. I can totally pitch in and help. Chloe and I can hang a couple days a week." She winks at the five-year-old who is excitedly bouncing in her chair at the idea.

"Are you sure?"

"Absolutely! It will give me something to do. Bonus for me, Chloe can work as my assistant taste tester."

"I guess I'm going back to work." Esther nervously sighs.

"It's settled!" Mary claps her hands and smiles, "Chloe, let's go check on Henrietta."

Esther's mind is a million miles away as she processes what transpired in her mother's kitchen. There aren't enough snickerdoodles to cover the empty feeling in Esther's stomach.

Chapter 12

Haddie & Maryssa

Maryssa tidies up her paperwork. She stands to stretch her aching shoulders and rolls her neck. Her eyes are exhausted from looking at spreadsheets and lists from suppliers. She will take a shower and try again later with fresh eyes. As she picks up the last paper from the makeshift desk in her bedroom, her phone begins ringing.

She immediately smiles as Haddie's face pops onto her screen

"Hey, Cuz! Wanna hear how my day is going?" Haddie cheerily chants into the phone.

"Hey, I'm glad you called. Between our busy schedules and missing our lunches with Dad, I barely recognize your voice." She pauses. "Wait a minute, you sound cheery, but that's not like you during finals week, so what's up?"

"Well, I was kicked out of PT school today. How is your day going?" Sarcasm dripping off of every syllable.

"WHAT?"

"You heard me correctly. I, Haddie Robinson Cashe. Overachiever and to-a-fault people pleaser was asked to not return to school next semester." Her voice is shaking now.

"Okay, slow down. Start from the beginning." Maryssa lays back on her bed, settling in for a long chat.

"So, did you see the news today?"

"I briefly saw a blurb about protestors, but I haven't had time to look. It seems par for the course with you guys, so I didn't worry."

"Well, this time, it was centered around my school. Apparently, the university hospital is doing some kind of cell testing. To be honest, I didn't even recognize what the protestors were against. Their signs didn't even match what they were chanting. Anyway, the PT school isn't involved in that area at all. I have no link to, nor any knowledge of what is happening. It is about one random study being conducted by some professor in the bio-science department."

"I still don't understand how something happening in the bio-science department has anything to do with you. Why are they protesting you then?" Maryssa is confused but now understands where Chloe gets her gift of telling dramatic stories.

"Exactly! I have no idea either, but it doesn't matter to the media vultures what they are protesting. It's like playing the game seven degrees of Haddie. If anything can be linked to me, they will find a way to link it. News outlets gave the protest prime coverage spots yesterday and today which added a level of attention the school was not expecting. It also intensified the attention directed at the university as a whole. They received bomb threats all day as well as pressure from parents and alumni donors. Now, it's an issue for me."

Maryssa rolls over and searches Haddie's name on the laptop lying next to her. "Whoop, there it is. Holy Toledo, Batman. This looks scary."

"I know. The dean. Let that sink in for a minute. The dean. The head of the School of Medicine called me during lunch yesterday and asked me to take off the afternoon until they could better assess the situation."

"Well, that doesn't sound like you are being kicked out, just a day or two off from class." Maryssa attempts to calm Haddie.

"Not in my world. In my new world, it means a lot more. You see, that's not the end of the story. He called this morning to tell me that I pose a safety concern for the entire university, specifically for the hospital. He went on to further explain they were already finding it difficult identifying a clinical placement that could meet my 'unique' security specifications."

"The dean sounds like a very serious, very uptight man." Maryssa chuckles.

"This is not funny."

"I'm sorry, you're right. What happened next?"

"We had to have a meeting. Everything involves a meeting around this dang place. Instead of talking about this with my husband, I had the entire United States government, up in my grill."

Unsuccessfully controlling laughter, "I'm sorry, but did you just say, 'up in my grill'?"

"Maryssa!"

"Okay, okay. I'm sorry. What happened at the meeting?"

"Obviously, I want to continue school and tell the press to bite me, but that isn't an option. If I continue school, I am a heartless witch who doesn't care about the safety of the faculty, staff, students, and patients. Not to mention, I will inadvertently be in support of any random study or research associated with the university as a whole. On the flip side, if I quit, I'm a weak woman who can't take the pressure of physical therapy school. Thus, killing everything women have fought for throughout history. There were multiple other arguments discussed, but those were the two most infuriating."

"Wow, women throughout history? I didn't realize you were so powerful." Maryssa pauses, trying to feel the weight of Haddie's dilemma. "You really can't win. No matter what you do, you will be either villainized or cheered. It truly is a lose-lose situation. Oh, Had, I'm so sorry. What did Jackson say during this meeting?"

"Well, at first he wanted to personally have the dean removed and thrown in jail. Rich, knowing Jackson well, asked the secretary to not make any outgoing calls until he or Madison gave the okay. Once Jackson calmed down and listened to them and his campaign director, we walked through other possible outcomes. He told me that it was completely my decision and that he would support whatever decision I made."

"I've always liked Jackson, even if I didn't vote for him last time." Maryssa holds the phone lovingly, wishing it was Haddie's hand. "So, what is the verdict?"

Maryssa pictures Haddie's sad but stoic face on the end of the phone. Her voice is resigned and sullen. "Since it's the end of the semester anyway, my professors are allowing me to take my finals remotely and record my grades. Effective immediately, I am taking a sabbatical from the program out of my deep concern for the safety of my colleagues and the university. I will begin full-time work as First Lady, focusing on the platforms of fighting cyberbullying along with championing sports and fitness education. Rich and his team are drafting the messaging. Now, I need to increase my staff to help with my *endeavors.* I can only imagine what that entails."

"I'm so sorry. I wish I had other words. More encouraging words. You probably should have called Nunnie instead of me. She always knows what to say."

"It's fine. I'm fine. I needed you to listen, and you did. At some point, I need to call my mom. I just don't want to give her one more thing to make her sadder. I'm worried about her concerns more than my disappointment. I need to call her and then study. I'll deal with the rest tomorrow."

"Hey Had," Maryssa draws Haddie out of her funk.

"What? You better not try to make me laugh again."

"I think we should add 'Bite Me' t-shirts to your clothing line. I'm picturing glitter and hot pink lips. You can design an entire line based on your daily outings. Lips wearing high heels and another pair with sneakers. Ooh, remember when you accidentally bumped into that news lady? You could make a pair of lips dressed in roller derby clothes."

The sound of laughter fills the void between them. Maryssa smiles, her work here is done.

Chapter 13

Beau

The air is unusually warm for December. Beau takes Chloe for a walk around the vineyard to gather wood for his gazebo project. The sun is stretching over the hillside, reaching it's rays out to prolong the day. Dusk is almost upon them. The wispy wind kisses their cheeks as the smell of pine needles fill their senses.

They walk hand in hand as Chloe tells him all about her day at school. Her friend Mercy is having a birthday party this weekend. Patrick laughed so hard over a joke that he spit chocolate milk out of his nose. Then the lunch teacher turned off the lights because they were too loud, so they lost five minutes off of recess. She is still not speaking to Jen Z, who is still, the meanest five-year-old alive. It seems kindergarten is a fascinating place.

Beau listens intently to every aspect of Chloe's day. He thinks about Lizzie and how she would have responded to Michael pushing Chloe on the playground. Beau wants to ask where this kid Michael lives, but he knew Lizzie would have had the right response.

Chloe's hand clenches his tighter as the sky darkens into dusk. Nature plays a symphony as they walk. The air smells so sweet. The cold ground crunches underneath each footstep. It was taking a while for Beau to adjust to the cold weather of his new home, but the beauty around him makes it worth the extra layers.

As they get closer to the farmhouse, Beau can sense Chloe's quietness. He stops and kneels down to face her. "Everything okay, princess?" Chloe lowers her head. He lifts it back up with his finger. "Your Mama used to always tell me that we face things together. That's what we do in our family. Whatever you need to say, say it. We'll deal with it together. Now, tell me what's got you so quiet all of a sudden."

Tears start forming in the corners of her blue eyes. "Daddy, does it mean I don't love Mama if I can't remember her?"

"Why would you say that, sweetheart?" Beau wipes her cheeks with his hand.

"Well, Jen Z. asked me why my mom never comes to school. She said she didn't think I had a Mama at all. I told her that my Mama is in Heaven, and then she asked me questions about Mama. When I didn't know the answers, she told me that I couldn't love her if I didn't even know her. I got so mad at her. I wanted to push her but then I remembered how I felt when Michael did it to me, and I didn't want to move my apple again. So, I just told her to mind her own business, and then I walked away." Beau's heart is breaking at the frustration emanating from his little girl. "It makes me mad that I don't know about Mama. I still love her, right?" Chloe looks up at her dad for the answer she needs.

Beau holds back tears of his own now. He places a hand on the side of Chloe's tiny face. "Of course you love your Mama. You will always love her. God just needed her in Heaven first, but He left part of her heart right here and right here." He points to her heart and his with his finger before wrapping her hands in his. He stares at his daughter for a long moment and sees Lizzie in her. He wishes so badly that he could trade places with Lizzie so that Chloe could have her Mama and Lizzie could be the mom he always knew she would be.

The moment stretches between them as Chloe searches her Daddy for more answers. "I'll tell you what, maybe it would help if we remembered stories about your Mama so you could know her better. I'm sure Nona, Nunnie, and Maryssa have plenty of stories too. Even better, I bet Nona will pull out her old photo albums. Now, what do you want to know about Mama most?"

"How did you meet Mama?" Chloe wipes her eyes and waits for his words to fill her heart.

Beau stands up and starts walking again with her hand in his. "Oh, that's a good one." He laughs at the memory. "You see, your Mama was one independent lady. She didn't suffer fools easily. I saw your Mama in one of my classes. I had to work up the nerve to talk to her because she was just so beautiful. I would sit near her on the lawn outside the student union, just trying to get her attention. I was determined to get her to talk to me, and she was determined not to."

"That's silly, Daddy. You are fun to talk to." Chloe giggles.

He smiles down at her. "Well, one day, I noticed something on her shoe as she was walking the hall to class. I tried to get her attention. I called out to her, 'Excuse me, miss,' but she wouldn't turn. I tried again using her name this name, 'Elizabeth,' but she kept walking. Finally, after the third time, she turned around and faced me. I had to catch my breath because she was so pretty. She looked me right in the eye and said, 'Look I don't want to hurt your feelings, but I'm focused on my education, and I don't have time to be hit on walking to class.'"

Beau laughs to himself at the memory. "Boy, she turned back around and started walking off, but I yelled after her, 'Thanks for telling me all that, but I just wanted to let you know that you have toilet paper on the back of your shoe.' I'm not sure if she turned back or not because I kept walking the other way to class. The next day, she came over to apologize. Somehow by the grace of God, she thought I was charming and funny. We started walking to class together and studying in the library. I used to write her corny notes and jokes on little pieces of paper and pass them to her. She'd start laughing and get us both yelled at by the librarian." Beau looks down at Chloe, who is smiling now.

"That's a funny story, Daddy. Good thing for that toilet paper." She belly laughs.

The two of them walk hand in hand as he tells her more stories about Lizzie. As they walk into the farmhouse, Beau fills Maryssa and Esther in about Jen Z. and asks if they have any stories to share about Lizzie.

Maryssa offers Beau a compassionate smile. She then takes Chloe's hand and starts pulling her into the family room. "Ooh, let me show you my favorite pictures from when we were younger. Your mama was older than Auntie Haddie and me so she used to talk us into playing maid all the time. She would be the queen, and the two of us had to wait on her."

Beau and Esther listen as Maryssa walks the little girl down the hallway and tells her stories. The heaviness of what just happened hits Beau like a ton of bricks. He sits down at the table and holds his head up with his hands. Esther comes up and places a hand on his back.

"Beau Baker, you are a good dad." She leans down and kisses the top of his head before she walks down the hallway to look at pictures and tell stories about her daughter.

Winter

Chapter 14

Haddie & Jackson

Travis walks into the room first. The entire house has been under siege by men in dark suits all week, but Travis's arrival signals a shift in the atmosphere. Chloe runs up to the man and hugs his leg. It's obvious he tries hard not to get on the ground and start playing with her. "Travis? Are you still keeping Auntie Haddie and Uncle Jackson safe from bad guys?" She asks with all seriousness.

"Of course I am, Miss Chloe. Are you still working hard in school so you can be a special agent like me?"

"Yes! I've decided to be a ballerina too. Can I be both? Maryssa says I can be both."

"Miss Chloe, you will make the best ballerina agent ever known." Smiling, Travis shifts away from the door before speaking into an invisible microphone. "All clear."

Haddie and Jackson climb out of a dark SUV and ascend the stairs of the farmhouse. Haddie taking them two at a time while Jackson's smiling eyes follow her the entire way. Haddie bursts into the room and quickly picks up Chloe. She swings the little girl around in circles. "I've missed you so much! I'm going to spend the entire day kissing you to pieces!" Haddie places kisses all over Chloe's face as the little girl squeals in delighted laughter.

"Good gracious Haddie Marie. I thought we were filming a blockbuster action-adventure movie with all of these men in dark suits and earpieces." Nunnie laughs as she tries to hug Haddie while the woman's arms are still wrapped around Chloe. She then reaches for Jackson but pulls back to look at Travis first. "Do I need a pat-down before hugging my new grandson?"

Laughter fills the family room. "Don't worry, we've already warned the agents to watch out for you. If you're not careful, I may add your name to America's Most Wanted." Jackson jokes as he leans in to hug the petite octogenarian.

"You're lucky we're here at all, Nunnie. We had to drive to Camp David then sneak off the property in the back of a catering van. I felt like I was on another reality TV show again, hiding from the paparazzi." Haddie shakes her head.

"As far as the American people are concerned, we're having a cozy Christmas on American soil. Maddie and Rich were concerned that Christmas in a foreign country wouldn't look good right now. It's still ridiculous to think that West Virginia is a different country. Of course, my entire life feels ridiculous these days, so I'm not the best judge." Haddie hugs Chloe once more in an attempt to forget her life as First Lady over the holidays.

Jackson, sensing the need for a change of perspective, wraps his arm around Esther and kisses her on the cheek. "I heard my favorite mother-in-law made some of her famous gingerbread man cookies. How can I get some of those?" The room clears of secret service agents as they all maneuver and settle into the kitchen where Nunnie has Christmas cookies and hot water ready for tea and cocoa. Chloe sits on Haddie's lap while propping her legs up on her uncle, oblivious to the fact that he is the leader of the free world.

Jackson finishes his first lemon cookie and reaches for a galette. "So, Haddie keeps trying to warn me about Christmas Eve dinner. Should I be worried?"

"No," voices sing in chorus.

"Malik gave me some suggestions and advice, but I'm not sure I should believe him. He had a sly smile on his face the entire time he talked about it. He told me the safest seat in the house is right in the middle of the table. Is that true? Haddie laughed when I told her, which worries me." Jackson asks in all seriousness.

"From my experience, you don't have a choice." Beau's voice booms from down the hallway. Fresh from the shower, his large frame walks into the kitchen. He places a hand on Jackson's shoulder, stopping the man from rising out of his seat. "Please, sit. I don't want Chloe mad at you or me for making her footrest move." He chortles as he leans down to place a kiss on Haddie's cheek. Resting his hands over the back of the chair and on her shoulders. "Now, back to your question. It's like a hazing ritual. No matter how far away from the center you try to sit, you'll be jostled around until you're plumb in the middle of the table."

"That sounds ominous. Why the middle? Is it the spotlight seat? Will they gang up on me and ask questions or grill me about my life?" Jackson chokes out laughter while asking.

"Worse." Beau grabs a cookie from the table. "The middle of the table is ground zero for serving. They want to watch you pass, fill, and distribute food for everyone at the table at breakneck speeds. You're the last to eat because you have to scoop out food as every plate passes you." Beau chuckles at the memory. "Your good friend Malik is the worst, which is funny because he should be compassionate, being an 'out-law' himself at one time. The first time I ate dinner with the family in Charleston, he gave me a dinner fork to scoop out spaghetti. I had spaghetti everywhere, including my shoe."

"Note to self, find an end chair before everyone sits down for dinner," Jackson says out loud. His statement is met with more laughter.

"Good luck with that one." Beau winks at Haddie, who is enjoying the banter at her husband's expense.

Stories and laughter fill the kitchen as aunts, uncles, and cousins straggle in throughout the day. A traditional Christmas Eve feast is constructed with all-hands-on-deck. It is an all-day cooking extravaganza.

Malik arrives with his new friend Victoria, and they pitch in as well. Wine bottles are opened. Music pipes in through old-fashioned stereo speakers. Everyone snacks on cheese and crackers, prosciutto, Calamata olives, and bruschetta. After four slices of bruschetta, Haddie warns Jackson not to ruin his dinner. He responds by telling her he can die happily now after eating the savory piece of Heaven. He moves onto the olives before being placed in charge of helping the kids set the table.

"So, we're only eating fish tonight?" He whispers in Haddie's ear. "No Nunnie Mary's famous meatballs? No lasagna from Malik?" Haddie giggles and shakes her head no.

"Christmas Eve is the Feast of the Seven Fishes. We only eat fish on Christmas Eve. You must have a bite of every single fish, even the smelts." Haddie warns, the last word in a hushed tone. She shushes him before he gets out another word. "Before you recite the history and origin you researched in preparation for this weekend, make sure you take time to enjoy it too." She kisses him on the nose and walks back into the kitchen.

As Jackson finishes setting the last piece of silverware with Chloe, Nunnie Mary begins directing the food to the table. Fried shrimp, baked cod, salmon, spaghetti with fish sauce, calamari, broiled scallops, and breaded smelts cover the table. Baskets of fresh Italian bread from the local bakery sit on opposite ends of the table. Bowls of salad sit in the middle of every plate. Bottles of red and white wines line the table.

The long farmhouse table has benches, allowing the table settings to be close enough to fit the entire brood. The aroma is intoxicating. The presentation, mouthwatering. Jackson is sent into the kitchen to fetch Nunnie Mary's special chair for the head of the table. When he returns, the only open spot at the table is dead center, directly in front of a bowl containing three pounds of spaghetti....with only a fork to scoop out the pasta. Jackson's head falls in defeat as the entire table erupts with joyous and raucous mirth.

Chapter 15

Haddie

"Had, pass me the sugar, please." Maryssa blows a wispy brown curl out of her face as she beats eggs and vanilla together in a bowl. Haddie adds the cup of sugar in as her cousin mixes the wet ingredients together. She then begins to pack brown sugar into the measuring cup before Maryssa even asks. The pair snickers at their mind-reading ability for each other.

Haddie and Maryssa revel in some quality baking time while Malik and Uncle Sam give Jackson a tour of the property. Ingredients line the counter of the farmhouse kitchen. Sunshine streaming in through the windows and reflecting off of the pale yellow walls. Christmas music wafts in from the family room where Nunnie, Esther, and Victoria are playing cards with Chloe.

"I really miss this." Haddie waves her hand around the kitchen at the mess they've made. "The two of us baking and talking. It has been so surreal going from our little apartment straight to the White House. Sometimes I still feel like I'm watching a Hallmark movie about someone else's life."

"Ha! In your case, it would be a Lifetime movie based on the assassination attempt and the cattiness of the *Future FLOTUS?* contestants. That cheerleader was vicious. She even pushed that one girl down a flight of stairs and blamed it on alcohol." Maryssa shakes her head.

"You mean the reality show *you* signed me up for without my consent?" Haddie stares back at her.

"Oh, you can't throw that back at me anymore, '*current FLOTUS*.' That argument became null and void the second you got married." Maryssa winks at Haddie with a big Cheshire grin. "You are officially welcome, by the way."

"I suppose you're right. Besides, not all of the contestants were catty. Annie actually stays at the White House one weekend a month to meet with Jackson, Madison, and Rich. We have so much fun when she works in DC. We're trying to plan a girls' trip over the summer with Priscilla and Rachelle. The other contestants were definitely colorful."

"Whatever happened to the wackadoo who freaked out and destroyed the bed and breakfast when Jackson sent her the veto roses?"

"Suzanne? You won't believe it. She was fired from her law firm after making a fool of herself. She then checked into an anger management rehabilitation center. Apparently, she is a completely different person. Annie heard she is teaching yoga in Colorado now."

"Ha! I'll believe it when I see it. She was crazy with a capital C. She wasn't even the worst one." Maryssa licks her finger while laughing.

"Sadly, the cattiness of the other contestants is nothing compared to the press. Good gracious. They are so malicious. They could tell me to wear a potato sack because it's fashionable then turn around and ridicule me for doing exactly that." Haddie throws the towel down in disgust. "I'm so frustrated with this whole mess. I knew I would be giving up my privacy, but I never thought people would be so mean." Haddie sits at the table and holds her head up with one hand. Her thick, curly, brown ponytail swaying behind her head.

"It's easy to say mean things when you're hiding behind your computer or phone. It's worse when they do it on television. They would never walk up to me in normal conversation and say those things. We grew up on the front end of this technology generation when you still had to be accountable for your actions. Now, everyone has a platform. It seems the louder and meaner they are, the more they're liked. I just can't win." Haddie sighs in despair.

Maryssa places the bowl on the table and pushes it toward Haddie as she sits. She starts rolling cookie dough before dipping the balls in sugar. "I remember how hard it was to read reviews about our shows in the newspaper. There was that one critic who moved from Quebec to DC and constantly compared our company with Canadian ballerinas. Remember him?"

Haddie nods.

"What prima was it who torched the Post onstage after that guy called her 'too stiff'?"

Haddie laughs. "I totally forgot about that. It was Stefania. The best part was that she was from Toronto. That was hilarious." Both women double over in laughter at the memory.

Maryssa attempts to speak while still laughing. "Maybe that can be another one of your platforms. You can kick start it by having a 'burn' party in the rose garden. You can burn all the newspapers and then sledgehammer all your electronics. You would definitely make a statement."

Still laughing, Haddie replies, "I'd probably wear the wrong shoes and have to do it again the next day." Tears start streaming down her face. What would one wear to a burn party? Sequins or no? Heels, flats, or gasp, tennis shoes?"

Nunnie walks into the room and sees her granddaughters in hysterics. "Either you slipped something into those cookies, or I'm missing out on a pretty good joke." She bends down to sniff the cookie dough then heads to the counter to refill her coffee mug. "The cookies smell fine, it must be the joke. I heard something about burning, parties, and clothing. Is Haddie moving forward with our cave clothes fashion line or are you two are planning some kind of coup?" She takes a seat at the table and begins unwrapping peanut butter cups for the cookies after popping the first one in her mouth.

"Not a coup, Nunnie. Just a little fun tangent. We remembered when critics would review National Ballet Ensemble performances. I never thought I would miss having a bad review once in a while. Now, I have them daily. At least the Ensemble choreographed my moves and costumes. Now, I feel like I'm flying blind. I'm just tired." Haddie wipes the leftover tears from laughter off her cheeks as she rolls another peanut butter ball.

Nunnie places her hand on top of Haddie's and turns the woman's face toward her. "My sweet girl, you can't allow others to change you. Those who are rooting for you to fail, don't care about your efforts and they'll never see them in the light of day. They'll only always find the flaws in the dark, but you see, the flaws are beauty marks that can shine in the light. Both of you were created for a greater purpose and were made as pretty, as smart, as wise, as talented, and as graceful as you need to be to do what He needs you to do. If you're too busy being someone else, the world will miss out on the beauty that is you."

"Nunnie, how did you become so wise?" Maryssa wipes her own eyes now.

"A long life filled with deserts and streams and a lot of time on my knees looking up. I learned to look for the beauty in both the barren and the abundant. Now, Miss Haddie. I want you to do something for me. You are going to read and write out on a piece of paper Matthew, chapter six, verses twenty-eight through thirty-three. You are going to keep that passage in your pocket and read it every time you need it." Nunnie unwraps another peanut butter cup. "Life is a journey. It's your choice whether you look down to watch out for puddles or look up to see the rainbows and feel the sun on your face."

Maryssa and Haddie gaze open-mouthed at their grandmother and marvel at her wisdom. The older woman snaps her fingers. "Let's go ladies. If you don't get those cookies in the oven soon, I'm going to eat all of your peanut butter cups."

Chapter 16

Malik

A light blanket of snow covers the land. Sunshine glistens off of the snow crystals as they begin to melt into the grass. The air smells of winter and pine. The truck pulls to the highest part of the property. The men climb out to get a bird's eye view of the vineyard. "This is spectacular!" Jackson marvels at the sight before him.

"Ma wanted this to be the spot where the house was built so she could see Heaven every morning, but Daddy told her that waking up next to him would bring the same effect." Uncle Sam laughs as he crosses his arms and leans against the pickup truck.

"I'm with Mary. This seems the perfect place to build a house." Jackson takes in the expanse in awe.

"Dad never said why. Dom thinks it's because he didn't want to spend money building a road all the way up here. I think he didn't want to count his chickens before they hatched. The vineyard was a dream. He was probably afraid it could burst at any time. You know, waiting for someone to pinch him from a dream. Didn't want to tempt the demons, as he would say." Sam rubs his chin.

"I'm surprised your mother didn't win." Malik chuckles as he rubs his hand over his face. "I've seen the way that man used to look at her."

Sam's smile stretches across his face. "That is very true. I think he changed her mind with the promise of both the barn and the pavilion by the lake to win her over to his plan. He definitely knew her well."

"I think it may have been the front porch swing." Beau offers. "Since we moved in, I've seen her sit on that swing at least once a day, rain or shine. Chloe sits out there with her after school. Chloe colors while Mary reads her Bible."

Silence envelopes them as they stare out over the land. Malik thinks back to all the family memories in that pavilion. Baptisms in the lake. Birthday parties. Graduations. Weddings. His own wedding. Mary and Sam would light up a dance floor. The way they moved together around the floor looked like a scene from a Fred Astaire movie. He and Ruth took ballroom dance lessons for months before their wedding trying to pull off a great dance. The classes didn't help. He ended up losing count and tripping over her train. It was evident that Maryssa got her graceful, gift for dance from her mother. There is something about being here on the farm and thinking about Ruth while his fiancé is back at the farmhouse with Ruth's family. Malik is overcome with feeling, of being accepted and loved as one of their own. He pulls out a handkerchief and dabs at his nose, trying to play it off as allergies.

"It gets me every time too, brother. Every, dang, time." Sam pats Malik on the back and walks around to open and pull down the tailgate on his truck. He pulls out a bottle of wine and four plastic cups. He pours the wine and passes them out to the other three men. "This is our newest wine. It will launch a family of wine made with a hint of hops. I don't know if I've ever been this excited about a release. This is my curtain call. I saved the best creation for retirement. Now, it's all up to Sammy and Maryssa to carry on the tradition."

The cups are raised in salute. Travis, who has been following from a distance, walks briskly toward the men. Jackson holds out his hand to stop him. "I think I'm fine, Travis. I'm pretty sure Haddie's two uncles haven't tricked me up here to poison my wine." Both Malik and Sam respond by offering ornery shrugs of their shoulders as if they're still trying to decide. "It seems that Beau has passed the test, I'm sure he can give me pointers."

Sam hands Beau a bench to sit upon, then hops up to sit on the tailgate. Malik follows in turn. Jackson leans back against the edge, in between the others. They each enjoy the scenery and the crisp taste of hops in the white wine.

"This is what I remember. Drinking wine from whatever cup was clean, and sometimes that didn't even matter." A wistful sigh escapes Sam's lips. "Before the fancy wine tastings and special glasses. Back when we could just enjoy the wine without all the steps. When it was Dad, Dom, and me with ladles out of a barrel." He pauses for a minute and takes another drink. "Don't get me wrong, I have grown to appreciate the beauty of winemaking, but sometimes I miss the simplicity of picking the berries behind our house and lugging them to Dad's cellar."

"Ah, those were good days. I loved blackberry season because I knew what came out of those beautiful fruits." Malik sighs.

"Malik, remember using that tin funnel to fill our own bottles by hand? We used masking tape to label the bottles and batches. Now, we have labels that are winning awards and being shipped all over the country, thanks to our distributor. Poppy's is already getting a buzz, and Maryssa is still two months from launching. The Vineyard is becoming her own brand. We've come a long way from Dad's cellar."

It's Malik's turn to reminisce. "I remember the funnel and that cellar well. Your sisters were the only ones your Dad would let write on the tape. He said our handwriting was worse than a baby." He laughs. "I'll tell you one thing I don't miss, that ridiculous stuffed snake. Who on earth has a snake stuffed?"

Sam laughs so hard, he almost spits out his wine. It's so infectious that Jackson starts laughing before hearing the story. Curiosity covering his face.

"Your sister didn't tell me about that thing, knowing that I'm terrified of snakes. I thought she was just trying to get fresh with me, she kept leaning closer, nudging me into the corner of the cellar. I looked up and Bam! Red eyes and fangs. I screamed, hit my head on the shelf, threw Ruth over my shoulder then ran. I have never run so fast in my life. She laughed the whole time."

The men are all laughing so hard that the truck shakes. Sam is doubled over holding his stomach. "That was great! I still remember you running down the driveway with one arm whirling around like a helicopter that could lift off at any moment. Ruth was holding on for dear life and laughing hysterically at the same time. That's when we knew you were all right. If you had left Ruth behind, you wouldn't have been back, that's for sure."

Beau breaks into the story. His own laughter causing his face to flush red all over. "That story is so legendary even John used to tell it. Anytime he heard someone mention they were scared of snakes, he would tell everyone about his brother-in-law Malik."

"And he wasn't even there when it happened! That is one epic story." Sam is all-out crying at this point.

"I thought I was a goner. I still have nightmares about that thing." Malik starts to pull himself back together from the laughter. "I was so mad at Ruth. It took months before I would go back into that cellar. When I finally did go back in, I stayed on the exact opposite side with a shovel in my hands." A few last hearty laughs escape the man.

"Your dad was a hoot. Laughter was never something lacking in this family. John and I loved hearing the girls tell stories from growing up. They had us in stitches with every story. I have to say, it's strange being on the farm without John."

As the quiet begins to descend again, Sam raises his cup in the air. "To John. A great man. A great father. A great husband and a dear brother. May he be drinking wine with the Father in Heaven!" A round of "Salute" follows and cups are finished.

Chapter 17

Esther

Maryssa drives Esther, Nunnie, and Chloe over to the barn in the dark. Mary holds a plate of lasagna in one hand and a bag of chocolate-covered biscotti in the other. The back road is bumpy coming from the house. With every jostle of her car, Maryssa mentions how grateful she is that the main road to Poppy's is paved. Chloe can't stop talking about her new room and how wonderful her Daddy is for building her a loft bed that looks like a castle. The little princess jumps out of her seat the second Maryssa turns off the engine. The three women follow behind as Chloe quickly ascends the outside stairs leading to her new home with Beau.

The lights are all on as the door swings open. Country music floats out of Beau's phone docked in speakers. The room has a woodsy, mossy, fresh mint scent. It is rugged and refreshing. The apartment is a simple, open area. The small kitchenette has enough space for a petite, square table. The living room blends right into the kitchen space with plenty of room for a leather couch and recliner. A sturdy, potbelly stove in the corner gives the room a country cabin feel to it.

The women glance around to explore the space. There is a quaint bathroom situated in the center on the opposite wall, two open doors on either side. The room on the left is clearly a man's bedroom. Gray walls, a navy plaid comforter on the bed. The other bedroom is brightly hued in light pink and lavender walls. The princess castle visible from the door.

"Chloe, which room is yours?" Maryssa asks the little girl, who is already halfway up the ladder of her bed.

"This one, silly!" Little girl giggles fill the entire space. She begins to bounce on the mattress as Esther carries in a bag with Chloe's bedding and stuffed animals. "Daddy can't fit in my castle. He's too big. He'll hit his head." More giggles, which are contagious.

Beau finishes tightening the screw on the curtain rod. He watches Chloe's face beam with happiness. "Daddy, you did a good job." She jumps off the bed and runs over to wrap her arms around his legs.

"I'm glad you like it G-dub," using the nickname Beau gave her when she was a baby.

Maryssa laughs, "What did you call her?"

"G-dub. Daddy said when I was a baby, I was super wiggly and giggly, so he started calling me giggly wiggly, that was too long so he called me GW then G-dub. He's very silly." Chloe giggles and her dimples deepen. He entire face glows when she laughs.

"Now that is the coolest nickname I think I've ever heard. Your Aunt Haddie and I used to call your Mama Lizzie Lizzard, but she didn't like that one bit." Maryssa shakes her head. "We thought it was funny until she started calling us Tweedle Dee and Tweedle Dum. We called a truce and banned nicknames forever, but we never would have done that if we had cool nicknames like you. Your Dad did a good job on that too."

"Lizzie Lizzard? That's funny." The little girl giggles again as she helps her grandmother pull out her sheets and comforter from the bag. The three women begin making Chloe's bed and putting away clothes in her dresser. Nunnie hands Beau the food. "Go eat before it gets cold. Let us help while we're here." She pats his shoulder as he walks past her to the kitchen table.

"Uncle Jackson promised to play princesses with me. Do you think Travis will too?" Chloe looks up and asks.

Nunnie coughs out a chuckle. "Who could say no to you?" She turns to the other two and quietly says, "If that happens, we need to record it. The press would pay good money for that."

"Mother!" Esther swats her mother's arm as she laughs.

Chloe keeps talking while the women work. She tells them about school and how she wants to learn to play football because Michael said girls couldn't play and she wants to prove him wrong. Then she switches gears to talk about how all the girls take dance, and she wants to take dance. She follows this up with a twirl and a bow.

Nunnie looks at Esther and is thinking about something. "You know, I think a friend of yours from high school owns a dance studio in town. She owns it with her daughter. Peggy Anderson, isn't that her name? You should call her and see if Chloe can take some ballet classes."

Esther stiffens at the name. "I actually saw her a few weeks ago when I was picking up Chloe. I had forgotten she was a dancer. She married Wes Anderson exactly *four months* after graduation if I recall. It was a quickly planned wedding."

Esther knows precisely how much time had passed, even after all these years. She moved to South Carolina on the day Peggy and Wes married. Esther drove directly to the bus station after sitting outside of the church. It seems she returned home in the same fashion in which she left, in tears.

Mary turns to Chloe and Maryssa while faking a whisper, "Wes Anderson was your grandmother's first love."

"Oooohhh, Aunt E."

"That was a lifetime ago. I hardly remember him." Esther playfully swats her mother attempting to change the subject off of Wes. "Chloe, would you like to take dance lessons? I can call the studio."

Chloe squeals and jumps up and down. "Yes! Yes! Yes! Then I can be a ballerina like Aunt Haddie and Maryssa! I need ballet shoes and a pretty pink ballet outfit too."

The three women watch the beautiful little girl as her brown ringlets bounce up and down around her face. Chloe stops bouncing, "Was my Mama a ballerina?"

Esther laughs out loud before responding. "No. Your Mama used to kick soccer balls around your Aunt Haddie's practice space. In fact, your grandpa had to put a strip of tape across the basement floor. He called one side swan lake and the other soccer land. If a soccer ball, leg, or arm crossed the line, the guilty party had to do the other's chores for the week. Nope, Lizzie was all about soccer, not dance."

Noticing Chloe's frown, Esther quickly recovers. "Haddie used to always tell your Mama that learning ballet would make her a better soccer player. Maybe you can take ballet and then play soccer in the spring. No one said you can't do both."

Chloe's smile returns. "I like that idea. I can be both." More dancing and twirling fill the space, but now they are accompanied by mock soccer kicks.

Esther is sure Lizzie would have tried to play football too if a boy told her she couldn't. Chloe would be just fine. She would chart her own journey through life. Just like her mother did.

Once the room is finished, they all stand back and look at the finished product. Chloe reaches for Esther's hand. "Nona, do you think my Mama would have liked this room? I know Grandpa would have liked it. He said princess was his favorite color." She snickers, covers her mouth with her hand, and whispers to Maryssa and Nunnie. "He was silly, princess isn't a color, but he said it was the color of sparkles and pinks and purples and any color that little girls like. He was very silly, like my Daddy."

Esther wipes away a stray tear before Chloe can see. "I think your Mama would have absolutely loved this room. I think princess was her favorite color too."

Maryssa notices Beau standing behind them in the doorway, a look of wistfulness in his eyes. He places a hand on his mother-in-law's shoulder. Maryssa looks at Chloe and asks if she wants to learn a few ballet moves. The two head for the open living room giving Beau and Esther time to grieve Lizzie and John.

***

Esther pulls out the calculator for the third time to add the last row of numbers. She opens the file folder again to double-check the column totals. Tapping her pencil on the desk, she looks around for another file folder, hoping she can find the missing link without disturbing Jo, again.

Esther works at the Rafaluzza Vineyard warehouse three days a week. Jo pops in a couple of times a week to help and make sure everything is on track with the launch paperwork. Jo spends a lot of time at home but is always available when E calls with a question.

The office is simple yet classic. Hannah decorated the space above the warehouse for Sam, Dom, and Jo. They have three other staff employees who help with the administration side of the vineyard, along with Sammy, DJ, and Frankie. The three Marchio children have office space along one wall with windows overlooking the vineyard. A conference room and kitchenette with a bathroom flank an open area with desks for their office team. Sammy is anxiously awaiting the official move into his dad's office soon.

Esther uses a desk right outside of Jo's office. The walls are a neutral shade of gray. They are lined with large prints taken of the vineyard and replicas of their labels. Hannah did an excellent job of mixing elegant with the warehouse vibe. Their office space sits atop the hub of activity. Below them lies a crush pad, destemmer, conveyor belts, fermenting tanks, along with various barrels and machinery. Esther is in awe of her siblings and how they have grown the family business.

Jo is the baby of the family. Mary used to call her the cherry-on-top baby until the other kids argued over who was the whipped cream and who was just plain nuts. Esther and Ruth were in high school when Jo was born and off to South Carolina as she entered elementary school. Jo grew up a tomboy, toted around by her two brothers. Jo told everyone she joined a sorority in college so she could know what it felt like to have sisters.

Watching Jo these past few months, Esther has realized how much she missed out on by living nine hours away from her family. Jo is a force. Always moving, organized, a little scattered brained but focused on her tasks. She manages kids and a household, works at the vineyard, volunteers for a national women's group, and still manages to get everyone to church and school on time. Esther is amazed by her little sister but actually knows her very little.

Jo spent the first week training Esther on the business and how everything works. Sam pitched in on the days Jo couldn't get to the office. Esther has mostly been working on inventory and sales projections. She has been able to keep up with the day to day paperwork, and some of the launch details but it's evident that Jo typically runs the show.

No one really talks about why Jo is spending so much time at home. Esther had been in her own world grieving and never felt comfortable prying into Jo's business once she started to reemerge into the land of the living. Their relationship is good but strained. They're more like work acquaintances than sisters. In fact, some of the women at work know more about Jo than E does, which makes her even more uncomfortable and sad.

Esther picks up the report she's been looking at for the past twenty minutes and walks into Jo's office. "I know you need to leave soon, but I just can't get these numbers to make sense." Esther offers the paper to her sister with a hopeful expression. "I know I'm missing something, but I can't seem to figure out what's causing the gap."

Jo takes the report and glances over the numbers quickly. With her pencil, she circles two line-items and hands it back to E. "I forget these two all the time. You need to add this year's and last year's numbers for it to work. You should be able to find the numbers you need in the file cabinet with last year's report." Jo smiles at E., "I should have told you. One more example of me getting into a routine and forgetting to share the details. Sorry E."

"That makes more sense. I should have thought of that." Esther looks over the paperwork with awareness now. "I'm sorry to bother you, I know you're in a rush today."

Esther pauses before leaving, contemplating. Hoping to extend an olive branch or open a door, Esther attempts to learn more about her sister. "Sam said you could only come in for a few minutes today, do you have plans?"

"Yeah, I have an appointment with Matty's doctor. This guy makes us sit in the waiting room for an hour sometimes, but if *we* are five minutes late, we have to reschedule." Jo offers a sad chuckle.

"Is everything okay with Matty? I heard that you are homeschooling him now and you've been driving to Morgantown a lot for doctor appointments. Is it serious?" Esther leans on the cluttered yet systematized desk, trying to build a bridge.

Jo searches her sister's face, warily, "It's nothing serious, medically. We're just trying to figure out what's going on with him. Some things were happening at school and at home. We had to pull him out so he could get the treatments he needs. The school was not cooperating."

"Is it the ADHD?"

"That is part of it. We think there may be some other neurological issues. We keep hitting walls with a diagnosis and finding people who will actually listen. There aren't many specialists who understand and treat these types of issues.

It's been rough. This doctor is supposedly one of the best in the region, so we're hopeful."

Esther places a hand on Jo's. The movement surprises them both. "I'm sorry I haven't been here for you, Jo. I can't imagine how frustrating it must be for you and Matt. At least when Lizzie was sick, we could trust the doctors. It doesn't seem like you have that."

A tear forms in Jo's hazel eyes. She brushes it away before it leaks. "It's been an interesting journey, that's for sure."

"Please let me know if I can help. I haven't been myself lately, but I'm sure we can muddle our way through things together."

Jo squeezes E's hand. "Thank you, E. That really means a lot to me. Sometimes I just feel like I'm trying to survive the day. Running here and there and keeping up with the kids and all the appointments. Learning to homeschool at the same time, I've been in my own bubble."

"Maybe we should merge bubbles." Esther laughs, wiping her own straggling tear.

"I'd like that."

A gesture, small as it was, profoundly moves both women. Years of separation, physical and emotional, begin shifting toward a place of healing. While the stolen moment is fleeting, it carries a promise. Sam's voice nearing from the hallway breaks their moment. The women collect themselves as they survey their surroundings.

Jo stands up when she notices the time. "Oh my. I need to go, but I'll have my phone if you can't find last year's files." She picks up her purse, phone, and keys before hugging her long-lost sister and runs out the door.

Sam peaks his head into Jo's office. "I'm not paying you to gab and stand around, you know." His faux bravado is followed by a wink.

"You're not paying me at all, darling brother. Speaking of which." Esther's voice trails off as Sam backs out of the office with a grin and a spin.

Chapter 18

Beau

The heat in the truck is coming out on full blast. The windows fog up around the edges. The radio is cranked up all the way to hear the weather forecast over the heater. There is no surprise when the voice out of the stereo announces a deep freeze impacting the entire northeast. The genius coming from the speakers encourages everyone to stay indoors for the next two days until the temperature rises above ten degrees. Being a southern-born boy, this weather is a shock to Beau's system. Thankfully, Esther was familiar with this arctic land they followed her to and had already purchased Chloe and Beau the right attire to bear the winter.

Beau turns off the engine and climbs out of the truck. He grips his jacket tighter around his chest as if that will make it any warmer. He pulls his knit cap down lower to cover his ears while watching his breath form an arctic cloud in front of his mouth. The covered Tupperware in his hand is fogging up from the opposition of hot and cold. He trudges into the front door of Poppy's and hears the sounds of clanging and pounding in the background.

The warmth is welcoming and reassures him that he won't have to face this formidable foe again until morning. He walks past the hostess and bar areas into the main dining room. Tony tinkers with a light fixture. They nod to one another. The main crew has moved on to the next project, but Tony left a few guys at Poppy's to finish up projects. Beau and Tony shuttle back and forth between jobs where they're needed. The restaurant looks amazing. The structure is a work of art, and Maryssa's design is coming together.

Maryssa sits on the floor with another woman holding instructions in one hand and a screwdriver in the other. He walks over to her. "Hey. Umm, I hate to be a know-it-all, but it might help if you held the directions right side up. That usually helps me put things together." He shrugs before offering her a smirk.

Maryssa rolls her eyes then glares back at Beau. "Smart aleck." She adds, "I'm taking that as an offer to help."

Beau shakes his head, "That backfired on me." He holds out the container in front of her. "I just left the house. Mary wanted me to bring you dinner. She told me to make sure you ate it before it gets cold. So please eat now. I don't want that woman mad at me." He grins and holds out his other hand, waiting for the instructions. "Here, you take this, I'll take that."

"Don't worry, I'm starving." Maryssa pushes off from the ground and swaps illegible papers for her grandmother's tiella. She opens the lid and deeply breathes in the aroma. "That woman is my idol. I'm going to get a fork from the kitchen. When I get back, you better have this entire table finished." The laughter carries over her shoulder as she turns to leave the room.

Beau starts un-layering. Gloves, hat, insulated jacket, scarf, and extra sweater come off piece by piece. Once finished, he holds out his hand to the woman sitting on the floor, staring up at him like he is dinner. "Hi, I'm Beau."

"Angelica. You know, like an angel." The blond holds his hand a little longer than he expects. "I'm Maryssa's manager. It's very nice to meet you." She tilts her head and smiles broadly.

He smiles back and glances at her warily. Her predatory stance takes him by surprise and causes confusion. "So, Beau, are you good with your hands?"

Beau's hesitation to speak causes a chuckle to come from Tony in the corner. He feels like a deer caught in headlights. "Yes, Ma'am." He glances down at the instructions to give himself a moment to regroup.

"Less talking, more working!" Maryssa calls from the door to the kitchen.

"She is a tough one." Angelica winks.

Beau laughs. "You should see her in a kitchen with her aunt and grandmother. It's downright dangerous." Beau studies the directions. "Let's see what we have here." He spreads out the paper and checks the hardware lying next to Angelica. He shakes his head as he tries to put the matching nuts and bolts together. "Why are we putting tables together exactly? I thought she got a furniture delivery yesterday. I assumed it was a full-service delivery." He picks up a table leg and examines the wood. "These will definitely be sturdy tables, I'll give her that."

Tony comes up behind them, tools in hand. "I'd stay and help, but tonight is my Mom's birthday. Missing dinner is not an option." Tony slaps Beau on the back. "Good luck with all this."

Angelica reaches over and squeezes Beau's arm. "It looks to me like he can handle it." Her smile is seductive and warm.

Tony laughs once more over his shoulder as he leaves the restaurant. "See you tomorrow, Muscles." More laughter.

Beau stands up to distance himself from Angelica. He's pretty sure she's flirting with him, but it's been so long, he's not really sure how to react. He takes off his hoodie. *Is it getting hot in here?*

Maryssa walks back into the main dining room toward the unassembled table. "To answer your question, I thought they were supposed to come assembled. Imagine my shock when the truck unloaded these boxes instead. Thank goodness the chairs came already put together. I would have stopped the delivery, but when I called the supply company, they said I would have to wait another month. I don't have time for that. So, here we are assembling tables. How lucky am I that my cousin married a carpenter?" She winks.

"Married? I didn't see a ring." Angelica looks confused.

"Widowed." Beau offers no more information. He doesn't want to share any part of Lizzie with a stranger.

Maryssa rescues him before Angelica gets out her next question. "Angelica, I know you have plans tonight. Thanks for staying so late to help me, but I have reinforcements now. Go ahead and enjoy your evening."

Angelica smiles directly at Beau while answering Maryssa. "I was just going to a party with friends. I can stay and help if you want."

The sounds of laughter come pouring into the room from the front entryway. Uncle Sam and Sammy walk in with tools in tow. "Someone call for the cavalry?" Uncle Sam's voice booms.

"Yes! Now that's what I'm talking about! Many hands make light the work." Beau walks farther away from Angelica in relief.

Maryssa jumps up and hugs them both. "Angelica, I think we have it covered, but you can come in tomorrow for a bit. I'd like to go over some of the wait staff applications." Maryssa turns to smile at the beautiful blond who is now downtrodden with disappointment.

Beau quickly adds, "This shouldn't take long at all now."

"Well, if you're sure. I can always come back later if you need help with anything else." Angelica stares longingly at Beau while offering a very friendly smile.

Uncle Sam, catching on to what is happening chokes back a laugh as he places his tool bag on the floor. "All right youngins, let's see if you can keep up with this old man."

Angelica gathers her purse and coat. She keeps looking back at Beau as she heads in the direction of the front door to leave. Once they hear the door close behind her, Sammy peers out a window to make sure the siren is outside then let's out a long whistle. "Well, well, well. It looks like our Beau here is quite the ladies' man. Tony and I have both asked Angelica out every day since Maryssa hired her and we get turned down flat each time. Thor just walks in with his chiseled good looks and has her hitting on him. Man, some guys have all the luck."

Beau shakes his head while looking down, but Maryssa sees the crimson flush covering his face.

"Can we talk about something else? The weather? The Steelers? The Panthers? Anything, but this topic?" Beau rubs his hand across his face and chuckles a little out of embarrassment.

"All right, all right. I'm just saying, she's a tough one to crack and Tony, and I have been working hard on that one. You may actually have a chance. She's hot."

"Seriously, Sammy? Hot? I'm shocked you and Tony are still single." Maryssa laughs as she pushes her cousin's arm. "On a serious side Beau, she did seem interested, and she seems like a really nice person. Next time, try a little more talking and a little less 'deer caught in headlights.' You might make a new friend." She winks at Beau.

"Says the other girl that Tony hits on every day. I'm not sure who he wants to date more, you or Angelica." Beau retorts.

Sammy vigorously protests. "Tony is just joking with her. First of all, he would never date someone he works for, he's just messing with Maryssa. Secondly, he would never break the guy code of dating your friend's sister, which in this family, Maryssa falls into that category. Don't even joke about that."

The younger three turn their heads in response to pounding on a finished table. The long rectangular, family-style table stands completed in all of its dark wood, elegant yet rustic beauty. "I'm up one to zero." Uncle Sam laughs. "Maybe I'll ask Angelica to help me, it sounds like her work ethic is a little better than the three of you at the moment."

Laughter roars between the four of them as they start picking up table parts and tools and begin working.

Chapter 19

Mary

Early morning sunbeams reflect off of the frozen blades of grass. The rocking chair squeaks with each pass over the floorboards. From the back porch, Mary has an expansive view of the trees in her backyard. One large oak staggered and planted for each of her five children. The trees protect the house from the hot afternoon sun and provide shade for the Rhododendrons lining the back of the house.

This is her favorite time of day. Mary wakes with Mr. Bubbles, the rooster, every morning. She sips her coffee and spends time in the Word. She'll be on the front porch swing as soon as the weather is warm enough. For now, she snuggles under a blanket in her sunroom.

The house is quiet this morning. Esther is still sleeping. Mary heard Esther tossing and turning all night. Maryssa went for a run after scolding Mr. Bubbles from the kitchen window. Thankfully, Maryssa bundled up on this frigid winter morning. Mary finds solace in the silence and sunrise. Her prayer journal sits open beside her. She knows the list by heart. Each child and grandchild has layers for her to cover. Mary prays for their faith, their futures, and their callings.

Mary Marchio is a praying woman. She was born right before the world went to war. Her father left for France when she was young and came home a war hero with a limp that would always haunt him. Mary's parents stressed the importance of education, so Mary and her three sisters all went to college twenty minutes away at Fairmont College.

That is where Mary met Salvatore Marchio. Salvo attended a dance at the college with a friend from his baseball team. He was two years older than Mary. According to him, he fell madly in love at first sight. Salvo attended college on a baseball scholarship. He was the youngest of six kids and the only one to attend college. Salvatore's mother died when he was ten, leaving him to be raised by two older sisters. He worked at the glass plant with his father and brothers during the summers.

Salvatore courted Mary from the night he first saw her. He met her after class and took her to dances on the weekends. Mary's sisters loved him, but her father was a tougher sell. Mary attended Salvo's baseball games, but things changed after a glass furnace at the factory ended his baseball career. He promised Mary he would make something of himself. He vowed to fill her life with dancing if she would agree to marry him.

After the wedding, Salvatore and Mary moved in with his father. Mary finished her last year of college while Salvo picked up extra shifts at the glass factory. The night he won land in the poker game changed their lives forever.

They built the vineyard together. Working the land, taking care of Salvo's father, and trying to raise kids. They spent the first ten years of their marriage exhausted and overstretched. They couldn't have done it without the help of Mary's mother, Raffaluzza. Mary's parents helped with the kids so Mary could teach during the day and work with Salvo in the afternoons. Mary and Salvo would come in from tending the vines to a waiting dinner.

Planting and harvesting time brought brothers and sisters, along with all of their kids to the farmhouse. Grapes and berries were pressed by stomping on the presses then strained and destemmed by hand. Salvatore's brothers collected old glass bottles from the factory for the first few years. By the grace of God, a regional grocery store chain began selling their blackberry wine. The rest was history.

Mary and Salvatore were a true romance. They were so in love with each other. They worked hard all day but ended every night dancing in the kitchen before bedtime. They built their house and their marriage on the Rock. Their foundation was unshakable, and boy did they have their share of earthquakes to shake them.

Salvatore left Mary with over fifty years of memories, five children, a thriving vineyard named after her own mother, and a lifetime of dancing. Mary has seen sickness and suffering. She has walked miles in the desert and up mountains. She intimately knows death and sorrow. More importantly, Mary knows the One who has walked with her.

As Mary rocks this morning and reads from the book of Ruth, she prays to the God of healing, the Redeemer. She prays for Esther and Beau and Maryssa and Malik and for Haddie and Chloe. Yes, Mary Marchio knows the sadness her daughter Esther wears every day like a heavy coat. Mary's father wore it like an unwanted war medal, and Salvatore's father wore it every day of his life when he looked at his children.

Mary also knows that God comforts us so that we can comfort others. The key is allowing that comfort to permeate all the holes left behind by the deepest depths of sadness and death. The healing balm God provides can fill the darkest pit where it hurts to even take a breath. Mary prays that Esther will allow God to lift the anchor that has her daughter chained in a pit of despair.

Mary rocks and prays for her family. The creaking of the floorboards is comforting. She sees Maryssa in the distance. Her granddaughter's steady pace brings her closer to the house. Yes, Mary has seen beauty arise from ashes countless times in her life, and she is convinced she will see it again soon.

Chapter 20

Maryssa

Maryssa's head jerks quickly upward after slipping from the hand that cradled it seconds ago. Sleepiness is her cue to stop for the night. She rolls her neck, then her shoulders. A quick stretch with her arms reaching high until she feels the tingling of her stiff muscles beginning to release. She has been sitting at her desk for hours trying to figure out the business software her cousin Frankie helped her to install today.

The morning began with a quick run at sunrise, thanks to her rooster alarm clock. She spent the morning training her kitchen staff and trying menu ideas with their input. Angelica stayed late to help Maryssa work on the menu layout but spent most of her time staring at the door looking for Beau. The younger woman lost her pep when Maryssa told her that Beau was working off-site. Angelica high tailed it out shortly after the revelation.

The highlight of Maryssa's day was picking up Chloe from ballet class. The little dancers with their black leotards, white tights, and pink ballet shoes filled Maryssa with sweet memories. When Maryssa arrived, they were finishing their lesson with a fun game. Ten tiny ballerinas were floating around the floor as butterflies. Maryssa chuckled as the other nine dancers had tight, neat buns while Chloe's hair had curls popping out in every direction. Just like Chloe, Maryssa's curls refused to conform.

As they descended the stairs from the dance studio, they were hit with the most amazing smell. Maryssa and Chloe decided they both deserved a cookie from the bakery on the bottom floor. Maryssa made a mental note to check local bakeries for dessert options until she could find a pastry chef.

Chloe and Maryssa played cards, then colored, and finished their evening helping Nunnie make dinner. Maryssa headed back to Poppy's after dinner to work on the new software. Falling asleep on the job was not in the plan. She doesn't know how Beau manages this balancing act every day.

Maryssa closes her laptop and smiles as she rises to leave. A slow twist of the trunk in both directions reminds Maryssa to stretch more in the mornings. As she turns off lights and closes doors behind her, she notices light emitted from the terrace doors. Her quick investigation reveals a hard-working Beau working into the night. She grabs her coat and slides the terrace doors open to the cold night air.

The noise catches Beau's attention, and he stops his sanding.

"Hey. I thought you were upstairs with Chloe. I didn't realize you were out here or I would have left on more lights." Maryssa sits on the side of an empty flower box that hasn't been placed yet.

"I'm fine. Tony left me one his spotlights to use. Chloe fell asleep as soon as her head hit the pillow." He holds up his phone, showing a child monitor app. "She hasn't made a peep."

"You know, I'm not opening the terrace until spring. I hope Tony isn't pressuring you to finish the bar now. It's so late."

Beau blows the sawdust off of the curve he just created before answering. "Nope. I just saw that your car was still here and figured I'd work a little too. It's kind of creepy out here when no one is around. I wanted to wait until you locked up and got into your car. Plus, after working on cabinet installation all day, this is just what I needed." He wedges a corner of sandpaper under a curve and smooths the rough patch. "Besides, it's been a long time since I've been inspired like this. I'd forgotten how good it feels."

She smiles. "You didn't have to stay for me, but I won't lie that I'm glad you did. I'll deny this if you repeat it, but I agree with you on the creepy part. Just don't tell Sammy or he'll tease me relentlessly."

"Ha, as if he doesn't do that already." Beau laughs, "But, your secret is safe with me."

"When I drove down here tonight, it made me feel better knowing you were upstairs. I love the peacefulness here, but it can get eerily quiet. I'm used to the city with all its cars, bangs, and other assorted noises. The weirdo in me misses the cacophony of city life."

"Cacophony? That's quite a fancy word for noise."

Maryssa pushes at his shoulder, laughing at herself. "Stop. I had a director who used the word all the time. I like the sound of it. It's not often I get to use it."

"Well, just so you know, the sounds are there, just different. Wait until spring when all the wildlife is moving and coming to life at night. That is my favorite part of camping, the nighttime music." Beau picks up another tool and goes back to work.

"I'll trust you on that one, camping is not my thing. I'm not a sleeping on the dirt kind of girl. And that music? It reminds me of bugs, lots of bugs that want to eat me. When we came here for planting and harvesting, cousins would come with tents and sleeping bags. I'd wait until everyone was asleep then sneak onto the back porch and sleep on Nunnie's porch swing." Her smile releasing a small laugh. "I used to feel bad for those poor suckers out there on the ground, getting eaten by bugs."

It's Beau's turn to laugh. He shakes his head at her. "All that tells me is that you need a camping coach."

"A what?"

"A camping coach." More laughter. "Someone to teach you how to find the best spot for a tent and the sleeping bag. It also sounds like you needed a better sleeping bag. Well, at least I know what to get you for your birthday."

"What? Did someone write a *Camping for Dummies* book?" Maryssa pulls her jacket tighter. Still smiling.

"I'll check, but no. I'm going to make you a container of my famous, all-natural, bug repellent. Some rosemary, lavender, tea tree oil. If you're really worried, I'll add some garlic and onions to it. That will definitely keep the bugs away from you and the vampires." He's all-out laughing now.

"Shut up, that sounds terrible. Apparently, I'd also be camping by myself, because no one could stand the smell of me. You seriously haven't sprayed onions and garlic on yourself, have you? That's some hardcore camping techniques."

"No, but I have pranked my brothers once or twice with it." Beau chuckles. "We used to go camping all the time in the summers. Boys. Pranks. It was all fun and games until you were the one getting tied to the tent while you slept. I realized that my bug spray was a commodity to my brothers, so I used it wisely. It was like having my own immunity idol."

"Tied to the tent? Are you trying to convince me to like camping or scare me even more? That sounds terrible." Their laughter trails off as Beau continues his work.

After a minute of silence, Maryssa's curiosity gets the best of her. "Do you miss them? Your brothers? It had to be hard leaving your family."

Beau ponders his answer. His hands still moving across the wood canvas beneath him. "Yes and no. I didn't grow up like you and Haddie and Lizzie. We weren't all that close growing up. We did our own things. Camping was more to get out of the house than it was for fun family bonding. My parents fought. A lot. They both had anger issues. They loved hard and fought harder. We couldn't hear the fighting outside in the woods."

"Beau, I'm sorry. I had no idea. I shouldn't have asked." Maryssa sits quietly, wishing she could erase her intrusive question.

"No, don't be, you didn't know. I wouldn't have said anything if I didn't want to." They sit quietly for a minute while Beau continues to sand. "My Dad worked a lot to build his reputation and get more construction jobs. My mom was home alone trying to manage a bunch of rowdy boys. She used guilt and comparisons to make us better kids. You know, the 'why can't you be more like so and so' approach? We all ended up being more competitive than we should have been. That's a lot of pressure for young boys. One minute wanting to trust your brother, the next trying to one-up him. It was hard."

Beau looks over at Maryssa with a sad smile and shrugs. "It is what it is, I guess. I didn't think anything of it until I met the Robinsons. John and Esther were nothing like my parents. I saw an unconditional love that I had never seen. They treasured both of the girls, and they did the same for Chloe and me. For the first time in my life, I felt loved for me, not what I did to earn it. That's why I came with Esther. She showed me love and faith that I couldn't let go of for Chloe, or me."

"Wow, Beau. That's a lot to deal with as a kid. I had no idea. Don't take this the wrong way, but you turned out pretty amazing considering all that."

"Thanks, I am pretty amazing." Beau winks before picking up another tool.

"Joke all you want, but you really are a great guy. Everything you did for Lizzie and Esther. You're so great with Chloe. I just assumed your mom was more Mrs. Brady than Mrs. Crazy. Doh, sorry. I didn't mean that. I'm an idiot." Maryssa quickly covers her mouth, trying to cover up the foot she just inserted.

Beau chuckles. "It's fine. My parents tried. They did the best they could. I don't think they had the best role models either. It was the blind leading the blind, I guess. Seriously, I love my brothers, don't get me wrong. I do miss them and my parents, we just don't have that closeness that the Marchios have. Not everyone has the perfect family life. Not everyone has a Mary at the helm."

"Ha! You're joking, right?"

"About Mary? No."

"No about our perfect family." Maryssa sits up straighter. "Not Nunnie, she is pretty awesome, but I do have some questions about her wild teenage days. But that's a whole different sidebar. You know about my Grandma Lavalier, right?" She stares at him in unbelief.

Beau looks at her warily. "Malik's mother? No, what about her?"

"She was a prostitute. You seriously didn't know?"

"Now, you shut up. There is no way. You're just messing with me." He laughs to himself as he looks back down at the wood.

"I'm dead serious. Grammy died when I was in second grade. She was such a sweet woman, a total Bible thumper. Her husband, my grandpa, was a preacher. My Grammy grew up in New Orleans. Her father worked on the docks while her mother cleaned houses. From what I've heard, my great-grandfather was quite fond of drinking and women. My great-grandmother died around the time the Great Depression was ending. My grandma was a small child at home with two older brothers. Her father never came home one night. Her brothers dropped her off at a fire station before heading out to sea for work. At fifteen, she realized the streets were better than the orphanage. She found herself in a shack with two other girls trying to feed herself. She started working near the docks and gained a few regular clients. At eighteen and pregnant, she wandered into a shelter ran by the church where my grandfather was a brand new preacher. The shelter let her stay until her baby was born. The only requirement was that she attend church regularly. They fell in love and were married before my Dad was even born. She spent her life trying to help homeless women find work and shelter."

Beau sits on his workbench, his mouth opens wide in shock. He shakes his head in non-belief. "I don't even know what to say. How have I never heard that story?"

Maryssa grins, "I know, right?" She slips off her chair and stands, trying to get her blood pumping from the cold. "See, not everyone has a perfect childhood. My Grandma Lavalier used to always say, "God puts you where He needs you, some places aren't so great, but He is, and He is all that matters. So, Beau Baker, it's not about where you've been, but what He will do with it that matters."

"You're starting to sound like Mary now." He steals a glance at her before collecting his tools.

"Don't tell her. She's already insufferable." They both laugh. "Well, I'm going home. It's been a long day, and it's cold. I'll see you tomorrow?"

He nods. Maryssa closes up the building as she heads home to her much-longed-for bed.

Chapter 21

Maryssa

There is one week before Valentine's Day. The restaurant is all hustle and bustle. Poppy's is scheduled to host friends and family for a menu showcase on Saturday. The waitstaff is being trained by Angelica. Maryssa is knee-deep in sous chefs and food orders. Tony and his crew are in and out finishing last-minute projects.

The outside of the restaurant is coming together, and the parking lot is completely paved. Tony will paint the lines tonight after everyone leaves. The inside is finished with only a few odds and ends that will be ready by the weekend. Seating is arranged, and lighting is being adjusted today.

Maryssa walks around the restaurant taking in all that is happening in her space. People and activity swirl around her. She is hosting an invitation-only Valentine's Day Dinner to promote Poppy's. She will use the next few weeks for a soft opening before spring when the vineyard opens for tastings and tours. As she looks around the room, everything is falling into place. Maryssa wonders what her mother would think of the restaurant? Of her life now. Maryssa closes her eyes and tries to see her Mama's face here in the room with her.

Her thoughts are shaken with the sound of her name being called from the doorway. Maryssa takes a break for a quick meeting with Uncle Sam. He asked to meet with her this afternoon with a business partner of his. She doesn't have time for a meeting, but she can't say no to Uncle Sam, who has done so much for her. He told her it would be worth it.

Her chef jacket is splattered with sauce, thanks to a run-in with an inexperienced waiter. Poor thing thought she would fire him on the spot. She shook her head and let him know that she came from a long line of klutzes, and he was just fine. The man almost hugged her. Her day had been one problem after another, but she was pushing through. As her Dad always says, "The kitchen never stops, it just improvises and keeps producing."

Uncle Sam walks in with an older gentleman and shows him around the restaurant. Both men are wearing dress slacks and wool coats. One of the hostesses take their coats and offers them a drink. Maryssa walks over, and introductions are made by Sam. "Maryssa Lavalier, this is Ben Stanley. He is the owner of our distribution company. Ben helped us catapult from local, to regional, and now to national venues with our sales. He helped us put Rafaluzza Vineyard on the map." Uncle Sam brags and pats Mr. Stanley on the back.

The older gentleman shakes his head in mock humility.

"It's great to meet you, Mr. Stanley. Please forgive my messy chef's whites, we had a kitchen-faux-pas while training new staff, and I seem to be a casualty." Maryssa offers a solid handshake like her father taught her.

"Call me Ben, please. Your uncle is too kind. Rafaluzza Vineyard has helped us branch out as well. It has been a lucrative relationship for us both." Ben Stanley's grey eyes match his silver hair. This man exudes confidence and power. Maryssa feels the need to match his posture and stance. "That's actually why I asked to meet with you today. Is there somewhere we can talk?"

Maryssa leads the way to the bar area. "We can talk in here, it's quieter. As you can tell the main dining area is still being put together. Is this good?"

The men nod as Maryssa directs them to a simple yet elegant high-top table. The sturdy leather chairs match the masculine and rustic theme of the room. The tabletop is dark cherry with a chalkboard tent for writing drink specials. Maryssa is so proud of this room. It reminds her of the restaurant she and Haddie would sometimes go to with other Ensemble members after performances. She sees it for the first time from an outsider's perspective, and inwardly beams with pride.

"So, Mr. Stanley." She pauses, "I'm sorry, Ben. I'm not sure how I can help you, but I'm all ears." Maryssa sits with the perfect posture of a ballerina and clasps her hands in her lap.

"Focused, I like that. Well, Maryssa, my company has made a significant amount of money helping to distribute regional beverages in the area. We've had a great deal of success in the eastern panhandle adding apple cider, apple butter, and now apple sauce to our distribution. We would like to expand our reach to include some food items that don't involve apples." He offers a snarky chuckle.

"Your uncle has been bragging about your menu for weeks. I am intrigued by your endeavor. I've done my homework, of course. Thanks to your father's connections, I presume, I've read that you were top of your class in culinary school and had an impressive internship under Jacques Boucher. Your stint at the White House is also marketable. With your resume and connections along with our production and distribution network, I think we may have a recipe for success if you pardon the pun." He leers with a sense of pride in his own cleverness.

Maryssa bristles when the gentleman alludes to her internship. She earned every single one of her accomplishments. In fact, she tried not to lean on her father's name or Jacques's for that matter. She sits up straighter as she converses with the man. "Well, Ben, my time at the White House was as a server and substitute dishwasher during school. While I definitely added to my education learning from the chefs, my job title was not as impressive. As for my internship, which I earned on my own merits, yes, it was an amazing opportunity. I'm still not sure what you are proposing? I haven't even opened the restaurant yet, let alone built a following."

"As intelligent as you are impressive." A sneer spreads on his face. "While you are an unknown at this point, my company is not. We would like to build on your resume and get in on the ground floor and help to launch your brand. Your grand opening, if marketed correctly, in conjunction with the reputation of the vineyard, could make you a household name in the region before you even officially open this spring. I can assure you, this venture will receive our top marketing strategies and promotions. We already have a head start with the vineyard launch this summer." Mr. Stanley studies Maryssa as she takes in the information.

"Wow." She draws a deep breath. "This is a lot to think about right now. I never in my wildest imagination thought I would receive such an offer at this point in my career. What types of items are you thinking?"

"I'll leave that to the expert, but I imagine starting with jars of sauce, marinara, alfredo, I hear your vodka sauce is to die for. Maybe a jar with toppings for bruschetta. Eventually, we would add some frozen entrees, ravioli, meatballs, lasagna. Obviously, you will work out the details with my VPs of food services and marketing. Of course, the main question is, are you interested in my proposal?"

Uncle Sam chimes in, "Maryssa, this is an amazing opportunity."

"Oh, I know. I'm definitely interested and very excited. My inclination is a resounding yes, but I need a day or two to process and think about which food items from the menu would work."

"Of course, of course." Ben Stanley slaps his knee and smiles in victory.

The three discuss timing and a few details to cover before their next meeting. Maryssa explains the layout of the restaurant and the terrace. Mr. Stanley asks her direct questions about projected costs and return of investment. She feels as if she is being tested. She wonders if Mr. Stanley's homework included the fact that her father owned multiple restaurants in South Carolina before moving to DC. It is evident that Mr. Stanley is an astute businessman who likes to be in control.

At the end of their meeting, Uncle Sam excuses himself to take a phone call from Sammy at the warehouse. Maryssa continues serving as hostess to her guest but is itching to get busy in the back of the house. "Ben, thank you again for this amazing opportunity. I look forward to working with you if this works out for us both."

Ben Stanley leans against the hostess stand. He is a little too close into Maryssa's personal space for her taste. The two of them are by the front door of the restaurant, closed off from both the bar and the main dining room. Maryssa feels uncomfortable and attempts to gracefully move out of the shared space.

"It has been a pleasure to meet you, Maryssa. Your family speaks very highly of you, and your resume is stellar for a new chef. I was impressed before I met you, but now I'm intrigued as well. I would love to get to know more about you. Maybe dinner or drinks sometime?" His grey eyes burn as he studies at her.

A small shiver runs up her spine to her neck. Not sure if this is a personal or business request, but feeling intrusive either way, she warily replies. "Well, ah, thank you for the generous invitation, but right now I essentially live at the restaurant. I barely have time to shower, let alone enjoy dinner or drinks." Praying the shower comment makes her less appealing. She walks behind the hostess stand and fidgets with the cord to the lamp, attempting to change the conversation.

He turns to face her. "I completely understand the stress of new business ventures." He reaches into a pocket and pulls out a card. "Here, this is my personal business card with my cell phone. Call me if you need a night out on the town for stress relief." He winks at her as she takes the card. His hand rubs her thumb in passing. The shiver is even more defined. She offers a slight smile and a prayer of thanksgiving when she hears her uncle's voice rounding the corner.

"There you are, Ben. Let's give Maryssa her restaurant back. I promised this wouldn't take too much of her prep time today."

Pleasantries and goodbyes are offered as the men depart the restaurant. Maryssa takes a deep breath and blows it out before returning to the main dining room. She peaks in the small party room where Angelica held waitstaff orientation. She bumps right into Angelica and they both laugh.

"Sorry, I was just checking to see if you needed anything before I head to my office." Maryssa peeks around Angelica's shoulder into the other room. "Are you finished? How was training?"

"It was great, actually. There are a few who will need to be monitored at first, but they are still promising. I'll feel better after we have a dress check and practice runs. Did my dad leave already? I was coming out to catch him?"

"Your dad?" Maryssa is confused.

"Ben Stanley. He was here, right? I'm sorry, I thought you knew. Sometimes I forget you're not from around here. Everyone knows everything in a small town." Angelica chuckles.

"Angelica Stanley. Duh. How did I not put that together?" Maryssa is in deep thought about the events of the past hour.

"Oh, no. You have that look on your face. Did my dad ask you out? I told him not to ask out my friends." Angelica apologizes.

Maryssa shakes her head incredulously. The confusion deepens. Feeling more awkward by the minute. "Well, umm, I think so. I wasn't sure if he was asking me out or being nice. I take it my first instinct was right?"

Angelica rolls her eyes and nods.

"I take it this is normal for you?"

"You have no idea. At least you're a few years older than me. Somewhere during my mid-twenties, I realized he was hitting on my friends. We made an agreement. He doesn't always keep it." Angelica laughs. "Don't let me discourage you. He's a great guy. Women love him from what I've heard. He likes to buy expensive gifts. I just didn't want to deal with my friends talking about their boyfriend with me. Gross." She scrunches up her nose in disgust.

Maryssa is a little surprised and even more uncomfortable than she was a few minutes ago. "I explained that I just don't have time right now. Speaking of which I really need to get to my office. Do you need anything from me before you take off tonight?"

"I think I'm good. I'm leaving now. A friend of mine has a band playing in Morgantown. I need to get ready. Have you seen Beau? I was going to see if he wants to come with me. Hey! If he does, could you watch his little girl?"

Maryssa is caught off guard. "Will I watch Chloe? Umm, sure. I'd need to finish up here first, but if Beau says yes, he has a Chloe sitter." Maryssa smiles and looks around the restaurant. "I think he's outside with Tony. They were going to prep the parking lot so Tony can paint lines for parking spots."

"Great! Hey, for what it's worth, you should totally go out with my Dad. The last girl he dated walked away with a trip to Paris!" Angelica bounces off as Maryssa turns towards the back of the house.

And I thought wearing a pot of sauce would be the worst part of my day. Oy vey!

***

The room feels warm and toasty. The smell of burning wood is comforting and homey. The last log is crackling and popping. Beau started the woodstove before he left for his date. Maryssa told him he didn't need to, but she is grateful for it now. The fire and a glass of wine helped her to relax after a long day.

Chloe fell asleep with her head on Maryssa's lap. Her brown ringlets still pulled back into a messy bun from their 'ballet class' tonight. Her purple tiara jammies are peeking out from underneath her pink unicorn fleece blanket.

Beau came into the kitchen shortly after Angelica ambushed him in the parking lot in front of the guys. Peer pressure from the crew and a pep talk from

Maryssa had him saying yes to a relentless Angelica. Beau reluctantly left Chloe in Maryssa's care and went on his first date in West Virginia.

Maryssa brought up pizza dough and some other essential ingredients to the apartment so she could make pizza with Chloe. They had the best time rolling out mini pizzas and topping them with extra cheese and pepperoni. Chloe made a smiley face with her pepperoni complete with ears. Afterward, they made butterscotch chocolate chip cookies and ate them right out of the oven.

After Chloe got ready for bed. They snuggled up on the couch and watched some cartoons before Chloe fell fast asleep. Maryssa, after checking to make sure Chloe was really out, changed the channel. Bringing up Baby had just started, and Maryssa melted into the couch. Her feet tucked up underneath her. It was just her, the wine, Cary Grant, and Katharine Hepburn.

Maryssa hears the truck door close and feet coming up the back stairs. She looks at her phone. It is a little after midnight. Beau quietly opens the door and sees Chloe fast asleep. His deep smile, reserved only for his daughter warms her heart. He puts his keys and phone down on the table by the door. He walks over to the couch, lifts Chloe's feet and exhaustedly sits down with her feet on his lap. She made a small sniffly snore as she shifted a little. Maryssa and Beau offer quiet giggles at her cuteness.

"Sorry, she was too cute to move. So, how did it go with Angelica? You could have stayed out longer. I was enjoying my evening with Cary and merlot." She smiles and winks.

Beau shakes his head back and forth. "No way. That was intense. I'm not cut out for the bar scene in Morgantown. The band was great, but it was really crowded. Not to mention that people don't even go out until ten. I'm usually in bed by ten. I stayed for as long as necessary to be social, but I cut and run by eleven-thirty. It was obvious that Angelica wanted to stay longer, so a friend of hers is bringing her back tonight." Beau rubs his chin in contemplation.

Maryssa tries to stifle her laugh. "Oh no, that's awful. Angelica seems really nice. Maybe a less crowded date will be better."

"Be careful what you wish for. I have a feeling she's going to ask you to babysit again next week. I told her I don't like to go out on weeknights because I need to have Chloe ready for school and she quickly booked up next Friday night. I honestly don't even know how it happened, but then again, I'm still trying to figure out how it happened tonight." Beau leans across Chloe and grabs a cookie from the coffee table. He eats the cookie in two bites. "Oh man, this is the best cookie I've ever eaten." He takes another.

"Well, I'm in for next weekend with Chloe. We had the best time tonight. She learned some basic ballet staples then we painted our nails. This was the most fun I've had in weeks. Chloe has her Auntie Haddie's sass, that's for sure." Maryssa takes a sip of her wine. "Other than the crowded bar, how was the date? Did you have a good time with Angelica on the drive up to Morgantown at least?"

"There definitely weren't any awkward silences, that's for sure. She fills up all the silences. She's nice and funny. She's just a little, I don't know." He pauses to think. "Too much for me. It was a nice drive. She's interesting and has traveled quite a bit. As far as dates go, it wasn't bad, just, a lot." Beau takes another cookie and settles back into the dark brown leather couch. "If it tells you anything, I drove in silence the whole way home just to give my ears a break." He shakes his head again then turns to Maryssa. "Here I am complaining when you gave up your Friday night. Thanks. I really appreciate you doing this. It was nice to get out a little. I just wish it wasn't so loud....and it didn't make me feel so old." They both laugh. Chloe stirs as they try to stifle the chuckles.

"No worries, I really did have a great time, and I'm glad you got out a little. Next Friday you should plan the date. Chloe and I can try homemade salsa and quesadillas. How sad is that? I'm excited about dinner next weekend? Maybe I need a date." She holds up her hand to stop Beau from laughing. "Don't you even say it, Beau! Not one word about it. Mr. Stanley is out of the question."

Beau holds his side in laughter, "We could go on a double date."

Maryssa drops her head into her hand. "Can you imagine?" She can't control her laughing. "I had to take a shower after that meeting. That was so gross and creepy. I know some women like older men, but that was really awkward."

Chloe rolls on her back, and Beau holds his finger to his lips to try and quiet Maryssa. She covers her mouth with her hand and points back accusingly at him. They both try to stop so as not to wake Chloe. The little girl pulls the blanket up to her chin and settles.

Beau glances at the TV as he grabs one last cookie. He whispers, "Oh, I love this movie." He chews the sweet goodness. "This is the one with the tiger, right? I watched this with John and E a while back, it's hilarious."

Maryssa reaches over and pats Beau's hand that is resting on Chloe's legs. "Seriously, Beau, I'm happy you got out tonight, even if it was loud." She smiles at him.

They both sit in silence as they watch Cary Grant and Katharine Hepburn chase a tiger around the woods.

Chapter 22

Haddie

Haddie still isn't comfortable walking the halls of the White House. Even late in the evening, there is still a hustle and bustle feel in this place. There are days she misses the solitude of her old apartment with Maryssa.

Haddie is on her way back from dinner with Uncle Malik and his fiancée. She still can't get used to her uncle having a fiancée. Uncle Malik is essentially Haddie's second father. She is so happy for him and really likes Victoria, but it's still weird. She reminds herself to call Maryssa tonight to chat about the whole thing. It all seemed to happen so fast. Haddie starts to wonder about her mom. Each phone call is the same, Esther trying to sound positive, but failing miserably. She needs to make a visit home soon. It's not like she has to worry about missing classes. She sighs at the overwhelming position she is in right now.

Haddie needed a break from these walls tonight. They ate at Victoria's restaurant in the center of the city. Haddie was pleased to see a table hidden in the back of the house, so she didn't have to deal with paparazzi. Uncle Malik is her only normalcy in DC. She relishes her visits with him. Now, she's back in the fishbowl.

Victoria's restaurant serves Mediterranean cuisine that is so authentic it's incredible. Haddie is on a specific mission now. She brought back a serving of baklava for Madison. That woman loves baklava. Haddie walks down the corridor of the West Wing to the chief of staff's office. She quickly ducks by Rich's door because she only brought one dessert back from dinner. Madison's secretary is long gone for the day, but it is evident from the partially opened door, that Madison is not.

Haddie lightly knocks while opening the door. "I was hoping you wouldn't be here tonight."

"And yet here you are, handing me something." Madison reaches out to accept the black Styrofoam container Haddie is offering. "I hope this is something good. I need a sugar fix."

"You need to take better care of yourself." Haddie scolds her new but very dear friend.

A subtle squeal of delight escapes as the container lid opens to reveal the golden piece of perfection. The sweet smell and flaky crust make Madison's mouth water. Her eyes filled with joy. She pops a stray nut into her mouth before diving in with the plastic fork.

"See? This is what I'm talking about Madison. We both know I love my desserts, but you shouldn't be worshipping a piece of food with that much intensity. You need a life outside of this place. Your boss is a real backbreaker." Haddie smirks.

"Hey! Victoria uses organic honey, that's a superfood. Isn't it?" She fills her mouth with another bite.

"I'm lucky no one saw me coming in tonight with this container. Tomorrow's headline would read 'FLOTUS Hates the Environment: Conspiracy with Greek Nationalists to Destroy Ozone.'"

Madison laughs and takes a sip of her pink, Smithsonian water bottle. "I would love to see Rich spin that headline. He would end up committing you to the planting of fifty trees in some remote national park."

"I'm sure it would include a personalized shovel and photoshoot. The big question wouldn't be on the species of trees but rather on whether I wore heels or flats." They both giggle at the irony and absurdity of it all.

An abrupt knock has the women looking at the door, which causes another round of laughter. "Seriously? Laughing at a man when he enters a room is a self-esteem buster. You realize this, right?"

More laughter. "Rich, I don't believe there is a force on this planet that could put a dent in your self-esteem." Madison finishes off the last bite just as Rich tries to reach down and grab her fork.

"Haddie, thanks for bringing me a special treat. Oh, wait, you didn't. Wait until I leak a story about you loving Styrofoam and hating trees."

Haddie falls into Madison as they both laugh themselves backward, deeper into Madison's silk couch.

"What? What did I miss?" Rich, genuinely concerned that he is missing out on a story. "Seriously? What?"

Jackson opens the door from the Oval Office and stands in the threshold watching the melee. Rich looks at him and shrugs in bewilderment.

"Honey? Everything all right?" Jackson saunters in and leans onto Madison's desk.

"Jackson, your wife is being mean to me."

"Again?"

The women pull themselves together as they get out the last few gurgles. Haddie stands to cross the room. She sidles up against Jackson and rests her head on his shoulder. "I'm sorry, Rich, but sometimes you make it too easy. Hey Babe. Are you headed upstairs or do you have more to do?"

Jackson wraps an arm around Haddie and leans down to kiss her head. "I think I'm heading up now. I'm starting to hallucinate. I sense the presence of baklava, but I know my wife wouldn't forget to bring me some."

Haddie pulls back and swats at Jackson's arm as he and Rich exchange their own chuckles.

"Attacking the President. Haddie, your rap sheet is growing. Too bad I don't have a camera." Rich sneers at Haddie.

"You two are insufferable." Madison tosses the container. "Haddie, I appreciate you."

"I know you do, and I, you" Haddie blows Madison a kiss.

"Madsi, did you set up that meeting we talked about for next month?" Jackson waits for an answer. Still determining if this is a good maneuver for him.

Madison, acting nonchalant to not worry Rich unnecessarily, "I have a call into his office." Madison stacks her papers and closes her laptop. "Haddie, thank you for the delicious and highly sought after baklava. I am truly honored."

Haddie winks at Madison Lyn then takes Jackson's hand in hers. "Come on, Mr. Cashe. Let's go home and let these two get some sleep. You may need to order Madison to leave the building."

"No worries. I'm leaving. I promised my father I would call tonight. He wants to discuss an article he read about the First Lady being an environmental terrorist."

"Hey!" Haddie rolls her eyes. "Next time I'm sneaking the dessert upstairs and eating it myself. You three are too much."

"You know I love you, Haddie." Madison walks to her desk and collects the leather briefcase tote her parents bought her for Christmas. Rich follows the sound of an intern in the hallway, talking about drinks. Jackson and Haddie stroll back into Jackson's office, arm in arm. A rare wave of melancholy washes over Madison. She wonders how long she can keep up this pace. For the first time, she wishes she had someone at home waiting for her.

Chapter 23

Beau

The smell of the exposed wood permeates the air. The floor is covered in sawdust and wood shavings. Tools made of high carbon steel rest beside him on the stool. Beau picks up the chisel to define the lines in his carving. He took advantage of the unseasonably warm weather today to start carving the posts for the gazebo.

The staff is preparing for dinner service inside Poppy's, but the terrace is quiet and peaceful. His view is of the vineyard and the lumber he's carving. Simple, natural beauty. He breathes in the clean air and wood scents.

Beau likes working with Tony and building cabinetry, but this is where his heart lies. Carving something beautiful out of a blank canvas. The art unfolding itself as he cuts and chisels.

He glances over his shoulder as he hears the terrace door open and footsteps approaching. His attention goes back to his work. Soft hands land on his shoulders and begin massaging the broad expanse. The gesture results in more tension, in opposition to the intended release it promises.

"You are so tense Beau Bear. You work too hard." Angelica leans close to whisper in his ear. The unnatural smell of apples in the winter wafts his direction, intruding on the red cedar scent. He tenses as she continues rubbing his shoulders.

They have been on two dates since the concert in a bar fiasco. Pizza and a movie ended with her friends texting the whole night inviting them to another bar. He dropped her off at Joe's Bar & Grill with the excuse he needed to get up early for work. Date three ended with him applying ice to a goose egg on his head. Indoor batting cages and bars don't mix. That night he learned she had never swung a bat in her life. Angelica flirts with him every time he comes to Poppys and sends him texts during the day. He has been trying to let her down easy, but she shows no signs of stopping her advances.

Her hands travel lower down his back, pressing firmly along his spine. He tenses and sits up straighter.

"So, I have been giving a lot of thought to our relationship," she coos.

Three botched dates is not a relationship. It's an omen.

She continues massaging. Her hands back on Beau's shoulders after sensing his tension. "I think our problem is that we need some alone time. You know, good old fashion adult, one on one time." Her sultry voice continues when he doesn't respond. "I'll make dinner. Some wine, candlelight, soft music, just you and me. No interruptions. No obligations. Just two people enjoying each other's company. We'll let the night go where it takes us."

And this is my stop on her highway of love.

Beau puts down his tool and brushes off wood as he stands to face her. She grins like a cat who just trapped her prey. She rises on tiptoes to wrap her arms around him. His strong arms gently catch her hands before they reach their destination. Her look transforms from victory to confusion.

"Angelica, I think you and I are in different places. You are a wonderful person..."

She jerks back her hands and quickly folds her arms. "Oh no, you don't. Tell me I'm not getting the 'it's not you, it's me' speech. You have got to be kidding me. I invite you over for dinner, and you break up with me?" She begins pacing and flailing her arms, talking mostly to herself. "This cannot be happening. What kind of man turns down an offer like this?" She waves her hands around her sumptuous body.

"Angelica, I'm sorry. You really are a great person. I have fun with you, but I don't see us becoming more than friends."

An awareness comes over Angelica. She knows the problem can't be with her. She cuts him off as she closes the distance she created. "Oh, Beau, I get it now. You're not ready yet. You're moving slowly because of your old wife. I totally understand. We can move as slow as you want. Just so you know, I'm not asking for any commitments. We can just have fun and see where this takes us. Come over for dinner tonight and let's see if we're even compatible." Her hands snake up his chest.

"Angelica. No." He finds himself gently removing her hands for the second time. "I'm not a casual, commitment-free, kind of guy. I'm an all-in, no intimacy outside of marriage, kind of guy."

She studies him for a second before her face turns mocking. Her harsh laugh takes him back. "You have got to be kidding me. Are you for real? How is that even possible?" She goes back to talking to herself as she paces back and forth on the terrace. "Go figure, I pick the one man in the entire world who has a conscience. What a joke."

He hears a string of mutterings as she walks back to the restaurant and the door closes behind her. His head drops in relief and resignation. Beau longs for the secure, soul entwining, overwhelming intimacy he had with Lizzie. The unbreakable, unto death, type of bond that shores up one another. Anything less feels empty and hollow. He picks up a chisel and tries to remember how that felt. It was a long time ago.

Angelica storms into the room as Maryssa folds napkins trying to find the right table decoration. "Everything all right?"

Angelica looks over and spits out one word, "Men!"

Maryssa clears her throat and tilts her head in the direction of the back table where Chloe is coloring quietly.

"Of course." Angelica absent-mindedly slurs before returning to her job of placing menus into their leather covers.

The women work in silence until Maryssa squeals in delight. "Aha! I did it!" She walks over to show Angelica a perfectly folded napkin in the shape of a rosette. "I was making the first crease wrong. It isn't hard to do when you actually follow the directions and do it right." She laughs at herself. "I'm going in the back to take pictures of each step." Maryssa walks while admiring her work of art. "Chlo, I'll be in my office if you need me."

Chloe smiles and answers, innocently, "K."

Angelica considers her situation and decides that she needs to win over Chloe if this thing with Beau will work. Beau might reconsider her proposition if his daughter likes her. It's worth a shot. She could be like a cool aunt or big sister type.

Angelica smooths her blush shift dress while walking to the little girl. "Hey there. Chloe, right? I'm Angelica." Angelica speaks slowly and adds short pauses between each statement as if Chloe is incapable of understanding. "I don't think we have actually been introduced. Do you mind if I color with you?"

"Sure. I only have one green. We have to share." Chloe hands Angelica a piece of paper and pushes over the crayons, so they sit in the middle of the table. "Do you like to draw trees? My grandpa taught me how to draw trees. They're my favorite to make. He's in Heaven now with my Mama." Chloe chatters on as Angelica assesses the crayon situation.

"I haven't drawn a tree in a long time." Angelica finds a brown crayon. "My friend gave me an adult coloring book and colored pencils. Sometimes, I color mosaic inspired pictures."

Chloe giggles, "What?" The girl looks at Angelica like she just spoke French.

Angelica tries to explain, but quickly gives up and switches tactics. "What are you drawing? Is that a pizza?" Angelica leans over to see the picture better. "Who are those people?"

Chloe puts down her crayon and lifts up the paper to show off her masterpiece. "This is my pizza. I like mine with pepperoni and cheese. This is Daddy. He likes sausage. He is making his pizza here with Maryssa." She turns to Angelica and crinkles her nose. "Maryssa likes lots of veggies on her pizza. I think it's yucky, but Daddy likes her pizza."

Chloe puts down the paper and rummages through the crayon box to find a yellow.

Angelica, taken aback, questions the five-year-old while filling in the trunk of her tree. "Does Maryssa make pizza with your Daddy a lot?" Angelica picks up the green crayon. "May I use this?"

Chloe nods. "We made pizza once. Sometimes we make meatballs in the big kitchen and eat them with sketti or on talian bread. Last night we made our own ice cream and watched the *Little Princess*. It was a really old movie about a little girl who had to go to a school because her daddy had to go somewhere far away. Then they thought he died so the main lady made her be the maid and the other girls were really mean to her, but she found her daddy in a hospital. Then they were together again. I liked it even though it was old. Daddy and Maryssa like to watch old movies. The ice cream was yummy."

Angelica stops coloring to soak in all the information pouring out of Chloe's mouth. Her never-ending sentences provide the missing clues that solve Angelica's riddle. "So, your daddy and Maryssa spend a lot of time together?"

"Yep, we all do. My Nona works a lot, so Maryssa picks me up from school a lot. She teaches me ballet, and then we eat dinner together. Nona and Nunnie eat too, but sometimes it's just me and Daddy and Maryssa." Chloe keeps coloring the sunshine in the sky. She has no idea the spark she just lit.

Angelica stands. "Chloe, thank you so much for letting me color with you. This has been a very informative play date."

"You're welcome. Don't you want to keep your picture? Your daddy can put it on his refrigerator." Chloe tries to hand Angelica the picture of the half colored tree, but the woman waves it off as she heads toward the kitchen.

"No, you keep it. I need to have a little chat with Maryssa." Angelica scowls as she walks purposefully through the kitchen to the chef's office. She knocks hard on the frame, startling Maryssa and making her jump.

"Oh my! You startled me. I didn't see you coming." Maryssa jokes. "What's up? Is everything okay?"

"Not really. I just had a lovely chat with Chloe. She told me all about how you three seem to be a happy little family. Seems that you've been spending cozy nights together eating dinner and watching movies. Silly me, when I asked you about him, I had no idea you had your own sights set on him. Seeing that you two are practically related an all. I had no idea you would be undermining me by having your own secret dates. A heads up would have been nice. You actually had me fooled when you turned down my Dad's advances. I thought you were different. I guess I was wrong about you. I should have been more careful. I didn't take you for the back-stabbing, boyfriend stealing type."

Maryssa stares open-mouthed at Angelica. She is frozen in place.

"You don't have anything to say for yourself? An apology? An explanation? Anything? I guess I'm the fool. I thought we were friends, Maryssa. Beau had me completely fooled, with his innocent poor widow vibe he puts off. It looks like it really wasn't me after all. Seems he's been getting his *dinner* elsewhere."

Maryssa finally puts Angelica's words together and stands. "Oh my gosh, Angelica, no. You have it all wrong. I've been teaching Chloe ballet in the evenings. Sometimes we'll just eat dinner together here if my grandmother and aunt have already eaten. It's not at all what you think. I'm actually a little offended that you think I'm that kind of person."

"Whatever. I quit. You can have him. He has too much baggage for me. I hope you two are happy." She turns to leave. "Good luck finding a manager in one week."

Maryssa stands in shock. Trying to make sense of the dramatic exhibit she just witnessed. She drops back down in her chair and gently bangs her head on the desk in mock defeat. *Good grief.*

Chapter 24

Maryssa

Early the next morning, Maryssa lies in bed. The sunrise isn't even high enough to wake the rooster or creep through Maryssa's window. It's not often she awakens before Mr. Bubbles. She stares at the textured farmhouse ceiling. The events from last night still ringing in her ears.

Angelica screaming in the parking lot walking to her car. Beau investigating and getting nailed in the head with a rock. Chloe crying when she saw the blood on Beau's face. Aunt E rescuing Chloe and getting her to bed.

Maryssa and Beau sitting in an urgent care center for two hours waiting on stitches. Beau repeatedly apologizing for Angelica's outburst. Maryssa reminding him that Angelica was the whackadoo and that he escaped a bullet. Meanwhile, feeling an odd sense of relief that Angelica was gone even though she would be in a panic to replace the woman. What a mess.

Of course, Nunnie was in the kitchen with tea when Maryssa came home. Her Bible on her lap, a scripture on her lips. "For I know the plans I have for you." Nunnie shared a story from her childhood to illustrate how God uses things that seem unfortunate for His glory. Maryssa sat silently listening as she drank tea and played back the events from earlier.

"Nunnie, how do you always have just the right scripture, at just the right time?" Maryssa asked her wise grandmother.

"Tis easy, my girl. Seek, and ye shall find. When the Word is your go-to for everything, you always know where to go to." She kissed the top of Maryssa's head then headed upstairs to her bedroom. Maryssa sat at the table, pondering Mary's words before heading to bed herself, willing the day to end.

A new morning brings a fresh perspective. Maryssa knows that God has a plan to prosper, not harm her. This was just part of the journey. She's seen harder days, but more importantly, she knows that God is good and faithful.

Maryssa decides to run. She dresses warmly and quietly tiptoes down the hallway so as not to wake the others. It is tempting to run by the chicken coop and wake Mr. Bubbles, but she resists. The cold air feels exhilarating. The dirt roads surrounding the vineyard are smooth from years of work. She runs the perimeter and makes her return for home when she reaches the crest of Nunnie's hill.

Maryssa's thoughts drift to her and Haddie from their professional ballet days. The hours were grueling. Their bodies took a beating, but their love of dance and fierce loyalty to each other made it seem magical. Haddie retired a year before Maryssa when she blew out her knee a month before their final show together.

At that point, Maryssa knew their days were coming to an end. Younger, more flexible, dancers were getting the coveted roles. Haddie's recovery period reminded them both that they couldn't dance forever. Haddie and Maryssa trusted God when it was time to move on, and she will trust Him now.

Beauty from ashes. God's path is perfect, even if the road seems covered in thorns.

Thoughts swirl through Maryssa's mind with a soundtrack of Tchaikovsky playing in the background. Watching Chloe learn to love dance makes Maryssa's heart swell with joy. The twirling. The leaping. Dance at its purest form. Maryssa feels an overwhelming sense of peace as she climbs the stairs to her room.

The peace is unexpectedly interrupted with the barrage of beeping from her phone. Maryssa picks it up off the nightstand next to the antique glass lamp.

"Fifteen texts. What is going on today?" She mumbles to herself.

```
JP:   Congratulations!!!!!

Simone:   Why didn't you tell me?!?!?!?

Marie:   Remember me when you make it big!
```

Maryssa continues reading the texts as they pop onto the screen. Confusion painting the room in swirls around her.

She clicks the link from Simone's text and reads the headline. "What the what? This can't be right."

Chopin's Spring Waltz begins playing on her phone.

His favorite piece.

"Did you have anything to do with this?" She blurts into the phone.

"Ah, ma plus chère, I see you have heard the magnificent news."

"Jacques, what have you done?" She falls back into her down pillow as her arm falls to cover her eyes.

"You are not happy? I simply did not want my time and energy to go to waste in a small family restaurant. You are too good for that. I'm too good for that. I mentored you for a reason. It wasn't to hide."

Maryssa stifles the scream building inside of her. She takes a deep breath before responding. "I appreciate everything you taught me, and I am grateful for your confidence in me, but, and am I saying this for the last time because it is getting on my last nerve, I am not hiding my talents. I am doing what your other interns did. I am starting my own restaurant."

Jacques cuts her off to remind her of the flaw in her argument. "Not in Rome. Not in New York. Not in Houston. Not where the world can see my work."

"Aaagghhh, you are insufferable. Might I remind you that I no longer work for you and I would appreciate it if you would stop acting as if I do? While you are at it, please shove the condescending attitude. I am my own chef. Yes, I learned a lot from you, but this is my time. My work. I'm not your pet project. This is mine, not yours."

"Yes! There is my passionate flower. I love your fire."

"Jacques. Please," Maryssa cries uncle.

"Please what? Stop wanting more for you? Pushing you for your best? Never." He grouches.

The silence in the air begins its calming work.

"My Dearest Maryssa, I am sorry for my tone. I called to offer my congratulations on your selection for the award. I simply want to ensure you receive the same accolades as your former predecessors. They are opening restaurants and writing books. They are traveling the world and writing their own futures. I want that for you. You are the most gifted of the lot, and I want things for you. I will not apologize for that. The Geoffrey Barton Rising Star Award, is the most prestigious award given to new restaurateurs. I have never been inspired to recommend anyone for the honor, until now. It will open doors for you." He pauses, "If you want it to."

Maryssa listens to his words. Her heart softens. "Jacques, thank you. This is an extraordinary opportunity and honor. I wish you would have given me some warning, but I am grateful. Just, please respect my decision and my work. It may not be the path you want for me, but this is where I need to be right now."

"Have you thought about recipes for the awards committee? I could help."

"I haven't even received the notification that I'm a finalist. I started getting texts, quickly saw the press release, then you called. I haven't even talked to my dad yet." Maryssa pulls the phone away from her ear to read the screen. "Speaking of whom...."

"Go. Enjoy your accolades. Give my best to Malik. Don't forget me, my darling. Ciao, Bella."

Maryssa takes a steadying breath to refocus as she slides the green button, "Daddy?"

"Maryssa Marie Lavalier, I am so very proud of you!" Maryssa beams at the sound of her father's voice.

"Why didn't you tell me?"

"I literally just found out myself. I started receiving a flurry of text messages then Jacques called. I haven't even received a notification yet." Maryssa grabs for her laptop to check her email.

Malik scowls, "Of course Jacques called. Ouch." Malik winces on the other end. "Victoria is here with me. She just pinched me. Apparently, I make a *face* when I hear Jacques' name."

"Congratulations, Maryssa!" Victoria talks over Malik. "You must be so proud. The Geoffrey Barton Award is such an honor. Well done, you."

Maryssa's cheeks are red and fixed in a permanent smile. "Thank you so much. So, I just pulled up the email. They must have sent it last night. This is the first year they are adding a television component to the award. They will film all the contestants and announce the winner live on reality TV."

"Well, that's some irony for you. Wait until Haddie hears this." Malik chuckles.

Maryssa reads the letter out loud while trying to process all of the information. "According to this, there were over five thousand chefs nominated. The list was narrowed down to fifty who were voted on by past winners. Oh, my goodness. I am one of five semifinalists."

Malik releases a slow whistle. "Wow, honey. I am so impressed."

Maryssa keeps reading. "A filming crew will come to Poppy's for footage and interviews. The awards committee will arrive later that week for an in-person interview and a demonstration of my work. They want to see a full service. They will announce the winner during a television special."

Silence falls over her, "Daddy, Poppy's isn't even open, yet. I can't pull this off in two months."

"Yes, you can. You can do all things, through Christ who strengthens you." Malik longs to hold his daughter. "Victoria and I will be there soon. Between the two of us, we know a thing or two about successful restaurants." He laughs at his own joke.

"Honey?"

"Yes, Daddy?"

"Maryssa, take the day to enjoy this. Let's talk tomorrow about the plans. Breathe. You are going to be fine. I'm so proud of you. Love you, Baby."

"I love you too, Daddy."

Maryssa stares at the words shouting at her from the laptop's screen. The blinking cursor, taunting her. Two months. No manager. Airhead hostess. Ongoing construction work. No terrace. A television crew. Maryssa falls back onto her bed.

For I know the plans.

"I'm glad You do God because I feel lost," Maryssa mumbles to herself as she stares at the ceiling.

Spring

Chapter 25

Esther

"Beau? Are you out here?" Esther calls out as she rounds the inside wall of the terrace. She peeks out toward the area between Poppy's and the building that houses the tasting rooms. The open space is framed by the vibrant green of the vineyard. It is the perfect spot for a gazebo. It will be a centerpiece for both the restaurant and the wine tasting rooms. Outside diners at Poppy's will see it from their seats like a piece of art in the distance.

Today is Esther's day to pick up Chloe from school and bring her to ballet class. She's been fretting all day about running into Peggy Anderson. It's bad enough watching that woman from a distance, but she is in no mood to plaster on a fake smile and pretend they are long lost friends. It has been over forty years, but that woman still makes Esther's skin crawl.

Peggy Lambert jumped on Wes Anderson the minute Esther broke up with him. His letterman's jacket was still warm from Esther when Peggy walked down the hallway wearing it. Flaunting it. Esther and Wes were going to run off to Atlantic City and elope. They would have been back in time for the first day of classes at Salem College. That's when a farm team of the Phillies came knocking, and he accepted, without talking to Esther. He claimed it was a better opportunity for them, but all she heard was moving to Virginia after graduation, away games half the week, and no Salem College. Wes promised he would come back for her, but Esther knew better. She broke it off and left for South Carolina with Ruth that fall, the very day Wes and Peggy were married.

Esther went to find Wes the night after they broke up and instead found Peggy Lambert *consoling* poor Wes over his breakup. She and Peggy had been friends until that point. Wes claims nothing happened, that he loved Esther, he was drunk and wasn't thinking. He begged Esther to get back together, but she refused. The following week, there was Peggy in Esther's old jacket.

Esther has avoided seeing Peggy up close at school. She hopes the same luck will follow her at the dance studio. Shaking the memories from her mind, Esther keeps moving. She doesn't need what-ifs on top of her sadness. She looks for signs of Beau.

Esther spies him on the backside of the structure. Beau is standing on a ladder working near the top on one of the posts. Esther watches as he works. His concentration is remarkable. There are six posts. Two are wrapped tight in plastic while the others are exposed. A large piece of plastic lays on the ground near Beau's tools.

"What are you working on over here and what's with plastic? Are you trying to hide a body? If so, I have a recommendation."

"Uh oh, that doesn't sound like you. We've known each other for a long time, and this is the first time you've asked me to hide a body. Not even Grandmother Eloise warranted that ask, and she deserved it. Should I be worried?" Beau laughs at himself.

"Maybe. It's been a long week." Esther stands with her hands on her hips. "Seriously, what's with all the plastic? I haven't seen you use this technique."

"It's not so much a technique as it is a preventative measure to keep prying eyes off my work until it's finished. I want this gazebo to be a family memorial of sorts. The plastic keeps the surprise under wraps, literally."

"Ah, I see. Didn't you just use a big blue tarp to hide Lizzie's gazebo when you worked on it?"

"Exactly my point. Your nosey daughter admitted to peeking quite often while I was at work. I don't trust you, or your mother, or Maryssa, or Chloe for that matter." He laughs more while climbing down the ladder for another tool. He walks over to place a kiss on his mother-in-law's cheek.

"Lizzie's gazebo was beautiful. She loved it. I don't know if I'll ever look at one without thinking of her." The sadness fills Esther's voice, which does not go unnoticed by Beau.

"I think this one will fill you with more happy memories. Isn't that what Pastor David used to tell us? Celebrate the memories we had instead of choking on the memories we don't? If I think about what Lizzie and I should have had together, that sadness takes hold and starts to strangle the good memories I cherish. This gazebo will honor her, probably more than the last." Beau searches his toolbox as he tries to pull himself back together. Both of them staring, looking beyond the structure itself.

"Well, I know one thing. The final piece of art will be magnificent when you finally unveil it." She smiles up at him as he ascends the ladder. "So, I'm picking Chloe up from school and taking her to dance class, right?"

"Yes, Ma'am. Tony wants me to finish the outside bar and decking on the terrace this week. I might be working late. Maryssa has pushed up the time table for the terrace because of her award nomination. Tony has me here full time until everything is finished. Maryssa said that Chloe can hang out in the kitchen with her if we need extra hands."

"Sam mentioned something about an award and a television crew. I hope everything is ready. She has a lot on her plate right now. Chloe and I should be fine this week. I'll just head to the warehouse earlier, so I can be there for school pickup."

"Thanks, Mom."

"I think Mama is making lasagna for dinner. I'll bring some to you tonight if you don't make it up to the house. I can't promise any of her apple pie will be left, but I'll try to snag a slice of that too."

Esther turns to leave. "All right, I'm headed to the school. Let me know if you need anything. Love you."

"Make sure Chloe's ballet shoes are in her backpack. If not, Maryssa might have them at the house. Love you too."

"Got it. Ballet slippers. Backpack or house." Esther walks back toward the front of Poppy's to her car.

"Hey, Mom!" Beau calls after her. She turns back to see him. "Just so we're clear, I would hide a body for you if you needed me to."

She laughs and offers a dismissive wave in her wake. "Goodbye, Beau."

"Bye, Mom!"

Esther relishes the crisp, cool wind flowing through her open car window. The sun is shining today and heating the air, but she is kept cool by the wispy breezes kissing her cheeks and blowing her hair. Her head is resting back on the driver's seat. She faintly hears the squeals and laughter of children coming from inside the elementary school.

Cars slowly fill the parking lot as the yellow buses idle in front of the school. Esther arrives early each day to beat the parking lot madhouse. Kindergarten is released ten minutes before the other children. The kindergarten dismissal doors are on the opposite of the building where the other parents wait. This allows Esther to collect Chloe without seeing many people and head home quickly.

Being home with her family is starting to pull Esther out of the blackness of her existence. Conversations with her mother and the familiar smells of the vineyard in early spring allow light to crack through the dark spaces like rays into a boarded-up house. She opens her eyes and surveys her surroundings. Young mothers waiting on the playground while younger siblings climb and chase. They talk in small groups while keeping watchful eyes on the herd of preschoolers. Esther pictures Lizzie as one of those mothers.

Another group of women, older, probably Esther's age mingles by the front doors. Would Esther be one of those grandmothers in South Carolina had Lizzie lived? Would she watch Chloe and another sibling or two while Lizzie worked? Would Lizzie stay home with her children? Would John come with her? They could have sat on a bench in the shade watching grandchildren play.

The wind draws her attention away from the grandmothers and back toward the playground. A little girl with long dark hair flits around like a ballerina. She is being chased by a little boy who aims pretend arrows at her feet. Esther smiles at their antics and changes the thoughts in her mind. *Take captive every thought.* Her mother keeps reminding her to take control of her thoughts and replace the negative with praise. Instead of longing for John and Lizzie, she thanks God for Chloe and Beau and Haddie and Jackson. She watches the ballerina float all over the playground as the boy gives up and begins climbing a small rock wall.

Esther jumps at the sound of her name being called from beside her window. Startled, she blocks the sunlight from her eyes with her hand and turns to the voice. Her heartbeat races as she desperately tries to catch her breath and compose herself before speaking.

You have got to be kidding me.

"Essie Marie, Is that really you?" The sound of her childhood nickname is unsettling and exciting at the same time. The man leans down into the open window and stares at Esther as if he's seen a ghost. Esther is sure she looks just as flabbergasted to see him.

"Oh my word, it is you. I heard you were back in town, but to run into you here is, well it's, it's just wonderful. Peggy thought she saw you here last week but wasn't sure."

"Wes Anderson, as I live and breathe, is that you?" Esther knows full well who this man is, but she still attempts to question it. Her red cheeks give away her cover.

The silver-haired man stares at her for a moment with a glimmer in his eyes. "It is me, in the flesh. Wow, you haven't aged at all. You still look as breathtaking as you did back when we graduated."

"Well, apparently you have lost your eyesight, but I appreciate your kind words." Esther glances in the direction of the school, trying to catch her composure. Looking back at the intruder, she notices his blue eyes haven't lost their deep color. "What are you doing here, Wes? Do you have grandchildren or children at this school?"

Still studying her, he chuckles at her comment. "Grandchildren. I only have one child, Lorraine. She is a lawyer in my father's old firm. Usually, Peggy picks up the grandkids, but she had an appointment today, so I'm pinch-hitting for the team." He pauses. "You look great, Ess."

Looking him straight in the eyes, reality snaps her back into the present. "I haven't been called that in decades. I go by Esther now, too much time has passed for nicknames. How is Peggy? How many grandchildren do you two have?"

"I just have Lorraine and her two kids. Peggy has two other children, a son and daughter, and seven grandchildren." Sensing Esther's effort to appear detached, the corner of Wes's mouth perks up in amusement. He responds to her look of confusion. "Peggy and I divorced shortly after Lorraine was born. She has been happily married to Dr. Mark Hartley ever since. I never remarried. It seems no one compares to that first love."

Esther blushes, not missing his comment. He continues studying her. "I saw your mother at the grocery store a few weeks ago. She told me about your husband and daughter. I'm so sorry. It must be a difficult time for you. You have a granddaughter, right?" She nods. "Your son-in-law moved here with you. I'm assuming you are here picking up your granddaughter?"

"Well, it seems you and my mother had a wonderful time catching up about me." She says with a fake laugh. "Funny she didn't mention it to me. Yes, I am here to pick up Chloe. She is in kindergarten. Speaking of which, I think it's about time for me to get her." Esther motions to the little children coming from the side of the building hand-in-hand with parents.

Wes opens the door and waits for her to step out of the car. The two take each other in for a second before Esther tries to leave. She closes the door and turns to walk to the school building. "It was nice seeing you again, Wes. I'm sure we'll bump into one another in this small town."

Wes reaches out and gently grabs Esther's arm. She freezes in her tracks but slowly turns to him. His eyes have always captivated her, so she averts her gaze to his hand on her elbow.

"Essie," he stops himself. "I'm sorry, Esther. Would you like to grab a cup of coffee or lunch sometime? I would love to catch up with you. Your mother is still as delightful as ever, but I'd rather catch up with you."

His sincerity moves her. She nods in consent, "I'd like that. You know where to find me. The house number is still the same. Now, I better go before Chloe gets worried." Wes Anderson watches her walk around to the side of the school building, laughing at the memories he has of Essie Marie Marchio.

Chapter 26

Beau

Beau tugs at the last piece of duct tape. He slowly wraps it around the post, securing the heavy plastic to itself. Pleased with his work today, he begins gathering all his tools. He brushes off the sawdust and tucks the ladder inside the gazebo for tomorrow. Spring evenings will welcome longer days. For now, he enjoys the sunset filled with oranges, purples, pinks, and yellows. A relaxed evening breeze blows and lifts Beau's wavy hair. He takes a deep breath of spring.

In the distance, the sound of a car comes nearer. He carries his tools around the building and sees Maryssa's Silver Dodge Charger driving into the parking lot. Seeing the tiny ballerina climb out of her muscle car makes him laugh every time.

Beau locks his tools inside the truck's toolbox. As he turns in the direction of Maryssa's car, something on the side of his truck catches his eye.

Along the length of the driver's side door is a long scratch. Beau shivers. The scratch wasn't there this afternoon when he parked.

Maryssa and Chloe climb out of the car and Chloe bounds over to Beau. She wraps her arms tightly around his legs. "Daddy!"

"Hey, Sweetheart." He leans down to pick up the little girl and places a kiss on her cheek. "How was your day?"

"It was great, Daddy. How was your day?"

Beau chuckles then places her on the ground. "It was good, honey. Thanks for asking."

"Nona said she was feeling tired, so Maryssa drove me home. We brought you some of Nunnie's zonya. I mean la-zonya and some pie. I'm going inside to get Beary the Bear. Is the door opened?"

"It sure is, sweetie. Beary is on the couch, waiting for you." Beau smiles as she runs around the barn toward the outside stairs.

"If I could have half of her energy," Maryssa muses.

"Tell me about it." He turns back to face his truck.

Maryssa walks over and checks out the spot where Beau's gaze is fixed. A slow whistle escapes her lips. "Oh man, you ticked off someone. That is a classic car keying right there, my friend."

"That's what I thought." He rubs his hand along the scratch.

"Did you botch a job?"

He glares at her, eliciting a small laugh. "Sorry, just trying to help."

"There is only one person I've managed to tick off since I've been in West Virginia. You don't think she would have done this, do you?" Beau rubs his chin in concentration.

"Angelica?" Maryssa shivers at the thought. "Surely not. No. She wouldn't. Would she?"

"I didn't think so, but not many people would drive out here when it's not opened yet and key a lone truck in this parking lot."

"Did you hear a car? See anything?"

"Nope, but I had the sander running a lot. I was back working on the gazebo. I'm overthinking this. Angelica wouldn't do that. Maybe it happened earlier, and I didn't notice it." His head shakes in disbelief.

"Doesn't Tony's brother own a body shop? He can probably buff that out pretty easily."

"Yeah, I'll call in the morning. I need to take a shower and eat something tonight."

Maryssa hands beau the bag full of leftovers as they both hear Chloe yelling from the stairs.

"Maryssa! Come up and see my goldfish! They want to meet you!"

Beau holds out his hand, inviting her in the direction of the stairs. "You can't offend Mr. and Mrs. Goldfish."

"Mr. and Mrs. Goldfish? You are a good Dad, Beau Baker." Maryssa walks with him around the building.

"Don't look at me. This is an Esther thing. I love her, but that woman cannot say no to Chloe. I'm already dreading the flushing of the fish ceremony."

Chloe and Maryssa feed the pair of goldfish as Beau unpacks Chloe's backpack and dance bag. He walks into her room and carries out a basket for the laundry room. Beau starts the water and tosses in a load then adds the detergent and fabric softener. Once in the kitchen, he looks through Chloe's school folder.

"Chloe, did you know you have homework? There is a coloring worksheet from your reading story to finish."

"Silly me. I forgot." She giggles.

Beau's voice is calm and caring, but Maryssa notices the exhaustion on his face.

"Hey, can I help you with your worksheet so your Daddy can take a shower and eat?" Maryssa offers, asking Beau with her eyes.

"Yes, please. We can use my new crayons." She jumps from the side table that holds the fish and runs into her room.

"You don't have to. I'm sure you'd rather be doing something else than coloring a Kindergarten worksheet."

"You were outside working on my restaurant all day. Please, let me help. I love hanging out with Chloe. Plus, Nunnie and Aunt E were already talking about bed when I left. They're probably both watching television through their eyelids as we speak."

Chloe emerges from her room with a pink, glittery pencil bag. "Here they are, my new crayons."

Maryssa follows Chloe to the kitchen table where the worksheet beckons them. She waves off Beau. "Go, we're fine. We have some coloring to do."

Beau takes a quick shower then emerges from the steamy bathroom wearing his favorite grey sweatpants and number one dad t-shirt. Maryssa and Chloe are snuggled on the couch, watching *Singing in the Rain*.

"Great movie. Did you finish your homework, Chloe?"

"Yep. Maryssa put it in my folder. Then Nona called to tell us that this movie is on and I should watch the guy dancing because he falls a lot and is really silly. Maryssa says it's coming up soon." Chloe doesn't take her eyes off of the television as she explains what's happening to her father.

Chloe asks Maryssa questions about the movie as Beau unpacks the bag of food sent from Mary. He removes the lasagna from the plastic container and places it on a dish for the microwave. Looking into the bag, Beau spies another larger container on the bottom of the paper shopping bag. He opens it to find two slices of apple pie.

"Ooh, what did I do to deserve two slices of pie?" Beau slaps his hands together, then rubs them in excitement.

Maryssa pops off of the couch, "What?" She crosses the room with a purpose. "Nunnie said all the pie was gone. How did you get some? Are you bribing my grandmother?"

Beau is laughing as he holds out a sticky note for her to read. Maryssa grabs it from his hands with flare. "Gotcha. Tell Maryssa one piece is hers. This is payback for eating my last cannoli." Maryssa wads up the note and tosses it onto the table. "That woman is sneaky, and dare I say, a little vindictive. In my defense,

I didn't know she was hoarding that cannoli. I thought it was fair game sitting in the fridge without a name on it. She still won't tell me who made it. It was the best cannoli I've ever eaten."

They both laugh as Beau begins eating his lasagna. Maryssa walks to the cabinet and pulls down two small plates then rifles through a drawer to find a small spatula and two forks. "I know I should be the bigger person and just let you have both pieces of pie, but I'm not. I've been craving this moment since I saw that woman peeling the apples this morning." Maryssa sticks a forkful of flaky, gooey goodness in her mouth. "Mmm, this is amazing."

Beau watches her enjoying the pie as he finishes his dinner and pulls the plastic container his way. "I know. My mouth has been watering for this since E mentioned it this afternoon. You're lucky you stayed. I might have eaten your slice due to my lack of self-control when it comes to Mary's desserts."

"I know what you mean. While I was in Paris, I was surrounded by the greatest of delicacies daily. Yet, all I could think about during my last month of the tour was getting home in time for Christmas to eat Nunnie's galettes. Granted, I couldn't indulge in all the food, all the time because I had to fit into my costumes, but still, you get the point."

"I do. I keep forgetting that you lived in Paris for a while. What was that like?"

Maryssa pauses her fork before stabbing another bite, thinking. "Paris was everything I expected it to be. It was exciting, wonderful, an adventure. I was young and wanted something bigger. I was in between productions when a director whom I had danced for in DC called. He was preparing for the spring season in Paris when one of his principal dancers went down with a fractured fibula. He needed someone to make a six-month commitment with the potential for a permanent spot. He thought of me. I went. I was immersed and loved it."

She waves her fork in the air. Talking with her hands to accentuate her point. "Paris was an inspiring place to visit, and I would love to go back one day, but I was ready to come home. I know that sounds weird for a ballerina and chef to say. Everyone assumed I would stay. I could have, they offered. I just wanted to be home with Haddie and my Dad. Does that make sense?" She shrugs.

"You are asking the guy who followed his mother-in-law to another state." He laughs at himself. "No, I totally get it. My brother Matt wanted us to merge with a commercial contractor in Atlanta. According to his numbers, the revenue would set us up for life after only a few joint projects. The kicker was that we'd all have to move. After a visit, I told him that I would support whatever decision they made, but I didn't want to leave our small-town life. I think my Dad was relieved too when the merger fell through at the last minute. I have nothing against big cities, it just didn't feel right for me. My brother is still bitter about the failed deal. Not everyone understands."

"Well, Jacques never understood. He constantly asked me why I didn't stay. He pushed and pushed for me to open a restaurant in Paris, or anywhere else really." She takes another bite of pie.

"Yeah, what is the deal with that guy? I only met him the one time when we visited Haddie and ate at his restaurant, but he seemed intense. He definitely was possessive of you. We all wondered if there was something between you two." He studies her response.

Maryssa rolls her eyes and shakes her head. "That is what everyone thought."

"It's none of my business, and you can tell me to mind my own business, but were you?"

"No! Good gravy, no. Not that he didn't try. Every day. I admire him, and I definitely have a major chef crush on him, but nothing romantic." She moves the last bite of pie around on her plate. "So, this might sound weird to you, but I've never really had a serious boyfriend at all. Haddie and I would both go on dates now and then, but, I don't know, we could just tell right off the bat if a guy was worth it. Worth the energy, the effort. We watched too many friends lose their identities, their ambition, their focus over guys who were clearly not meant for them. The second I met Jacques, let me clarify, the moment Jacques actually noticed me, I knew he would never be my helpmate. He wasn't safe. I don't mean that in a physical way, but an emotional one. He would have swallowed me or drawn me in ways that weren't in my character. Haddie called it the 'icky test.' If the hair on the back of your neck raises even once during a conversation with someone, run. God gave us that sense for a reason." She shakes her head again before forking the last bite. "Is that answer clear as mud?"

"Again, you're asking the wrong guy. The girl who instantly failed my 'icky test' apparently keyed my truck. Right now, you and Haddie are looking pretty superior in your dating records." Beau places his head in his hands in mock defeat.

"I totally forgot about your truck. I had no idea Angelica was crazy. Do you really think she did it and if so, what are you going to do?" Maryssa sits back in her chair, feeling stuffed with apple pie.

"I'm going to fix it and move on with my life. What else can I do? I just hope she finds someone else to torment, I mean date. Let's not talk about Angelica. She's giving me the ickies right now."

"Right? I'm glad we found out now. She is one violent crime away from a made-for-TV-movie." Maryssa shivers.

"Agreed. Moving on, are you ready for this weekend? What exactly is the difference between a soft and grand opening anyway?"

"The soft opening gave me weekends to try out the recipes and specials. Plus it was good practice for the wait staff to serve friends and family before we opened to the public. Up until now, it's been invitation-only. This has been the dress rehearsal for the real deal this weekend. Sammy opens the tasting rooms and starts vineyard tours too so there will be more people. Hopefully, we'll be like a fluid ballet ensemble this weekend." She grins in anticipation.

"Is everyone coming in, your Dad and Haddie?"

"Daddy and Victoria will be here on Thursday. Haddie and Jackson will arrive on Friday, but leave early Saturday morning for security reasons. I feel ready. I'm excited. Mr. Stanley has a table reserved for Saturday evening. He was so excited about the Geoffrey Barton Award that he pushed back the product launches to capitalize on the media coverage. I think the first items will hit stores the week before the award show airs. I'm more anxious about that than the award and the opening combined. The man is staking a lot on me. I hope he doesn't regret it."

"Are you kidding? That man should be thanking his lucky stars for you. Once the show airs, your name will be a goldmine. That should be the last thing on your mind."

Beau picks up their plates and carries them to the sink. He turns back and leans against the counter. "No offense, but I'll skip the Saturday night service. Just in case Mr. Stanley brings his daughter as his plus one. And I think I'll park my car by the pond." They both laugh.

Chapter 27

Maryssa

The sound of *My Girl* being sung by the Temptations streams from her phone. Maryssa quickly wraps her wet hair up into a towel and leaps across the bed to reach her dresser. She grabs her toe after it bangs off of the bedpost. "Hi, Daddy," she says while hopping.

"Honey? Are you all right?" Malik Lavalier's voice brings her comfort.

"Yes, I'm here, I just hit my toe. How are you?" She sits down on her bed and gets comfy up against the pillows.

"I have Haddie here with Victoria and me." Malik pauses to hear her response.

Maryssa sits up, sensing something more than just a call with her father. "Okay, is there a reason we're all gathered here together today or am I just lucky? Should I be worried? Does Haddie want the purple couch back, because she's not getting it? In fact, it's at Beau's apartment so she'll have to steal it from her darling niece." Maryssa rambles, avoiding the real purpose of the call.

"That's just cold. I don't want the couch back, but using Chloe is a new low for you." Haddie jeers.

"I was lying about that anyway, it's still in the basement, but you can't have it."

"Sweetheart, it's not bad. Relax. Victoria and I have a question to ask you. Haddie is here to offer you moral support if you begin to panic over the time table aspect."

"Just spit it out, Daddy. You're scaring me." Maryssa chews on the top of her thumb. Waiting.

"Maryssa, as you know, your father and I need to nail down our wedding plans. We have chosen the venue, but we're not quite sure they are available in such a short time frame. This is where you come in." Victoria's voice is calming and sensible.

"Oh. Is it someone I know? I'll be glad to call. Just tell me where, when, and how many people and I'm on it." Maryssa nestles back into her pillows.

"Poppy's Place. Four weeks. One hundred and twenty-five guests." Malik cringes as he anticipates her response.

Silence.

"I think you broke her, Uncle Malik."

Silence.

"I'm sorry, what?" Maryssa is sitting up stick-straight on her bed.

Malik's voice is soft and controlled. He speaks slowly, allowing her time to absorb the information. "We want to plan a wedding this May at Poppy's Place. According to the *Farmer's Almanac*, the weekend we've chosen is supposed to be warm and dry. We would like to get married on the terrace and have our reception in the restaurant. Mary has already reserved your church for us if the weather turns bad, but we definitely want Poppy's as our reception venue." Malik takes pause to gauge his daughter's reaction.

Silence.

"The guest list will be intimate friends and immediate family." He nervously laughs. "You know what Nunnie says, 'Immediate family on the Italian side is two hundred.'"

"Maryssa?" Haddie interjects. "Are you there or have you passed out and need assistance?"

"Four weeks? Are you two mad? Poppy's only just opened." Maryssa stands and begins pacing in her bedroom. A deluge of thoughts and anti-arguments prepare to pour from her brain and mouth.

"Daddy, you were here to see the soft opening or what I like to call the Valentine's Day Debacle and worse, the April flood. There aren't bugs to work out, there are giant, superbugs. I have a camera crew coming in six weeks. I have to work out my recipes for the awards committee. Last week, I had a pipe burst because the dishwasher broke the pin." Maryssa is just getting started. "I lost my main hostess slash manager because she's crazy jealous of Beau. I can't find a qualified new manager anywhere. My current head hostess calls me Ma'am like I'm fifty. The terrace still needs work. I don't know if my staff can handle an event of this size. I haven't even finalized my catering menu yet. Mr. Stanley needs help with the distribution products."

"Maryssa," Malik tries to pull her out of her tirade.

"I'm still trying to build a relationship with the local growers and food suppliers. That's a lot of food. We would need hundreds of Italian cookies. I don't even know if my dessert vendor knows how to make a good galette. We need galettes. Good galettes. They need to have perfect consistency, sweet, but not too sweet."

"Maryssa," he tries once more.

"Then there are the flowers. I don't have relationships with florists yet. You are in DC. I'll need to be the point person for flowers. Who should I call? Ooohh, there is the lady from church, I think she creates wedding flowers. What about music?"

As Maryssa is pacing, a notecard slides under her door. She bends to pick it up and read it.

"Maryssa?" Malik is confused by the sudden silence.

"What is this? 'Therefore I tell you, do not worry about your life, what you will eat or drink; or about your body, what you will wear. Is not life more than food, and the body more than clothes? Look at the birds of the air; they do not sow or reap or store away in barns, and yet your heavenly Father feeds them. Are you not much more valuable than they? Can anyone of you by worrying add a single hour to your life?' Matthew six twenty-five through twenty-seven." Maryssa stares at the door. "Haddie Marie! Did you call Nunnie and tattle on me for flipping out?"

"Nope," she replies sheepishly. "I texted her."

Victoria's sing-song voice floats through the phone. "Maryssa, we simply won't settle for anything less. You have the best venue. Your food is exquisite, and that's coming from two top chefs. Every new restaurant has to work out giant bugs. I literally had giant bugs in my first restaurant. You are an up and coming culinary artist. We want the best venue for our wedding, and Poppy's is it. We have complete faith in you. We are willing to do whatever it takes to make this happen."

Maryssa catches a glance at herself in the mirror. Towel still wrapped on her head and a Bible verse in her hand. She takes a deep breath. "I can see that you are going to be one of those bossy stepmothers, aren't you?" Maryssa laughs. She hears laughter on the other side of the door.

"Poppy's. Four weeks. I'm on it."

***

Madison

The Cabinet Room is a reverent place for Madison Lyn. The eighteen-foot ceilings with the original sconces and overhead lighting from the previous eras provide the perfect ambiance for important discussions and historic meetings.

Hundreds of men and women have sat in these leather chairs. Brass plates proclaiming their titles. Their placement around the table, announcing their position's introduction into the Cabinet. Each chair identical, but one.

Madison Lyn walks quietly and directly to the one chair in the room which is exactly two inches higher than all of the others. She walks behind President Jackson Cashe as she slips a paper between his arm and the Secretary of State's. She stands back against the wall to await a nod of okay or a shake to nix the plan.

Jackson waits until the Secretary of Education finishes his opening comments and begins reading from a report. Jackson unfolds the paper Madsi has just handed him and leans back to read the contents of her shorthand; a language only he, Madsi, and Rich can decipher.

Yes. Next time you are in town. No eyes or ears. In Vino Veritas. No schedules. No names.

Jackson watches the Secretary of Education intently while folding the note and tucking it into an inside suit pocket. Only Madison notices the nod and slight smile forming on the corner of his mouth.

Chapter 28

Frankie Jo

Francesca Marchio, Frankie, is dressed for success. Donning her favorite dark gray, wrap dress that ties on her hip. She looks professional yet sophisticated. Her look is complete with tall, suede, black boots and her black and white polka dot scarf. The polka dots remind her of Lucille Ball. Frankie loves Lucy.

She pulls into the parking lot, takes a deep breath, and grabs her purse, portfolio, and a box from the passenger seat. Frankie is not leaving until she gets this job. She walks in with all the confidence she can muster as she passes through the hostess area. A slow whistle stops her short and makes her turn.

A man she has secretly had a crush on since she was old enough to crush, comes out from behind the hostess stand. Tony, her brother's roommate, grins at Frankie while trying to fix an exposed wire hanging from a hole in the wall. "Looking good, Frankie. Big date?"

Frankie rolls her eyes. "Don't electrocute yourself," she sweetly replies with a sardonic grin. Continuing her determined pace while forcefully blowing off another one of his passes.

Frankie's intended target is sitting at a dining table with a coffee cup and muffin, flipping the pages of a bridal magazine. Maryssa looks up and smiles broadly.

"Hey, Frankie! Wow, you look amazing. To what do I owe this surprise?" Maryssa stands to offer a hug and kiss to her younger cousin.

Frankie loves a good hug. "Maryssa, do you have a minute to talk? I have a proposition for you."

"Uh oh, you're not going to ask me out, are you? The last time someone had a proposition, it came with a very creepy dinner offer." Maryssa shivers with the memory of Ben Stanley.

"No, definitely not, but I really need to hear that story." Laughing at the thought, Frankie sits down and puts her portfolio and a pink box on the table.

"Ooh, this feels official. What's up?" Maryssa sits back down and moves her magazine out of the way. She is intrigued.

"I would like to apply for the manager position." Frankie starts off strong, pointedly announcing her desired outcome.

"Well, I was definitely not expecting that. Let me unpack all of the information and process." Maryssa studies her younger cousin. "What about the vineyard office? I thought you were learning the business side from Aunt Jo and Sammy. I mean, isn't that why you got your business degree? Wouldn't your background and skill set be a better fit at the main office than running a restaurant? Not that I don't want you here, but honestly, I don't think I can afford you. Not to mention that you are way overqualified."

"Daddy has pretty much retired. Which means everything at the office has been streamlined to Sammy. He is already running the show, so to speak. Don't get me wrong, I enjoy it, but I'm not exactly involved in business decisions. I've been learning from Aunt Jo, but with Aunt E there now, I'm not really doing much. The vineyard is Sammy's baby. He has worked really hard since he was in high school. He has earned running the vineyard. Besides, that's not where my passions lie. I can still help the aunts, but I want my own thing." Shaking her head to refocus from the tangent. "I have dreams that don't involve the day to day operations of a vineyard."

Maryssa is curious and confused. "Okay, so what is your thing, and how does being the manager here help you? Are you interested in the restaurant business?"

"Not exactly, but an aspect of it." Frankie draws in air and confidence before sharing her secret with another person for the first time. "I'm a baker. I love to bake. Cookies, cakes, pies, cheesecake, but my all-time favorite thing to do is design cakes. Here, look." She opens the portfolio and pushes it across the table to Maryssa.

Page after page showcases a different cake. Each creation looks like it came out of a magazine. The intricate details are mesmerizing. Each cake, its own work of art. Some with sugar flowers, some with real flowers. Rough surfaces, smooth surfaces, one with latticework. The images on par with those from the bridal magazines on the table.

"Oh my goodness, Frankie. I had no idea. Wait, are these all made with buttercream? No fondant?" Maryssa stares at her amazed.

Frankie opens the box to reveal a large variety of petit fours and cookies.

Frankie nods, pride peeking through the nervous smile. She turns the page. "This is my favorite. It has Italian buttercream with a blackberry preserve filling. I thought your dad would love that one. Here, try something."

Maryssa picks a chocolate cake with peanut butter icing and chocolate shavings. The moist cake melts in her mouth while the salty peanut butter balances the richness of the fudgy chocolate. Maryssa moans in delight. She picks up a galette next and looks questioningly at Frankie.

"Yep, that's Nunnie's recipe. Don't rat me out, I'm not supposed to have it. Uncle Malik thinks he's the only one with a copy." She grins.

Maryssa clasps Frankie's hand. "I am in a state of shock. These are magnificent. Why haven't you told anyone? Does Nunnie know?"

"She is the only one. I started baking with Nunnie. It soon turned into an obsession. I use her buttercream recipe. She says it came over on the boat from San Giovanni and I'm to guard it with my life." She giggles like a schoolgirl, finally able to share a secret. "I didn't tell anyone because I don't like attention. Sammy is the extrovert like Daddy, I'm not. Nunnie encouraged me to tell you. She called to tell me that you were stressing about your Dad's wedding cake. I guess now is as good a time as any to start this new adventure."

"She is right. I've really been struggling with desserts in general. There has always been a pastry chef in every restaurant I've worked in, but I'm using a vendor for Poppy's until I can hire someone." Realization dawning, "Did you say something earlier about cookies?"

Another giggle. "Yes, on the cookies and I know you need a pastry chef. So, here is my proposition. Let me be the manager. I can help you run Poppy's so that you can focus on the food, and I can wet my feet in the food industry pool while learning from you. Instead of paying a vendor, pay me. I can bake before the restaurant opens and manage during business hours. What do you think?"

"Are you kidding? Yes! Absolutely! You are an answer to prayer." Maryssa pulls out the cell phone from her pocket. "Let's call Daddy and ask how he feels about Italian buttercream with blackberry preserve filling."

Frankie exhales and releases the nerves she didn't realize she was holding. A smile slowly growing on her face. A small waving movement catches her eye.

Tony pokes his head around the corner and mouths "Congratulations" to Frankie with an added wink.

Franke rolls her eyes at him again, but her smile is unmistakable.

Her attention is immediately drawn back to Maryssa's voice, "Daddy, I just nabbed you the best baker in the state for your wedding cake!"

Chapter 29

Esther

The *Farmer's Almanac* got it right. The temperature is set to hit seventy-two degrees with a slight breeze. The smell of new grass intermingles with blooms opening from dogwood trees and rhododendrons along the property. Green covers every inch of the farm. A blanket of dew creates a shimmer when hit by the rays peeking out from sunrise. Ruth would have been in love with this day.

The porch swing creeks with each passing, front to back. The coolness of the early morning requires a blanket around Esther's shoulders. Spring has always been Esther's favorite season. Today, ironically, her thoughts are flooded with memories of Ruth. Spring takes Esther back to the dreams of her youth. Planting with her father and playing outside with Ruth. The endless nights surrounded by fireflies. The crack of baseball bats hitting balls into the air. Sam played baseball since he was small and Dom followed suit. Their father coached, so the family always seemed to be sitting on bleachers. Of course, Esther would have gone just to watch Wes play. Sam was not thrilled with his sister dating his teammate. That didn't stop Wes from pointing to her in the stands before stepping up to the box.

Esther shakes the thought from her mind. How did the rabbit hole start with the weather and end up with her high school sweetheart? She sips her tea as the front screen door opens with a creak.

Mary Marchio walks out onto the porch and takes stock of her sprawling view. The woman, wearing slim cotton pants and a fitted, cardigan sweater, still looks as fit and stylish as she did in her youth. She carries her Bible and a cup of coffee to the swing.

"Well, good morning. I thought you were still asleep." Mary settles herself into the swing and pats her daughter's knee.

"I couldn't sleep. I kept dreaming about Ruth." She rests her head on her mother's shoulder.

"Ah." The woman absorbs the sentiment and melancholy in Esther's voice. "Ruth would have loved today. She relished big family events, and weddings were her favorite. She loved the flowers and the music and everything tied in pretty bows." Mary sighs.

"I know," Esther sniffles.

"It never gets easy. Losing a child."

"Tell me about it. Now I'm a daughterless, sisterless, widow."

Mary remains quiet, trying to hear what Esther is really saying. Praying for the words that might offer healing and understanding.

Esther wipes her cheek. "It's just so hard to breathe sometimes. I wake up alone. I go to bed alone. I pick up the phone to call Ruth, but she's not there anymore. My granddaughter is growing up without a mother. I'm just tired of feeling so empty. I keep waiting for God to take away someone else from me."

The women swing in silence. The gentle sway is soothing. Tears slowly yet steadily stream down Esther's face.

"Esther, honey, I'm worried about you. You seem to be wallowing in the pit instead of healing."

Esther sits up and stares at her mother. "How does one heal from losing a child? A sister? A husband? I'll never heal from this. It's, it's, it's devastating. How do I get out of a pit, when I keep getting swallowed by it?"

Mary reaches over and takes her daughter's hand. "You forget. I have lost a child. I have lost my soulmate. I have lost a grandchild. I have lost siblings, parents, dear friends. I have lost too. I know your pain deeply. I realized a long time ago that I had to make a choice. I could relish the memories and celebrate their lives, or I could die with them."

"I think I would rather die with them. Each day seems to get harder, not easier. Whoever said time heals all things was a liar."

"Esther, that is my point. You already are, every day you are dying with them. You are too busy looking at the graves and missing life."

"Mama, I can't believe this is coming from you. Maybe I shouldn't have come home. I didn't realize I was going to be judged the entire time." Esther huffs.

"This isn't about grief. Somewhere in the grief, you took a left turn. I watched you after Lizzie. I watched you help Beau and Chloe. I know grief and mourning, this is different. This is about you being filled with anger instead of faith. Over the years, I have learned the difference. I'm not sure you have."

Esther bristles, oozing with defensive weapons. "I have faith. God is punishing me for leaving home for all of the sins in my life. I must have done something to tick him off because he keeps taking people from me." Esther looks up and shakes her hands into the air. "I surrender! Whatever I did to make you angry, I apologize." She drops her head and weeps into her hands.

Mary reaches over and rubs Esther's back. She prays for the right words to say. She has watched her daughter spiral down into a pit of depression for months. *Please, Father, give me Your words.* "Esther, I understand how you feel. I have battled with the questions and fear. I have felt the knots in my stomach and the overwhelming pain that makes it impossible to even breathe. In my life, I had to make a choice. I can't praise God and trust His promises with one side of my mouth and curse him with the other. God doesn't hate you, dear child. He isn't punishing you. If you believe in Him, you have to believe in all of Him. He is good, all the time, especially in our tears."

Mary looks down at her daughter. "It's there, in the deepest darkest nights that He is ever-present. Every time I've hit my knees in anguish, He was already there waiting for me. I know your hurt. God never wastes a tear. He is always working for our good, even when it doesn't feel good. It is okay to hurt and to cry and to miss them. God knows how you feel. Remember, He loves you so much, He watched His own Son die on a cross for you. He knows what it is like to lose a child. He promises comfort. At some point, you have to decide if you will accept His comfort and trust Him."

Esther's shoulders shake with sobbing. She leans into her mother's embrace. "Mama, it's just so hard. I can't take it anymore."

Mary holds Esther tightly as they rock. Esther empties herself. After a few minutes, Esther's breathing steadies. A tissue wipes away the residue from her waterfall of emotion. They listen as birds sing from the trees near the pond. The creaking of the porch swing adds to the melody. Esther wipes her nose.

"I just feel as though I'm drowning some days. Losing Lizzie and Ruthie within months was devastating. I think I was running on adrenaline. Just moving. Never stopping to think. Then John died, and I hit a wall. I don't know what to do."

"This, honey. You do this. You talk, you pray. You heal. A little bit at a time. You will be changed, but only you can determine what that looks like."

Mary leans over and kisses the top of Esther's head. "I miss them too. I wish so badly that Ruth was here today, but she's not. She's in Heaven with a bird's eye view of a day she would love. Today we are celebrating life. Instead of missing Ruth, today we will celebrate with the two people she loved the most. Maryssa and Malik need us. We love the people God needs us to love today. Healing happens when we stop picking the scars."

It's now Mary's turn to wipe her damp eyes. Esther leans her head back down on Mary's shoulder. The swinging becomes cathartic. The silence ends with

Mary's soft humming of her favorite hymn. The sun rises higher in the sky, illuminating the family farm for another day of celebration.

***

Maryssa

"Maryssa, stop! I have this. Go. Get ready for the wedding. This is my job now. The staff is ready. Your team is prepped and ready. The cake, well, the cake is just exquisite. Not to toot my own horn, but toot-toot." Frankie's mind drifts to her gorgeous creation of sugary, creamy bliss.

"I know. I know. You are right. I can't help myself. This is our first big event. Deep breaths. Okay. I'm going out now." Maryssa frantically spins in circles. "Where did I put my bouquet?"

Frankie picks up the bouquet of pink peonies and lavender freesia and hands it to Maryssa. The lace bow compliments her bridesmaid dress perfectly. "Maryssa." Frankie smiles and shoos her cousin from the kitchen.

"Thank you." Maryssa squeezes her cousin's hand in appreciation. Frankie has become Maryssa's right-hand woman for the past few weeks. Relief and trust help to release the tension in Maryssa's shoulders. She takes a deep breath as she wraps her hands around the fragrant bouquet.

As Maryssa walks out of the kitchen and through the restaurant, she admires the tables. Frankie worked with the florist and Victoria to design spectacular centerpieces and favors. Each guest will leave with a tree seedling to plant. In the center of each table sits a tall vanilla pillar candle surrounded by small potted plants of white violets and dark purple freesia. Individual seed packets tell guests their table number. Dim lighting creates an intimate and classy ambiance for the affair.

Malik and Victoria opt for a social hour before the wedding so they can greet their guests. Maryssa heads to the terrace to check on the cocktails and appetizers. Beau sees her approach and trots over to open the door for her. Chloe skips across the expanse to embrace Maryssa's waist.

"Oh, my. Aren't you the most darling of wedding guests?" Maryssa stares down at Chloe's beautiful curls pulled back into a ponytail with a bow that matches her yellow dress.

"Nona bought me a new dress. Daddy fixed my hair. My shoes are from Christmas, but Daddy says they match so I can wear them again." Chloe twirls to show off her dress.

"Your Daddy did an outstanding job. You look absolutely perfect." Maryssa winks at Beau.

"Hey you two, you're not supposed to look better than the bride. I might need to elope." A voice comes from the doorway behind them.

Victoria is stunning. Her tight black curls are pinned back on one side with a large Magnolia flower. The lace, high-neck, halter sheath dress is embedded with tiny crystals throughout the design. The tips of shimmery champagne shoes peek out from under her gown.

"Victoria, you look so amazing." Maryssa walks over to give her future step-mother a cheek kiss so as not to smudge their makeup. Chloe adds, in awe, "You look like a real-life princess."

"Those are high compliments coming from the two of you," Victoria replies. "Maryssa, the restaurant looks just perfect. You have exceeded all my dreams for this day. Every detail is flawless. Thank you so much." She squeezes Maryssa's hand.

"You'll have to thank Frankie for the decorations. She took the lead and made it happen. Have you seen the cake? It looks like a picture from a bridal magazine. I'm so excited for the family to see her debut. Who knew all that baking talent was hidden in the vineyard warehouse?" The women giggle.

"I, for one, cannot wait to eat some of it later. After eating her sample cakes, I'm a big fan already." Malik pats his stomach and grins as he approaches the group.

Maryssa beams at her father as she leans in to kiss him. "Hi, Daddy. Don't you look dapper."

"Daddy says I have to stay away from the cake. He says that little girls who like to twirl are dangerous to special wedding cakes. He said I can twirl, but not near the cake." Chloe twirls once more.

"Your Daddy is a very smart man. I am actually relieved you are here early, Miss Chloe. I need to check the Italian cookie table before everyone arrives, and I might have a few extra needing to be tested. Do you think you could help me?" Maryssa winks at Chloe then takes the girl's small hand in hers.

They turn to the door and head inside the restaurant. "A cookie table and a cake? This is the best wedding ever."

Maryssa stifles a laugh. "An Italian cookie table is an important tradition at a wedding. It's an entire table filled with special cookies. It began a long time ago. While Italian brides were preparing for their weddings, the women in their family would gather together to bake cookies from the old country to celebrate the big day. There are pizzelles, snowballs, cream puffs, rainbow cookies, thumbprints, and my favorite, the lemon cookie with icing. Mmm, yummy."

Chloe stares up at Maryssa with wide eyes.

"My Aunt Roxie used to make the most delicious lemon cookies. I loved it when she came in for weddings and let me help. Watching her and Nunnie together was so much fun. They would spend all day baking and telling stories from when they were young. Those ladies were something else." Maryssa taps the tip of Chloe's nose.

"Is it like when we bake together in Nunnie Mary's kitchen? And you and Nona tell stories about my Mama and Aunt Haddie?"

"It's exactly like that. Remember last week when Nunnie asked us to carry up her raspberry preserves from the basement?" Chloe nods. "She was getting ready to make her thumbprint cookies. Wait until you try those. They are so delicious. There is a little dollop of preserves in each cookie. I've seen you scarf down your toast with preserves. You'll love those cookies." The two walk hand in hand through the restaurant to taste test cookies.

A string quartet softly plays as guests begin to arrive for the wedding. Victoria and Malik mingle with family and friends as Maryssa's waitstaff serves everyone. Trays filled with bruschetta points, antipasto skewers, and mozzarella wrapped in prosciutto pass through the growing crowd. Glasses filled with an assortment of Rafaluzza wines are being enjoyed. The weather is absolutely perfect for an outdoor wedding. The sun is shining down on the terrace. Floral garlands surround them as rows of chairs face the vastness of the vineyard.

Chloe regales the guests with a detailed description of the cookie table and Frankie's cake. She twirls for everyone to see as Beau and Chloe help to direct people to the chairs. Malik and Victoria excuse themselves to the restaurant. Music fills the air. A gentle breeze floats the scents of lavender and freesia throughout the chairs.

With the last of the guests seated, everyone takes their place. Pastor Emil stands facing the crowd, holding his Bible. As the pastor of their church in DC, he was honored to make the drive to West Virginia to marry his two dear friends. Maryssa carries her bouquet while slowly walking toward the canopy. Chloe waves at Maryssa from her seat and Maryssa winks back at her. Malik and Victoria walk up the aisle together, taking their place in front of those they love most.

They are married in front of a sea of green, on Ruth's family farm, on a day that Ruth would have loved.

Chapter 30

Jackson

Jackson Cashe sneaks away from the wedding reception shortly after the cake is cut. He brings a piece, or more fitting, a peace offering for his meeting at the vineyard offices. Madison Lyn ensures the meeting site is secure from any uninvited guests. Secret Service sweeps the building before Jackson emerges from The Beast, his tank of an SUV. He carries two plates of wedding cake. Madison opens the door. Jackson follows her down the hallway to a conference room overlooking a portion of the vineyard. They are tailed only by Travis. Madison opens the conference room door. Inside sits one man at the table.

The Governor of West Virginia, former United States Senator, John Marchio, stands as the president enters the room. "President Cashe." The elder statesman extends his hand forward as Jackson places a cake plate down on the table. "I'm nervous now. Should I be worried? Did someone tell you that dessert is my weakness?" He laughs as Jackson shakes his hand.

"On the contrary, the cake is a gift for agreeing to meet under these circumstances." Jackson pulls out a chair to sit. Madison closes the door behind her, leaving the two men alone to talk.

John angles his chair to give President Cashe space while still facing the man. "I must admit, the invitation was intriguing, but the cloak and dagger element upped the ante for me. One can assume this meeting is an attempt to entice my support during the Reunification Summit next month." He pauses to gauge Jackson's response. Jackson, unreadable, instead takes a bite of his cake while pushing the other plate toward John. "However, unless you are planning on making multiple secret trips to all the governors, that seems unlikely. So, you are either on a fool's errand, or you have something up your sleeve."

The Governor lifts up his fork and pokes at the buttercream icing.

"Well, Sir, I hope I'm not on a fool's errand, and I can promise you that my sleeves are empty." John appreciates Jackson's show of respect as well as his honesty. He always liked the young politician and felt it was a shame he couldn't work with him any longer once the two nations separated.

"Well, you definitely have my attention. I'm all ears."

"I'm not sure if you have noticed, but my wife has me seeing issues from different angles these days. She has opened my eyes if you will. Instead of seeing down party lines, my vision has widened to see people over policy. That is the reason I pushed for the summit. I think it would be valuable for us to revisit the issues that divided us as a nation. Were we divided by policy or politics? To prepare, I need to understand and educate myself on the real issues instead of the hot button topics we all argued to death in the media. At one point, I thought I understood, but now I'm not so sure." Jackson stops and looks the man straight on before continuing. "John, I have always admired your service. You were one of the good guys in Washington. I am coming to you for insight. I want to learn from you. What really divided the nation? More importantly, what will it take to unify?"

John studies Jackson carefully. "You are serious, aren't you? You want to know my opinion and nothing more? No alliances? No pretenses, merely for the purpose of learning?" John waits while Jackson nods in affirmation as he chews another bite. John settles back in his chair and lifts a forkful of cake. "What do you want to know?"

Jackson smiles. "Everything, but let's start with the main crux keeping us separated. I know there were disagreements over insurance reform, immigration laws, taxes, welfare, the list is endless. What I learned from my time in Washington is that any topic can be argued from either side depending on which side held the votes. My first question to you is why? Why does everything need to be all or nothing? What happened to the art of compromise and communication?"

John laughs, sarcastically. "Maybe you should have asked a philosopher or historian. Do you want world peace too?" He laughs.

"If it is on the table, yes." Jackson chuckles at himself. "I want to understand the differences instead of arguing from one side."

"That's an easy answer, Jackson. Unfortunately, the solution is out of our hands. The answer to your question of why is freedom. However, freedom is defined differently by people. Republicans wanted the freedom to make their own decisions and choices for those under their care. The manifestation of this is in smaller federal government and more state rights. The Democrats wanted to ensure the rights and freedoms for everyone regardless of race, sex, religion, nationality. The manifestation of this requires federal laws and regulations, ensuring that everyone is treated equally. Essentially, one group saw freedom as governing themselves while the other saw freedom as governing everyone to protect the rights of all. Both sides used freedom of speech as their war cry. Anyone rallying the company line was righteous and speaking truth while the other side was immoral. This isn't anything new, Jackson. These are the same arguments that plagued our Founding Fathers as they broke free from England and began crafting a new government. More government versus less government. That is the foundational basis, but I have my own opinion of the crux, as you put it. I am interested to hear your perspective, as a younger politician during the Separation. What do you think caused the irreparable damage?"

"Honestly, I don't know. I'll tell you what I do know and what I've been struggling with since the Education Bill. I know the two-party system is the largest culprit. However, this has been in existence, as you said, since the founding of our country. Think about it, they settled their debates with duels. Not that I blame them on occasion." Jackson smirks which John returns with a snicker. "I do know that behind closed doors, without cameras or audiences, willing people can find ways to compromise. I saw this firsthand with the Education Bill. The divide wasn't so great when we took one item at a time and worked out the solutions."

Jackson rubs his chin before continuing. "That points to the media. Which, I partly blame for oversaturation and the creating of drama for ratings and money. I do agree that the inundation of coverage makes it impossible for people to stay detached. Nevertheless, the bias in media, contrary to their arguments otherwise, has always been prevalent in America. Newspapers as far back as the Revolution supported one party over another. My wife, Haddie, is passionate to place all the blame on media coverage, but I've learned to live with it. I have yet to find a true, unbiased source, but I don't believe that it is the cause. Most people choose to educate themselves by finding multiple sources in this day and age."

John interjects with a smile, "Just remember the majority of coverage is skewed in your favor."

Jackson laughs, "So I've been told."

"I agree with you on both points. Yes, the media and two-party system were both main contenders in the fight, but neither was a new phenomenon. You also must remember that our country has been divided before and met the same fate. History does, in fact, repeat itself. I sense that you have been studying this exact topic."

"You would be correct. I have spent time reading letters from both Washington and Lincoln as well as FDR. How did these men unify a nation during times of need? What causes half of a nation to cast votes of no-confidence in their government? Do they have regrets? Can this be repaired? Surely, we must be stronger together than apart."

Jackson picks at his half-eaten piece of cake. He's deep in thought. "When I created the Education Bill, with input from every side, it felt good. It felt right. There was compromise. It was poetic. It wasn't perfect, but it was a start. We discussed the concerns and issues from different angles and made decisions based on common ground and common sense. It was fair. It makes me wonder if the political party system interferes too much. It's one thing to agree with a group of people who work together. Its an entirely different story when a person cannot make their own decision based on their state's wishes or their gut feelings on a vote."

John shakes his head as he begins to chuckle. "Jackson, be careful, you're starting to sound like me now." The older gentleman sits up in his chair and leans toward Jackson. "Do you know why I am a Republican? Why I pushed for the Separation? I did it because I was tired of fighting the same fights with the same people. We weren't accomplishing anything. We were constantly playing tennis on the same court, with the same outcomes depending on who served last. It's no secret where I stand on federal versus state government, but do you know why? The masses vote on their federal politicians and look where that gets us. Democrats pass massive legislative changes. Republican voters respond then there is a deadlock for two years. Republicans take over and pass legislation then the Democrats respond with their votes. Another deadlock and the cycle continues. Nothing changes. At the state level, if I sign a bill, I have to talk to the actual people it effects on Sunday mornings or at the next county fair. State politicians can't hide in Washington. We live in the state where we govern, not in Washington. The grassroots movement is important because it encourages every person to have a voice and make a difference. This might shock you, but I agree with you that our country needs a stable federal system. We need a strong cabinet with departments that aid and support on a national level. Within reason, of course. This federal system should aid, not enable. We also need senators and congressmen and judges for checks and balances. It must work together and not in opposition. I agree with you that we would accomplish more with compromise rather than with accusation. Sadly, as you know, it usually ends with grandstanding instead of genuine discussion."

"After working with the teacher unions, the homeschool associations, and the charter school groups, I tend to agree with you. Not everyone walked away with sweeping victories, but everyone left the table feeling good and with something to show for it." Jackson rubs his chin. "John, it felt good. For the first time in my career, I felt as if I truly made a difference. It mattered. You know what really struck me? Before I met with the party leaders, I called Rich's mother. She's been a fourth-grade teacher for thirty years. I asked her for a list of things that would help her in the classroom. You know what she said?" Jackson pauses in the moment.

"No, but you have me on pins and needles, based on how it seems to have impacted you." John chuckles.

"She said, 'Jackson, dear, I need *you* out of my classroom. Let me teach the children in my classroom. Stop telling me how to do it and stop telling schools how they should spend the money. Politicians have no business telling teachers how to teach. Let me do my job by trusting me.' John, it hit me. She was right. I'm not an education expert. Obviously, Hayman Barnes wasn't an expert. I'm laying all my cards on the table here, John. I struggle with how to balance federal regulations with real people and real problems. I'm worried we have lost the balance with the Separation."

John settles back into his chair and watches Jackson, contemplating his next words. "Between us, while the Allied States is thriving in many ways, we are struggling without the very federal support system we rallied against. With that said, I still believe that the current federal system was teetering between support and intrusion. There is a fine line between ensuring the rights of some while taking away the rights of others in the process. California has different needs than West Virginia. Let West Virginians decide how they are governed. Now, before you get started with a debate, this goes both ways. From my experience, both sides of the aisle agree on the core issues. What's that saying, the devil is in the details?"

"So how do I fix that? How do I get people back to the table to talk?" Jackson is perplexed.

"You invite them. Start small. Take away the cameras and the fuel. Choose leaders who work well together and have shown diplomacy over their careers. Leave out the grandstanders and showman. Think outside of the box. Review the current system. What departments do we need as opposed to which are here because that's the way it's always been?"

The man continues. "The problem is that both sides want to appear as the authority so instead of agreeing, we accuse. We cry foul. The focus needs to switch to candidates instead of political parties. Jackson, start the way you did with me. Honesty and open-mindedness go a long way. Invite people to the table and present unified proposals to the people. Control the narrative and the players through cooperation. Make compromise the new way. Lead by example."

Jackson taps his finger on the solid oak table. "Think outside the box. No media." Jackson repeats John's words as they marinate in his mind. "No grandstanders." He chortles. "That will be the most difficult part, I think."

"You may need to look for leaders at the state level. Maybe some tried and true business and community leaders. If you are serious, you need to change the entire conversation. You are going to face a lot of opposition, especially from your own party. You will offend everyone not invited. This will create new enemies."

"Can I count on you to come?" Jackson earnestly beseeches the man.

John laughs. "Taking me down with you?" He shakes his head, then extends his hand. "If you handle a summit like you did this meeting, then I would be honored, Mr. President."

"Well, I guess the worst they can do is try me for treason, right? Will you offer me asylum?"

"West Virginia is a great place to live." John smiles before lifting another forkful of fluffy delight. "Now, who got married, and how is your beautiful wife?"

The men engage in personal chit chat while they finish their cake. They catch up on old friends and share their favorite Washington haunts. John regales Jackson with stories of his grandparents living with Haddie's great-grandparents when they first arrived in America. They discuss the common surnames that are all traced back to Fiore, Italy. Jackson remembers how much he misses having conversations without maneuvering elements. As they shake hands and John heads for the door, Jackson remembers something from the beginning of their conversation. "Wait, John. You never told me your opinion of the crux."

The gray-haired gentleman slowly turns back in the direction of the table. His face exemplifies a calm peacefulness that Jackson envies. "Jackson, I am a Christian. I believe that Jesus Christ is the Ruler of all Nations. The King of kings. He is my authority. I spend time studying the Word every day before I leave my home. Every issue I must deal with, I seek His Word first, and I vote accordingly. The Bible recounts stories of battles and wars, sin and Holiness, the rising and falling of nations. This mess we're in now isn't new, and it will continue regardless of what we do as politicians. We live in a world filled with lonely and hurting people. Every person longs for freedom. I have learned that the only true freedom is found in Him. World peace will come, but it won't happen because of us, it will happen in spite of us at the appointed time. If you want the answers, seek the Truth."

Jackson sits quietly. John leaves the building and climbs into his waiting car. After a moment, the driver steps out and hands Travis a well-worn book and tells him it is for President Cashe. The car drives down the road as Jackson exits the building. Travis hands Jackson Governor John Marchio's personal Bible. Inside the cover, in John's handwriting, "If you want true peace, start here."

Chapter 31

Beau

Maryssa Lavalier and Haddie Robinson Cashe have pulled over some great pranks throughout the years. In elementary school, they traded dessert coupons from Maria's Ristorante for homework passes. They have sweet-talked their way into extra servings of pie at their favorite diner in DC. They have even name-dropped to get into sold-out shows at the Kennedy Center. Sneaking out a window to lose a Secret Service detail, tops anything they've done before tonight.

"Shh, your panting is going to get us caught." Haddie scolds Maryssa as they army crawl behind Nunnie's garden shed. The two women are dressed from head to toe in black. Once they reach the edge of the vineyard, they duck through the first row and take off at full speed towards the converted barn. The red tin roof of Poppy's appears in the distance. They laugh and keep running. Once they reach the clearing, they spot Beau leaning up against his old pickup. He sees them pop out from the vines and shakes his head as he nods in the direction of the truck. The three of them climb into the cab of the pickup and Beau peels out of the parking lot.

"You two realize how ridiculous you look, right?"

Haddie pokes her brother-in-law in the shoulder, "Just drive."

"The last time I was in a pickup truck was when Mama made me go to homecoming with Michael Albright."

"Oh my goodness, I totally forgot about that night." Maryssa begins laughing. "Didn't he try to kiss you?"

"He did kiss me! I was checking for something in my purse, and when I looked up, his lips were right on mine. It was awful. My first kiss was a drive-by slobbery mess. I actually gagged. Then I spent the rest of the night clenching the passenger door." Haddie reflexively gags at the thought. "I hate pickup trucks."

Beau protests, "Hey, don't judge a perfectly good vehicle based on some bad-kissing, dorky, high school kid."

"I'm with Beau on this one, Had. I love pickup trucks. I loved those old movies where bucket seats didn't exist, and the girl slides right over next to her cowboy." Maryssa dreams out the window.

Now it's Haddie's turn to laugh. "You really need a date. A real date, not a good book about vampires or werewolves. I think Cary Grant ruined you."

"We all have our ideas of romance. Look at you, you're married to a walking encyclopedia." Maryssa leans over the seat to poke Haddie's shoulder.

"You can tell a lot about a man from his truck, that's all I'm sayin' on this issue. Maryssa, your dream guy needs to drive an older model, they all come with bucket seats these days. Sorry." He grins at her through the rearview mirror.

They drive for twenty minutes down a dark and twisty two-lane highway. Haddie conducts surveillance the entire drive. Maryssa isn't sure if Haddie is more fearful of her service detail finding her or a random photographer.

They pull onto a gravel path and slowly inch down the tight makeshift road. They pass under a thick canopy of trees and pull up behind Sammy's pickup truck. They wearily climb out slowly into the pitch blackness of night. They follow voices down toward Tygart Lake. Haddie feels nervous but relieved to have lost her service detail. They would have had a fit over this adventure. The gravel road, if you can call it that, turns to dirt then narrows even more into a path. Just as they crest a small hill, they see lights on the dock.

Sammy sees them first and shouts, "Welcome to Wildcat Hollow!" The three crafty evaders balance themselves as they walk across the docks and try to climb onto the pontoon boat waiting for them to leave.

"I thought we were taking your boat?" Maryssa asks Sammy.

Frankie bursts out laughing, "If we did, we'd end up broken down in the middle of the lake."

"Hey!" Sammy is affronted by his sister's snarky reply.

"Am I wrong?" Frankie pulls out a chip from the bag she's holding and pops it into her mouth.

"Dad's boat is bigger," Sammy backpedals.

"She's right," Tony admits to the new passengers as he unties the ropes linking them to the dock. "We bought a used boat last year from a buddy who moved to Colorado. We've only had it out three times. The first time the engine flooded. Next time the battery died. The final blow required us to rewire the whole dang thing. So, we cleaned off Sam's boat instead."

"Technically, we're not even supposed to be here, so if we get arrested, I'm saying they kidnapped me." Frankie deadpans while eating another chip.

"Arrested?" Haddie panics and tries to climb back off of the boat. Beau grabs her around the waist and prevents her from leaving.

"I'd sit back down unless you want to go swimming in the dark." Beau points to Sammy, who has already coasted the boat out five feet.

"Relax, Haddie. We're not going out that far plus we're tucked back here in the 'holler.' The conservation officer will never see us." Sammy blows off her concerns and keeps coasting.

"Famous last words. If I'm the headline tomorrow, I'm backing up Frankie's kidnapping story." Haddie plops down beside her cousin and reaches for her own handful of salty chips.

The lake is lit by a full moon and a blanket of stars. Maryssa holds onto the railing of the boat and breathes in the chilly air. The night smells of moss and earth. It is so refreshing and cleansing. "What kind of fish are in the lake? Maybe I can add some seasonal local fish specials this summer."

Tony takes his eye off of Sammy's driving and looks at Maryssa. "Walleye, crappie, perch, carp, there are a lot. There's a lot of catfish too. Just ask your cousin. According to Sammy, he caught a twenty-five-pounder last summer, but no one was around to see it before he set it free."

"It was the right thing to do. A beautiful fish like that needs to live free, not end up in my freezer." Sammy puffs out his chest.

"Uh-huh. I'm sure that is exactly what happened. Sammy just oozes humility and compassion." Maryssa throws a pillow at the back of the captain's chair.

"Hey!" Sammy protests as they all settle in and laugh.

As soon as the boat is hidden behind a tree in the bend of the lake. Tony opens the cooler and passes out bottles of water and soda. Sammy turns his chair and grabs the bag of chips quickly from his sister before she realizes what's happening. They sit quietly for a moment enjoying the symphony around them, crickets, toads croaking, fish splashing as they get to the water's surface. The wind rustling in the trees along with animals creeping on the ground, make a surround sound system for them to enjoy. The sounds are soothing and reassuring.

"It's so calm and peaceful." Maryssa takes another deep breath and wraps a blanket around her. "I remember this when we were younger. After spending our days working on the farm, we would come out to Uncle Sam's cabin. We would camp and swim. I'd forgotten how grounded the lake makes me feel. It reminds me of childhood."

"Lady Maryssa, shall I grab a scroll to copy your artful words of wonder for the lake. Err, laketh." Sammy mocks her as he waves his arms in adoration for nature.

"Frankie, do you have an extra pillow to throw?" Maryssa asks as they all laugh.

"I'm with Maryssa," It's Haddie's turn to reminisce. "My favorite childhood memories revolve around you lunatics and summer. Remember that time Lizzie was floating lazily in a raft and Uncle Dom threw a stick right next to her and yelled 'water snake'?" Haddie holds her sides from laughing so hard.

"Or that time you ended up with poison ivy all over your legs because you were running away from a turtle? Who runs that fast from a turtle? A tuurr-tle." Sammy speaks slowly to emphasize the irony.

"My favorite memory was when the three of you got busted with DJ for trying to TP houses." Frankie drinks her water while watching her older cousins.

Haddie drops her head in her hands from embarrassment. Beau speaks up this time. "Ah, I've heard this story. Didn't you guys drive all over town looking for toilet paper?"

"Oh my. I forgot about that. It was the summer before Haddie and I started school in DC. The Michigan family came down for a funeral or wedding or something big. Sammy just got his driver's license. We went into every fast food restaurant in town and took as many rolls as we could neatly tuck under our jackets." Maryssa, Haddie, and Sammy are laughing so hard at this point they can barely speak.

Frankie finishes the story so Beau and Tony can enjoy it. "These idiots thought they were so clever. They drove back to the farmhouse for some reason when Nunnie busted them. She knew something was off and walked around the barn. She found them sitting in the car, surrounded by rolls of toilet paper."

"I don't even think she said a word to us. We just drove back into town and returned every last roll." Haddie remembers. "She didn't tell our parents, but big mouth Frankie did."

Tony is laughing along with them as if he were there that night. "Now that's a headline. First Lady Haddie Robinson Cashe was a thug during her teenage years."

"You have no idea. I'm just waiting for the right price. I have so many embarrassing stories on her. I will be rich and retire with Dad." Sammy leans back in his chair and folds his hands behind his head while stretching his legs out in front of himself.

Haddie nails him right in the forehead with a pretzel. "Do, and I'll tell everyone here about Lesley Donaldson."

Sammy sits up ramrod straight as the others jeer and beg Haddie for details. The banter continues for over an hour. They talk in groups and together, never missing a beat to build up one another or call someone to task. Beau watches them. An outsider who has worked beside them for months is now part of the conversations.

Cousins who have been separated by time and distance come together like no time has passed at all. Beau relishes this night. The next generation weaving the stories. Love, laughter, loss, and longing are all intertwined to craft the tapestry of the Marchio family legacy, and he is part of it.

The ringing of Maryssa's cell phone startles them all. She laughs and hands the phone to Haddie without answering it first.

"Hi Honey, is everything all right? Did you make it back to DC, okay?" Haddie says in a fake groggy voice.

"Hello, Darling. Sorry, did I wake you? I just wanted to call and tell you goodnight, and I love you."

"You are so sweet. I love you too, honey."

"Oh, I was curious about something."

"What's that, Babe?"

"I was wondering why Chloe is wearing your tracking bracelet, while you and Maryssa are nowhere to be found at the farmhouse."

"Umm, well, I, we." Haddie begins to sputter.

"Sweetheart, I believe the word you are looking for is 'Busted.'"

Chapter 32

Esther

*T*his is a bad idea.

Esther fidgets with her charm bracelet. She checks her face in the rearview mirror one last time. Taking a deep breath, she grabs her purse from the passenger seat. Already five minutes late, she walks slowly from the parking lot to Main Street. Hoping that he assumes she isn't coming, and already left.

She turns the corner and sees people sitting in chairs along the main road outside of the café. A group of teenagers blocks her view of the tables. As she gets closer, a thick head of silver hair catches her eye.

This is a bad idea. I should go before he sees me.

Wes Anderson stands the second he spies Esther. His broad smile reminds her of summer; fresh-cut grass, baseball games, and ice cream. She breathes deeply and tries to return his smile.

He meets her on the sidewalk and awkwardly leans in to offer a friendly kiss on the cheek. Esther's insides are a mess. She is nervous and anxious. Trying to control her inner shaking, Esther offers a prayer for peace and takes a calming breath. She slowly hangs her purse on the back of the chair to give her more time. As she settles, she looks up, right into bright blue eyes.

"I wasn't sure you were going to show up today." Wes laughs, uncertain.

Esther chooses transparency. "To be honest, I wasn't sure I was going to either." She smiles and shrugs.

"Well, I'm really glad you did."

"You did call the house multiple times to ask," Esther smirks at Wes. "My mother made me come so you would stop calling."

His face launches into a jolly smile. "Now I know you're lying. One, your mother loves me, always has. Two, you still have that tell when you're trying to hide the truth."

She stares at him in unbelief as a young waitress comes to their table with plates.

"I ordered us their famous peanut butter brownies. If you didn't show up, I was going to drown my sorrow in chocolate." He shrugs.

Esther orders her coffee, and the waitress leaves them alone.

"You still drink your coffee with more milk than coffee?"

Honesty seems to be coming easier and easier as Wes talks. "It's a little unnerving, or maybe I should say annoying how you think you know me so well. It's been forty years, Wes." Esther settles back into her chair and crosses her arms.

"Your grandmother Marchio always gave you coffee milk when you stayed with her. You drink your coffee that way because it reminds you of her." Wes returns her pointed look with a checkmate look of his own.

Esther shakes her head and smiles. "So, Wes, what is it you've been doing with yourself all these years?" She picks up her fork and takes a bite of her brownie. The moist, creamy, decadent taste catches her off guard.

"It is good, right?" He watches her and smiles.

"What have I been doing? Recently or for the past forty years?"

"Both."

Esther watches Wes intently as he tells her all about the insurance business he owns. He is partially retired and only works with a few long-time clients. He couldn't bear to go into law like his father, even after his baseball career tanked. He announces baseball games for the high school team on the radio and helps with a few baseball clinics across the state. He is a doting father and grandfather and never remarried after he and Peggy divorced.

Esther asks questions along the way but only to keep the conversation from turning to her own story. She notices the lines around his eyes and across his forehead. He has aged well. He is distinguished yet still very much youthful. His laugh still comes from his belly and his entire face lights with his smile.

Esther catches herself smiling and enjoying his company as guilt begins to creep over her. She tries to listen to Wes while frantically trying to remember John's favorite tie. She compares John's smile to Wes's while thinking about the first time John made her his famous chili. Warring thoughts in her mind catch her off balance. A car horn shakes her thoughts back to the present as Wes waves to a passing SUV.

"Speak of the devil. That was Steve."

Esther looks at Wes, confused.

"He's my business partner I was telling you about. You remember Steve Lambert, don't you?"

Esther sits up straight in her chair and stares directly into Wes's eyes. "Wait a minute. You mean to tell me that your business partner, and I believe you said best friend as well, is Steve Lambert? Peggy-Lambert-Anderson-whatever-her-last-name-is-now's brother? That Steve Lambert is your business partner? The business you started *after* you divorced and moved home?"

Wes nods.

"Well, if that doesn't beat all. I mean, I've heard of amicable divorces before, but this must be a first." She sits back and studies the man carefully. "Now I'm intrigued. You and Peggy are friends?"

He nods.

"You and Peggy take turns helping with your grandkids?"

He nods.

"You and Peggy spend holidays together with your daughter and Peggy's new family?"

He nods.

"And your business partner and best friend is her brother. And this all happened after your divorce?"

He nods.

Esther shakes her head in disbelief.

"And I play golf with her second husband if he needs a fourth at the last minute."

They sit, staring at one another for a moment. Both assessing the other.

"I never, in my wildest dreams, thought I would be asking you this question, but, why on earth did you and Peggy ever divorce?" She picks up her iced coffee and takes a big gulp, trying to piece this all together.

Wes Anderson stares right into Esther Marchio's hazel eyes. He pauses before he says, "You."

Esther begins choking on her drink. She coughs and coughs until she can finally catch her breath. She's not sure if she's angry, shocked, curious, or being played. "Me? You can't be serious?" Her shocked tone elicits a worried look to cross Wes's face.

The man looks down at his empty plate and pulls out his wallet. His digs out a yellowed picture of Esther.

"I didn't plan on getting this deep on our first date, but I guess we're going there now."

She sputters, "This is not a date. This is two old friends getting together for coffee. Technically we're not even friends."

Esther feels badly as soon as the words escape her mouth. The hurt look on Wes doesn't go unnoticed.

"Whatever the reason you are here, I would like to tell you the story if you want to hear it." He pauses, waiting for her to nod.

"Esther, the night you left me, I was devastated. I thought you would be so happy for me. I thought we could get married and eventually you would move to wherever the team settled me."

"You never told me that. You just told me you were leaving for a farm team in Virginia and that you'd be back at the end of the season."

"I just assumed you knew I wanted to marry you. I wanted to buy you a real ring first."

Esther sits up, trying to maintain her composure. Her emotions are too raw for this right now. "That still doesn't explain your divorce."

"Peggy came to me that night, I had been drinking, a lot. My pride was hurt, I was confused. I thought you knew I wanted to marry you and when you left, I thought that was the end of us. Peggy was your friend. She was telling me how you only wanted me because I was the captain of the baseball team, and you assumed I would be a lawyer like my dad. You didn't want to follow a loser baseball player around the east coast."

Esther shakes at the implications. "Wes, you know I would never have said any of that."

He cuts her off, "Please let me finish." She nods.

"I know. I knew then. Peggy admitted it after we were married, but it was too late by then. Regardless, things got carried away that night, and I slept with Peggy. I was so embarrassed. I knew you would never forgive me. I couldn't even forgive me. I started dating Peggy and then left for baseball. She called me on the road and told me she was pregnant. I came home that fall. We got married and moved to Virginia."

Wes searches Esther's face for her approval to continue. He plays with his napkin for a minute.

"Peggy and I made it work, but neither of us was happy. One night, she came to me in tears. She told me what she had done. She heard what happened that night and she came to find me. Her father was an abusive alcoholic, and she wanted to get out of town. I was her only ticket. She admitted to lying about you and told me that she had been having an affair with Lorraine's pediatrician and was leaving me for him."

He rubs his chin, far off in his own memories. "The sad part was that I wasn't angry at her for cheating, I was relieved. That was the first night the two of us really talked. Over the years we had grown to respect and appreciate one another, but there was never love. She told me that she knew I carried your picture in my wallet. At first she resented you and me, but then began to resent herself more. She started seeing a counselor and knew she had to tell me the truth."

Wes looks into Esther's eyes. "The truth is, I never felt that I deserved you. After that night, I knew I didn't. I let my pride and ego ruin all of my dreams. I can't be angry at what happened. If things didn't work out the way they did, I wouldn't have Lorraine or her kids, and they are the greatest gift in my life. I wouldn't have gone into business with Steve. I know my life turned out the way it was supposed to, but you have always been the greatest regret in my life. When I ran into your mom at the store, it was a spark of something that I hadn't felt in forty years."

Numbness has overtaken Esther. She can't formulate words. Her emotions and his words are swirling like a hurricane in her heart. She closes her eyes before tears can escape. She takes a deep, steadying breath and looks back into his eyes.

"Wes, I don't know what to say. I didn't expect all of that. I don't even know what to think about all of this. I'm at a disadvantage. You dropped a lot of information on me."

Wes reaches across the table and takes her hand in both of his. "Esther, I just needed you to know. I needed to apologize for failing you. For letting us both down. I don't know what this means either, but I feel like we're getting a second chance."

"Wes, I-I can't. I'm not ready. I was married to John for most of my life. I loved him deeply. I can't do that to him. I'm not ready." She shakes her head and wipes a tear. Her heart is torn and shaken. She feels shredded and confused.

"I understand. I do. I just would like to spend some time with you. Getting to know you again. I'll take anything you'll give me. Maybe you can at least consider me a friend to have coffee with?" He winks, acknowledging her slight from earlier.

"Esther, I've spent the last forty years regretting one night. I'll spend the next forty trying to make up for it if you let me."

"Wes, I can only offer you friendship right now. I don't have anything else to give. I gave my broken heart to John, and he healed it. I don't think it can survive much more." She looks at his longing eyes and sees the hurt. She understands hurt. "If you're willing to be a friend, I could use one of those."

Relief and promise flood his deep blue eyes. "I'll take it."

Chapter 33

Beau

After a long hard day of framing a new kitchen with Tony's crew, Beau is exhausted. He is still getting used to the weather in West Virginia. One day it reaches eighty degrees and the next it is in the fifties. He passes the road to the family farmhouse and heads to the entrance of the vineyard. A split rail fence separates the property from the country road. He turns at the stone post holding the black slate sign for Rafaluzza Vineyard. He and Tony secured the matching sign for Poppy's last month. This road will take him to the vineyard's tasting rooms and Poppy's. It is a tree-lined drive, just like the family farmhouse. Esther asked him earlier to meet them at Poppy's after work. Tonight, Maryssa wants to thank the family for their support with a dinner. The film crew arrived yesterday. The judges for the Geoffrey Barton Award arrive in two days.

Beau passes the building that hosts the tasting rooms and vineyard store on the right side of the road. As he drives into the parking lot, Poppy's is luminous with the setting sun lowering behind it. He marvels at the magnificent structure and smiles. Beau smiles for Maryssa's vision, and he smiles for sharing a part of the construction and the structure itself. The two-story building is crowned with a red tin roof which matches the other buildings on the property. The original structure was a massive barn with a kitchen and bathrooms. It was inspired by the log cabins Esther's father had loved. The Marchio family used it for family gatherings and reunions. It was perfect.

Maryssa took the original design and enhanced every element without changing the intimate design of her Poppy's dream. It looks like a French chalet in the middle of West Virginia. Tony's crew replaced the roof and spruced up the landscaping. The building itself was extended using the same type of logs and stain. Stone accents were added to create an upscale restaurant exterior. The back wall of the restaurant is enclosed by windows so guests can enjoy a view of the vineyard.

A hidden staircase on the left side of the building leads to Beau's apartment on the second floor. Off to the right and rear of the building is Ruthie's Terrazza. Beau is proud of the terrace as it mostly consists of his woodwork. He led the decking project and installed the carved railing himself. He also built the outside bar by hand and carved the bar top. The piece of resistance is the gazebo that he has been hand carving in the evenings. It is still hidden under a tent where he has been working on it. He will stain and seal it this week. The gazebo is inspired by the family he has come to know and love even more over the past few months. The family who took him in along with Chloe and gave them a new life.

Beau pulls into the parking lot where he helped paint the lines. He finds the farthest spot on the left and takes a minute to run up the stairs to shower and change. Chloe should already be downstairs helping Mary, Esther, and Maryssa. Thirty minutes later, he is walking into the front door of Poppy's to the sound of laughter. His grateful heart smiles at the sounds. As he passes the hostess stand and the bar and waiting areas, the threshold of the dining room boasts large wooden beams and ambient lighting. Large metal chandeliers complement the natural light streaming in from the windows. The tables are covered in either black or deep burgundy tablecloths. An assortment of small potted plants and herbs in hand-painted clay pots are arranged in the center of each table.

Beau's attention is drawn to the long, family-sized table near the kitchen door. Everyone is here to celebrate Maryssa. The entire Marchio family. His family. Malik and Victoria arrived today. Haddie and Jackson won't be here until after the camera crew arrives, but the rest of the clan is celebrating. Chloe sees Beau and runs full speed into his waiting arms. His arrival is noted with cheers and greetings from the table. Some are already sitting while most are walking back and forth carrying platters from the kitchen.

Uncle Sam and Uncle Dom fill glasses with wine and water. The younger cousins run around the restaurant as their mothers caution them to watch out for the tables. Aunt Jo's teenage son sits at one end of the table, intently reading a book. Frankie carries out a beautiful chocolate cake with raspberries on top. Everyone works together in a simplistic harmony. He is reminded of their well-used verse, "Many hands make light the work." A calmness that he hasn't felt since Lizzie passed rushes over him. He takes his place with the family and begins to help prepare the meal.

Once the food is on the table, and everyone is seated, Maryssa clinks her spoon against her glass. "I want to thank each and every one of you for all of your encouragement and support. Not just tonight, but every day. You have attended countless ballet performances, graduations, birthdays, and many mundane events in between. I am beyond blessed to be in this family. Poppy's is more than a restaurant, it's a celebration of our family legacy." Maryssa raises her glass in the air. "Here's to Nunnie and Poppy and the legacy of love they have taught us all. Salute!"

A round of "Salute" fills the air as Nunnie Mary wipes a stray tear. She lifts her glass as well and offers her own toast. "To Maryssa and all my grandchildren who will carry on after us! Salute."

The family eats and laughs for hours. The platters of food are taken back into the kitchen, and leftovers are sent home as stragglers leave. Sammy, Uncle Sam, and Uncle Dom are talking about the health of the grapes while the others help Maryssa clean the kitchen. Uncle Sam excuses himself when he unexpectedly receives a phone call. The last of the kitchen helpers walk back into the dining room to collect children, purses, phones, and leftover boxes. Maryssa begins turning off lights when Uncle Sam returns. Everything seems to freeze with the baffled expression on his face.

His wife Hannah, visibly worried speaks first. "Sam, what's wrong?"

"That was Ben Stanley. He just left a meeting with his financial advisors. It seems they want to go a different direction with their distribution outlets. They will continue to carry the Rafaluzza brand for the remainder of the year, but will be phasing out our wine and will not be moving forward with our national launch or with Poppy's restaurant line." The older man shakes his head and rubs his hand across his chin.

"Can he do that, Dad?" Sammy asks.

"It seems he can because of a loophole in the contracts, though I'm not sure I agree. I'll call our lawyer in the morning, but fighting it out in court may not be worth the cost." He looks straight on at his niece. "Maryssa, I'm so sorry. I just don't understand. Did something happen between you and Stanley's daughter? He said something about voiding the contract based on 'no confidence' in the chef. He wouldn't go into details, but I remember hearing that his daughter quit."

Beau's face is as white as Uncle Sam's now. *Surely, she wouldn't sabotage the entire family because of me.*

"No confidence? Is he serious? I can have a list of chefs all over the country send emails tonight vouching for her skills and work ethic!" Malik is fuming.

"Daddy, stop. Uncle Sam, to be honest, I still don't know what happened with Angelica. She stormed into my office one night all upset. I tried to call her several times, but she wouldn't return my calls. She actually blocked me from calling or texting and from all of her social media. I mailed her final paycheck with a little extra for all she did for me."

Maryssa pauses, unsure of sharing this next bit of information. "And, well, something did happen with Mr. Stanley. It was very minor. I didn't mention it to you, but he sort of hit on me after our meeting. It wasn't overt, more flirting than anything else, but I assured him I was focused on growing the business. I've spoken to him several times since then, and he seemed fine, so I don't think that's the reason."

Sammy attempts to cover his laughter at the thought of Ben Stanley hitting on Maryssa. "You're kidding, right? He's what like 70? That is so gross."

"He did what? What is this man's name?" Malik is livid. He stands up quickly at the table, almost knocking over his chair. Victoria places her hand on his arm, trying to calm him. "The nerve of that man! I would like to have a word with him." Malik is rambling and plotting at this point. "This is completely unacceptable. Unbelievable. Give me his name, I'll fix this."

"Stop, all of you." Maryssa raises her voice slightly over the family mob. "Dad and Sammy. I can handle unwarranted and unwanted advances. I've been doing it for years. Men love ballerinas. I can handle myself. I don't need you fighting my battles. Uncle Sam, this was not your fault. I won't lie, I'm disappointed, but that was not my priority. My priority is Poppy's, that is where my focus needs to be right now. I'm more concerned with the vineyard. Does this mean the end of your national launch?"

Sammy is cocky now. "Oh, cugina, don't worry about us. I've been telling Dad we could do better than the Stanleys for years. We have other distributors who would love to carry our line. Dad always said we needed to be loyal to the Stanleys. Turns out, they're not so loyal in return."

"Maryssa, Sammy is right. We'll be fine. I just hate that you put so much effort into designing and planning for nothing." Sam rubs his jaw.

"Sam, this might be my fault. Angelica and I." Beau guilty begins his story but is cut off quickly by Maryssa.

"Stop! Seriously. This has nothing to do with us. The Stanleys obviously have an issue not getting their way. I don't want to be in business with them if this is how they behave. It's childish." She holds her chin high while tamping down disappointment. "Victoria, please take my father to the hotel before he grabs a pitchfork and torch. Beau, take Miss Chloe to bed. Uncle Sam, we can talk tomorrow. Nunnie, Aunt E, let's go home."

An hour later, Beau has bathed and dressed Chloe for bed. Her wet curls are tied in two messy braids. They have read her favorite book twice. He helps her arrange stuffed animals around her bed. Uni the Unicorn goes right beside her pillow. The pink blanket with dancers on it is pulled right up under her chin. They say her prayers. She blows a kiss to her Mommy in Heaven. As Beau is getting ready to leave the room, Chloe calls his attention back to her. "Daddy, I think it's my fault."

He walks back to her bedside and kneels so he can see her face. "What's your fault, Sweetheart?"

"Maryssa and that man not selling her food." A single tear slides down her face.

He quickly wipes the tear. "Honey, you couldn't possibly have had anything to do with it. Why would you think that?"

"Gelica came over to color with me one time when I was at the restaurant. You were working outside, and Maryssa was in the kitchen. I made a picture with me, you, and Maryssa playing together. Gelica started asking me stuff about you and then she got really mad. She went into the kitchen and was using her outside voice to Maryssa. Then she ran out, and Maryssa came out of the kitchen to check on me, and she was sad or mad. I'm not sure which, but she wasn't happy like normal. Then Gelica hit you in the noggin and made you bleed. See, I made Gelica mad now Gelica's dad is being mean to Maryssa." The sweet little girl finally finishes her argument then looks to her Daddy for forgiveness.

"My sweet, sweet girl. You had absolutely nothing to do with what happened to Maryssa. Angelica and Mr. Stanley are both grownups. You were just coloring. I don't want you to worry one more second about this. You heard Maryssa tonight. We have a big celebration this weekend for her and her restaurant. Let's focus on that like Maryssa asked. You did nothing wrong, do you understand?"

She nods.

He stares down at her for a moment. She is such a miracle. "Now, you get some sleep. We have a big week ahead, okay?" She nods again as he brushes her hair away from her face. He leans down to kiss her forehead then leaves the room.

Beau walks across the room to the kitchen for a glass of water. He thinks about Angelica and Chloe and Maryssa. She must be so disappointed. This is the last thing she needs to worry about during her big week.

The picture Chloe drew that night of the three of them is pinned to the refrigerator. He remembers that night. He felt terrible upsetting Angelica but forgot all about it when he went inside and saw Chloe's pictures. She asked to put the one with the three of them on the fridge. Now, he's relieved that he turned down Angelica when he did. The last thing he needs is a crazy girlfriend. He rubs his forehead in remembrance then heads for bed.

He sends a quick text to Maryssa.

`Beau:  You've got this, don't worry about the Stanleys. It's their loss.`

His phone chirps in response.

`Maryssa:  Thanks, I needed that.`

The next morning Beau walks from his bedroom into Chloe's and finds an empty bed.

Summer

Chapter 34

Missing

Haddie runs frantically down the hallway. Phone clutched tightly in her hand. Weaving around people. An intern drops papers on the floor as Haddie crashes past. "I'm so sorry," she shouts over her shoulder in his direction.

Mrs. Pennington jumps to her feet in surprise as Haddie streaks by her desk. The other secretary turning to the sound of the commotion behind her. The door to the Oval Office swings open wide as Travis reflexively reaches for his weapon. Her voice, shaking and gasping for air, pierces the quiet conversation. "Jackson, it's Chloe."

Scattered shock makes way for confusion and the need for clarity. Jackson crosses the room in seconds as Haddie crumbles into his arms. Travis, always in command of the situation, walks toward Haddie behind Jackson.

"What is it, Haddie?" Worry etched into his face. He quickly assesses her body for signs of distress or danger. "Are you okay? What's wrong with Chloe?'

Haddie squeezes Jackson's arms tightly, pleading with her eyes for him to grasp what is happening. "She's missing, Jackson. Beau went to wake her up this morning, and she was gone. They're all looking for her now. Chloe is missing." Tears well up in her eyes once the words are spoken.

Jackson turns to Travis. "Send everyone to look for her. I want the national guard, the army, the marines. Everyone."

Travis straightens his posture. His eyes fill with compassion and understanding. "Sir, you know we can't do that. Chloe is on foreign soil. We can't order military movement inside of the Allied States. Let me make some phone calls with the local officials." Travis speaks slowly, hoping common sense speaks to the president. He looks in the direction of Madison Lyn for backup.

Jackson surveys the room as the facts swirl in his head. He is the President of the United States. Chloe, his niece, technically, lives in another country. They are five hours away from Haddie's family and the search for Chloe. Madison and Rich are now standing. The communication team, frozen in their seats, watching how Rich will respond. Travis appears to be willing Jackson to see reason.

Haddie, crying.

Chloe, missing.

Jackson straightens up and composes himself. Wrapping his arm around Haddie, he turns to Madison.

"Madison, call President McCalister and let him know that I will be traveling to the Allied States territory of West Virginia two days early for personal reasons." He shouts to the open door. "Mrs. Pennington, I want Marine One in the air in five minutes. Marcus, please, quickly pack bags for Haddie and me. Travis, I suggest you call every agent available to travel. The First Lady and I will be walking through the mountains of West Virginia looking for our niece. Everyone else, that will be all for today. Enjoy your weekend."

Jackson enfolds Haddie into his arms as he waits for his office to clear. Travis and Madison exchange glances but know better than to argue at this time. She heads to her office to grab her briefcase and her emergency overnight bag. Haddie and Jackson stand still as they wait for the sound of whirring propellers.

***

The sacred morning calmness is replaced with flashing red and blue lights. A steady stream of pickup trucks and minivans enter the property. The entire Marchio clan is walking, canvassing the vineyard with police officers and volunteer firemen. Mary, Esther, and Hannah are making phone calls to kids from school and to area hospitals. Jo and her husband Matthew are quietly talking in a corner. Friends from church bring food and coffee before joining the search.

Beau and Maryssa began walking the fields before the police arrived. As soon as Marine One lands in the parking lot of Poppy's, Travis jumps out first and heads directly to the command center to coordinate efforts with the local police. Jackson finishes his call with President McCalister as Haddie is escorted down the stairs and into the restaurant. Madison carries three bags into the restaurant behind Haddie. She won't be much help searching the fields with her four-inch heels, but she will be there for support wherever needed.

Poppy's is filled with people. They aren't here to eat, they are here to help find a missing child. Tables are moved to the walls allowing the police to spread out and assign search parties. Packages of water bottles fill the center of the room. Flare guns are assigned to group leaders while batteries are being charged for two-way radios. Haddie rubs her eyes. The scene looks like something out of a movie script. Jackson comes up behind her and kisses her head. He points to the table of women sitting with phones. Esther rushes to Haddie as they cross the room.

The two don't need to speak a word. The heavy emotions they share are expressed in soft sobbing as they embrace and hold tight to one another. *Not Lizzie's daughter.* The room spins around them. People moving and speaking. Phones ringing. Doors opening and closing. Jackson doesn't leave Haddie's side. Madison approaches, giving the family space. Jackson waves her over.

She attempts a quiet debriefing to Jackson. "Travis is working outside with the sheriff. Three teams are canvasing the vineyard. Three more, including a canine unit, are scouring the forest behind the vineyard. Haddie's uncles and cousins are riding ATVs searching the property. There is another party getting ready to walk the main road in a few minutes."

Madison's face softens as she watches Haddie and her mother. "Jackson, I know you want to help search, but Travis and the police feel that you being out there could actually take away from the search. If you stay inside the restaurant, that will allow more agents to look for her instead of watching out for you. Not to mention, civilians wanting to snap selfies with you."

Jackson nods in agreement. "I know Madsi." He squeezes her hand. Relief fills Madison knowing she doesn't have to physically restrain her longtime friend from joining a search party. She continues, but speaks softly, not wanting to upset Haddie and Esther. "There still is no trace of Chloe. They aren't sure how long she's been missing, but they think it was before five this morning. It rained from five until shortly after six. The dogs lost her scent at the apartment door, and there aren't tracks in the mud. The rest you know, Beau was the last person to see her last night. She was upset about the Stanleys and Maryssa. Police are headed to question the Stanley's, but they don't believe there is a link."

Esther and Haddie begin walking over to Nunnie Mary and the others. "I'll be over in the corner. I'll update Rich and make some calls. Let me know if you need anything." Jackson squeezes Madison's shoulder before turning to follow his wife.

The search party continues to grow throughout the day. The search primarily focuses on the vineyard, the forest beyond the property, and the main road. Madison and Haddie carry out food for the volunteers. Jackson Cashe walks around the room, filling coffee mugs.

Haddie chuckles to herself before turning to Madison. "I think I'm spending too much time with you and Rich. Sometimes I look at Jackson, and all I see is a photo op."

"I'm glad you said it. I felt guilty having that thought during such a terrible time." Madison squeezes Haddie in a sideways hug. The two lean their heads together. Jackson sees them and offers a wink.

Haddie watches as a tall, older gentleman walks into the room with purpose. He scans the room quickly before walking directly toward Esther. He places a hand familiarly on her back, causing her to turn to him. She enters into his waiting hug. The gesture gives Haddie an odd feeling of longing for her father and curiosity about her mother as a woman. The man obviously knows her mother well. Based on the waves from the family, so does everyone else. Jackson walks over to Esther and shakes the man's hand. Esther seems to be making introductions.

"Earth to Haddie. Haddie?" Madison follows Haddie's gaze to Esther then back to Haddie's face. "I take it you don't know that man hugging your mother?" Haddie moves her head back and forth, still observing. "Well, you know Jackson, he'll know everything about the man in five minutes."

Just then, Maryssa walks into the door. She is disheveled and exhausted. Haddie rushes to her and grabs her into a tight embrace. Maryssa can't even cry. She is so overwhelmed with emotion. She only stares and offers a feeble hug in return. Haddie pulls back and stares at her. Maryssa's hair is falling out of her messy bun. She has a leaf stuck inside of a brown curl. Haddie pulls it out and searches Maryssa's eyes for any sign of hope. Maryssa just bows her head. They walk arm in arm towards Esther. The man stands to the side as Esther joins the girls.

"Nothing. No sign of Chloe at all. Beau is still looking. I came back for coffee and food for Beau. I'll wrap some up for him and bring it back to the front line. He is pale and frantic. I doubt he'll eat, but some food will help keep up his strength."

Maryssa collapses into the nearest chair. Haddie sits beside her as Esther fixes a plate of food. Haddie grabs a bottle of water from the table and passes it to Maryssa. Maryssa drains half of the bottle in one drink. "It's muddy out there from all the rain. The dogs can't even find a scent." Maryssa offers as an explanation.

"We heard. It's killing me to sit inside, but I know I'll just be a distraction." Haddie returns an explanation. They sit in silence for a minute.

Jackson walks over and rests his hands on Haddie's shoulders. "Travis should be inside in a minute for another update." Jackson leans closer to Haddie and whispers only to her. "In other news, apparently your mother's high school sweetheart has resurfaced. I don't know all the details, but I'll get them." Haddie drops her head in her hands. That information is too much to bear right now. Jackson stands and waves at Wes Anderson. Esther returns with a plate for Maryssa and a bag filled with food for Beau.

Esther sits. She is wringing the napkin in front of her. She is beside herself. "I've called her teacher and every child in her class. I've called the kids from her Sunday school class. I don't know what else to do. I even called the mother of that Jen Z girl."

Maryssa takes a bite of the pepperoni roll then moves the chips around on her plate. "They won't be much help. That Jen Z is vicious. Even if she did know something, she probably wouldn't tell you anyway. I'm so sorry. Apparently, I'm mean to five-year-olds now. I've just heard so many stories about that girl. Poor Chloe. I don't remember girls being that mean so young, but I could be wrong."

"Are you kidding? Remember in kindergarten when Janet Reeves called you 'Marysshrimp' for months because you were the shortest kid in the class?" Haddie recalls, "She stopped when you walked up to her, flipped your hair and told her she was just jealous because dynamite came in small packages."

Maryssa froze. She quickly finished chewing, gulped down some water, and stood abruptly while touching her phone. "Oh God, please," Maryssa offers a prayer. "I think I know where she is now. Stay here, I don't want to scare her." She puts the phone to her ear as she runs to the door. "Beau, meet me at the farmhouse."

Maryssa runs through the parking lot and jumps onto Sammy's ATV sitting in the grass. She takes the dirt path hidden in the field between the vineyard. The hills are bumpy and muddy. As a kid, she'd made this ride many times, but never before in such a panic. Trees off in the distance, she sees police cars next to the woods. She cuts through the backyard and parks right beside Nunnie's garden. Nunnie planted five tall oaks around the house. She hated "boring" yards with no character. Maryssa begins yelling for Chloe and stops underneath each tree to search it from the ground. Branches and thick green leaves canopy the fading daylight around her.

At the third tree, she hears a small whimper as she approaches. She ducks under the low lying branches and peeks up into the heart of the tree. There she sees a little girl with her favorite purple hoodie and Beary. She exhales in relief, but braces for the excavation of a scared child. "Chloe, may I come up there with you?"

A whispy "yes" trapped in silent sobs is returned.

Maryssa drops her flashlight in the direction of the road as a makeshift flare for Beau. She picks the best branch and pulls her body up onto the mighty oak. She maneuvers the limbs like a pro. Apparently climbing trees is just like riding a bike. Halfway up the sturdy tree, Maryssa settles on a branch that is below yet angled near the one holding Chloe.

"Hi." Maryssa assesses Chloe's physical condition before tackling the child's emotional state. "Are you okay?"

Chloe nods. Tears streaming down her tiny face.

"Are you scared?" Maryssa's face softens once she realizes Chloe is safe.

Chloe again nods.

"Do you want to talk?"

Chloe shakes her head.

"Can I guess?"

Chloe nods.

"Are you upset about Angelica?"

Chloe shrugs.

"Do you think it's your fault, about the Stanleys and my food?"

More tears. Chloe nods as her shoulders begin to shake.

"Sweet girl. Nothing could be farther from the truth. Everything works out the way it's supposed to in life. I'm not worried or upset. It threw me for a loop, but I know it wasn't part of the master plan. You were honest when Angelica asked about your Daddy and me. You can never go wrong telling the truth. Angelica is a big girl, and so am I. The only thing I'm upset about is that you carried this weight on your heart. You mean the world to me, Miss Chloe. The only thing I care about right now is you."

Chloe leans into Maryssa and buries her head in Maryssa's shoulder. The little girl is still sniffling when the police car barrels up the road. Beau is opening the car door before the cruiser comes to a stop. He runs to the tree and begins climbing.

Maryssa yells down as she holds Chloe tightly in her arms. "Don't climb. You'll bring down the whole tree. We're coming down to you." She looks at Chloe, wiping the girl's cheeks. "Are you ready, Chlo?" The nod in response prompts Maryssa to shift on her branch to give them room to move. She helps Chloe down the tree where Beau snatches the girl the second he can reach her body.

Beau crushes Chloe into his chest and buries his head in her curly brown ringlets. He is crying and breathing in the little girl's scent. Chloe wraps her arms tightly around her daddy as the sobs begin to rack her tiny body. Maryssa watches as the police chief radios the good news into the command center. The silence settles into Maryssa's bones. The exhaustion hit her like a brick wall as the adrenaline drains. She leans against the tree to keep her upright.

"Chloe? What happened? Didn't you hear everyone calling for you? I was so worried." He pulls back to look her over for any sign of harm or marring. Beau stares directly into her big hazel eyes, waiting for an answer.

She wipes her eyes and nose. "I climbed up in the tree then it started raining, so I wanted to wait 'til it stopped but then I heard all the sirens, and it scared me. I thought you would be mad and I'd be in trouble. I was going to wait until the lights and sirens left then come home, but more cars came, so I stayed up here." Her small voice quivers as the words spill out of her mouth. "I'm so sorry, Daddy. I didn't want to make you mad. This is all my fault." She buries her head again as he holds her securely in his arms. His right hand holding the back of her head.

"It's okay, Honey. I'm not mad at you. I could never be mad at you. I love you. You are safe now. Don't be afraid. I'm here now." His words, a soothing balm washing away her fear. The police chief walks over to them with a blanket. Maryssa walks to meet him and takes the offering. She walks behind Chloe and drapes the blanket around the girl's shoulders. She locks eyes with Beau. Both sets of eyes speak volumes between the two without a word spoken. They walk toward the police car and climb into the back seat.

***

Poppy's has cleared out significantly since Chloe's return. The Sheriff is speaking with Travis as deputies load up their cars and head back to the station. Local volunteers hugged and waved before leaving for their own homes. Beau took Chloe upstairs to their apartment for a bath and bed. She was overwhelmed by the number of people searching for her. Esther and Haddie brought food to her. Aunts, uncles, and cousins help Maryssa put the restaurant back together. Chairs and tables are arranged as tablecloths are lined up at the corners.

Jackson helps Malik and Victoria clean the kitchen and store food. Malik and Jackson have grown closer over the past year. Malik stops working as Maryssa walks into the room. His open arms welcome his daughter right into them. Maryssa collapses into her Daddy's embrace. "There is just something about a Dad hug. It makes everything better." She exhales as he kisses the top of her head.

"How are you, sweetheart? You were out there the entire day with Beau. You must be exhausted." He rubs her back, gauging her wellbeing.

She mumbles her response into his chest. "I'm fine. Tired, but fine." After a minute, she pulls away and turns to fit herself right into the crook of her father's left arm. "I'm just so relieved. I feel terrible for Beau. I know he is going to beat himself up over this, but he couldn't control it. Chloe is a little girl with big feelings. She misses a Mama she never really knew. She was acting out in the only way she knew how to at the time." Maryssa stares into space as the events run through her thoughts.

"How did you know where she was, Honey?" Malik squeezes her shoulder to bring her back to the present.

She shakes the memories from her vision. "Remember that time in kindergarten when Janet Reeves had the whole class calling me Marysshrimp?" She waits for her dad to acknowledge that terrible time. He offers her a sly smile in return. She swats his chest. "Daddy! How could you forget that? It was awful."

She begins to recount the sordid details for Victoria and Jackson. "She was a mean girl at school, and I stood up to her like Mama told me to do, but it still really hurt. I was so embarrassed. When I got home from school, I ran right to the back yard and climbed up the old Elm tree in the corner. Daddy must have seen me run out, and he climbed up to talk to me. He listened to my story and let me know how special I am and reminded me that Janet Reeves didn't have the power to control my life. At that moment in my life, I felt loved and valued. Apparently, that special talk didn't mean that much to my Dad." She pokes him.

"In my defense, I remember the tree and the talk. I just forgot the specific crime of Janet. She was a constant thorn in your side. That girl had issues." He laughs and pulls Maryssa closer.

"All right, you're forgiven." She laughs, then continues her story. "Anyway, Chloe has her own Janet Reeves in her life. This little girl Jen Z is so mean to her. So, I shared my story with her and my Daddy's wisdom. We started talking about all of the trees in West Virginia and how great they are for climbing. I forgot all about it until Aunt E mentioned that she called Jen Z's mom. All of a sudden, it just hit me. I prayed the whole time on Sammy's four-wheeler that she was up in one of Nunnie's trees. No one thought to look up into the trees, and she was scared, so she stayed quiet when the police were checking the property." Maryssa takes a deep breath. "It was a long shot, but I felt it in my gut. What a scary day."

"I'm sure Beau is relieved to have her home. He'll probably never let Chloe out of his sight." Victoria folds the dish towel she was using to dry coffee mugs.

Jackson takes the dry mugs and places them on a tray for shelving behind the bar in the beverage center. "Haddie wants to move them in with us so that Chloe has twenty-four-hour Secret Service protection. I'm ready to assign Travis to her. I don't know how Beau is going to let her go back to school without sitting outside the building and staring in the window. Forget about her teenage years, I can't handle five."

"Beau is a great dad. He'll know how to balance the strongest layer of protection with giving her enough room to fall and get up again. He is amazing with Chloe. He wakes up at the crack of dawn to get her ready for school. He packs lunches, washes clothes, and always has those adorable ringlets styled just right. He works hard all day and still finds time to take care of Aunt E and Chloe. Nunnie is convinced that he has a twin who tag teams with him. On top of everything else on his plate, he still managed to carve out my outside bar and the gazebo. I'm still dying to see the final product." She shakes her head in amazement.

A look passes between Malik and Victoria. Jackson pauses to study Maryssa then begins to smile. "Well, I'm on my way back to the house. I need to see Madison before she leaves for DC. I'll drop these glasses off in the front. Can I do anything else?"

"No, Mr. President. We can manage." Maryssa chides him. "Wait, leave one of those mugs. I think I'll bring a mug of hot chocolate up to Chloe. She loves when I put a peppermint stick in it."

Malik looks down at his daughter in wonder. "You have become very close to Chloe, haven't you?" Maryssa nods.

"I try to help as much as I can. Beau does so much. It's easy for me to help since I'm always in the restaurant. Chloe and I practice ballet, then we bake together. Now I have her watching old movies with me. We even pop our own popcorn. Maybe I should bring up popcorn too." Maryssa begins moving through the kitchen, pulling out some chocolate and a pot to warm oil for popcorn.

Victoria walks over to the massive gas range. She gently places her hand on Maryssa's back. "I know how chefs are with their kitchen, but may I help? Let me do something for you. You have been walking and searching all day too. I'll make three mugs of hot chocolate, and your dad can pop the popcorn. Why don't you go upstairs and relieve Esther and Haddie? We'll bring up the goodies when they are ready."

Maryssa notices Victoria's eyes for the first time. They are warm chocolate, like brownies. Her cheeks are round and rosy. Maryssa sees the kindness in her face in a new light. She smiles, not only at Victoria's thoughtfulness but also for her father, who found a new partner. "Thank you, Victoria. That is so sweet of you. Everything you need is in the storeroom. The peppermint sticks are with Frankie's baking supplies." She squeezes her step-mother's arm and walks toward Beau and Chloe.

Chapter 35

Beau

The morning begins early for Beau. Chloe fell asleep in his arms last night on the couch. He didn't dare move her. Haddie made Esther leave to get some sleep when Maryssa came up to relieve them. Victoria and Malik sent up hot chocolate, and the three of them watched Mary Poppins together. Chloe's eyes were sealed shut before the first "Chim chim cheree." He asked Maryssa to stay longer. He wasn't ready to be alone after the traumatic day. She must have waited until he fell asleep. She cleaned up the mugs, and covered them in a blanket before heading back to the farmhouse.

Chloe stirs with the sunrise. She shifts on Beau's chest and rubs her eyes. Her curly head turns to the other side of the couch and takes the blanket with her. Beau watches as she curls into a ball. Chloe has the tenacity of Lizzie and the feisty spirit of the Marchio women he has come to know and love. Beau rubs his chin admiring the long line of women in his daughter's life. He stands and stretches. The kinks and stiffness, reminders of yesterday, ripple out of his muscles. He walks to the coffee pot and finds it already set and coming to life. He realizes Maryssa must have set it before she left last night. He smiles at her thoughtfulness.

He heads to take a quick shower while Chloe is sleeping. He needs to help the family get Poppy's ready. The Geoffrey Barton Awards Committee will arrive for dinner service today. The staff will arrive shortly to begin preparations. He wants to work on the gazebo this morning before the activity starts.

The smell of fresh pine fills his nose as the steam from the shower clears his head. Pine needles fall out of his hair when he washes it. Remnants of his frantic searching. He washes away the memories of the past. The pain, the sadness, the haunting memories.

Chloe lives under the veil of a ghost. It is time to move forward for her and for himself. They will celebrate Lizzie's life and legacy, but the future is Chloe. West Virginia is a fresh start for them both. Leaving home was the first step. They are in a new home, a new beginning, a new life.

He turns off the water and opens the colorful fish shower curtain. As it opens, a squirt gun falls into the base of the tub and onto his foot. He laughs as he picks it up and places it back on the ledge. Maryssa and Chloe ambushed him one night when he came home from a late-night of working on her gazebo. He walked in while Maryssa was helping Chloe take a bath, they both turned on him and started firing water directly at him. Their aim impressed him as much as the prank itself. He heads to his room and quietly dresses, being careful to let Chloe sleep.

He hears a knock on the front door just as he walks out of his bedroom. Esther peeks in as he waves her inside quietly. He nods toward the coffee pot, and she smiles and nods in return. Chloe is still sleeping as Esther quietly pulls out a chair to sit at the table. Beau carries over two mismatched mugs of coffee, sugar, and milk. They sit in silence for a minute, mixing their creamy coffee. Esther chuckles softly as she looks at the son-in-law who followed her three states away from his home.

"The two of us are the only ones who never drank black coffee. Eloise insisted on giving me black coffee every morning. No matter how many times I told her. She couldn't fathom anyone mixing her favorite drink with anything at all. Then you came, and I finally had a partner in my crime to take down her precious java."

"I think she finally gave up when I moved into the garage. I remember the first day I pulled out the milk and sugar for the table. She rolled her eyes and left the room." Now it is Beau's turn to softly laugh. "No offense to John, but I definitely won the mother-in-law prize with you. Eloise is a real peach, as my mom would say."

Esther covers her mouth to keep the laughter from roaring out and waking up Chloe. They drink their coffee as they sit, both deep in thought. Esther looks over at her sleeping granddaughter and then back at Beau. He is kind and loyal, far beyond anything she could have expected that first day Lizzie brought him home. If anyone won the lottery, it was Esther. It was time. Time for a new beginning.

"What time did Maryssa leave last night?" Esther coyly takes another sip.

"I'm not sure. Mary Poppins was on tv last night, and Chloe wanted to watch it. She fell asleep, Maryssa must have stayed until after I fell asleep myself. I'm glad she stayed, I wasn't ready to be alone after that. You can thank her for our coffee this morning. She must have set it up when she cleaned up the hot chocolate mugs."

"You and Maryssa spend a great deal of time together with her always at the barn and helping Chloe with ballet. You two are great at tag-teaming with Chloe. Chloe loves having her around all the time."

"She does. I think it's a combination of the ballet lessons and the extreme amount of sugar they consume together while baking." Beau snickers then pats his non-existent pot belly. "I'm not complaining about the baking, I think I've made out pretty well on that deal."

"Haven't we all? Maryssa always makes sure to bring me a full container of goodies. I'm going to need to go on a diet soon." Esther grins then drinks more of her liquid gold. "You both also really seem to have a lot in common with the old movies and love of mini-golf. The three of you seem to golf once a week."

"I think it's more sheer competitive grit we both share more than the actual sport of mini-golf." Beau snickers. "I felt bad the kids had to witness our showmanship over putting last week. Speaking of old movies, did you see that the Robinson Grand Theatre downtown is showing Bedknobs and Broomsticks next week? We need to take Chloe, she'll love it."

"You and Maryssa should take her. Maryssa loves Angela Lansbury. I love that theatre. When I was younger, that was the only place in town to watch movies or have recitals. Ruth, Jo, and I had our dance recitals on that stage." Esther twists her mug in her hands.

"I have been thinking a lot about Ruth lately. And John and Lizzie. I've been thinking a lot about death and life. I'm not sure if it's the new buds on the vines or the flowers in bloom, but the new life all around us is inspiring me to look up instead of backward."

"I was thinking the same thing in the shower. I'm just not sure how to keep Lizzie alive for Chloe without making her live with a mother who is a ghost." Beau touches Esther's hand, "I'm sorry, I didn't mean."

"Stop, Beau. I know what you meant." She reassuringly pats his hand.

They both sit and stare into their mugs for a moment. The sun's rays are creeping into the windows and brightening the room with light. Chloe shifts and offers a tiny murmur to the morning before rolling over and flopping an arm off of the couch.

"I remember sitting with Ruth in the hospital one day. I flew up to help Malik get her to and from treatments. She was so strong. Much stronger than me. I was lamenting about how Lizzie might not see Chloe grow up and how she might not see Maryssa get married or have children." Esther pauses and takes in a slow, deep breath. The memory feels so close and recent that it still burns as the words escape. "She held my hand and let me go on and on about my sorrows. She turned to me and said, 'E, this isn't our home. I'm just lucky that I get to go home first. Don't cry for Lizzie or me. We'll be dancing in Heaven'." Esther wipes her eyes. "Can you imagine? My sister, dying of cancer, still found a way to make me smile."

"Lizzie used to tell me the same thing. I think Ruth and Lizzie both got that idea from the book Nunnie Mary bought them about suffering or blessings or being blessed through suffering." Beau softly laughs. "I hated that book. Lizzie told me to read it if she died. We got into a fight about that and ended up waking Chloe from a nap. I think I threw the book away after the funeral. After your intervention in my apartment, I remember searching for it and thinking that she was dancing and I was searching. Talk about irony."

"One thing I've learned about God over my lifetime, He loves using irony to teach lessons," Esther adds more cream to her mug. "I forgot that Maryssa likes her coffee strong like her mother did."

"I hadn't noticed. I guess I've gotten used to her making me coffee at Poppy's."

The corner of Esther's mouth rises slightly. She takes another sip to hide it. "Speaking of blessings, Maryssa has been great for Chloe. Ballet and baking have really helped Chloe's self-esteem. Plus, Maryssa gets Chloe's special brand of sass." They both smile at the thought. Esther drinks more creamy coffee before making her next move.

"Maryssa has been a blessing to you too, it seems. Poppy's is filled with your woodwork. It's nice to see you get back into it. It's almost as if you have new inspiration to create." Another long sip.

"I guess you're right. It has been nice. Maryssa has given me blank canvases essentially. She wanted original woodwork and just let me do whatever I felt would work. I can't wait to show everyone the gazebo. I just have to secure one piece of wood that has been bothering me. Then I'm finished."

Esther slowly places her mug on the table and looks directly at Beau. "Yes, it definitely seems as if you and Maryssa were meant to be a team. Isn't it 'ironic' how God worked it out the way it has for us this year? Moving back to West Virginia and Maryssa being around to help us with Chloe and you getting your inspiration back? I've seen a spring in your step, as well as hers lately. It's nice to have a teammate." She stares at Beau, wondering if he is picking up on her not so subtle remarks.

"E, why do I feel like there is something more to this conversation?" He studies his mother-in-law, waiting.

"Beau, I think you know. I have seen you date a woman here and there from church or work, you have even humored a few older ladies at church by going out on blind dates with their granddaughters. I won't lie, it was difficult at first, watching you date. After a while, I began praying for the right woman for you and Chloe. That wasn't easy, but I trusted. Once John died last year, I selfishly wanted to keep you and Chloe mine forever. Then, once the fog lifted, I saw. I have been watching you and Maryssa and Chloe for months. You bring out the best in each other." She takes his hands in hers.

"Esther."

She cuts him off again so she can finish.

"Have you ever watched a kitchen staff work during dinner service?" He shakes his head. She continues.

"It is a sight to behold. When we all worked together at Maria's Ristorante, I would stand back and watch Malik in the kitchen and John in the dining room. A good kitchen staff listens to one another and appears to float around each other like the choreographed dance numbers Haddie and Maryssa would perform on stage. Sure, there are collisions and spills, but the dance continues. Dance, cooking, music, they are all art forms in which it only works when it's working together. The seamlessness comes from a respect and knowledge of one another. There is trust, and trust is hard to find. I see that beautiful choreography with you and Maryssa. It's time Beau. You need someone in your life who can give you more."

Beau stands and leans against the counter. He stares at a sleeping Chloe. "For just a minute, let's say that I agree with you, what does that even mean? How do I know she feels the same? For all we know, she thinks of me as family only." Beau rubs his forehead, trying to absorb all the words.

Esther rises to stand beside him. "I have watched and listened. She feels the same. Trust me."

"I don't know, Mom. If I share my feelings, and she doesn't feel the same, things will get weird with the family. That will be hard for me, but Chloe can't lose her relationship with Maryssa."

"Do you trust me?"

Beau looks at Esther like she has lost her mind.

"Nevermind, I know you do." Esther winks at Beau and begins talking. "I have a plan."

Chapter 36

Maryssa

Two dippy eggs, three pieces of bacon, and one slice of Italian toast sit on a glass dish. Silverware and napkin, waiting. A travel mug, filled and sealed tight, sits neatly beside the plate. Nunnie Mary flips the page and folds her newspaper just as Maryssa bounds through the doorway to the kitchen. The smell of fried bacon hits her first. Maryssa freezes to take in the room and instantly calms.

"Sit, bella. You need to eat." Nunnie puts down the paper. Maryssa knows that tone. She also knows it is pointless, possibly dangerous, to argue. When an Italian grandmother tells you to eat, you listen.

Maryssa pulls out the chair and holds up the sticky note in her hand. "Romans eight twenty-eight stuck to my bathroom mirror was a nice touch. I'm surprised you limited yourself to one sticky note." She chides her grandmother.

"Just wait until you get to Poppy's." Mary winks. "Now eat. Today is a big day for you. You need fuel."

Maryssa bites into the crisp, thick bacon and moans. "Thank you, Nunnie."

"I got up with Mr. Bubbles this morning. I jotted down a few of my favorite verses for you during my time with Jesus. You could be finding sticky notes for months." Nunnie heartily laughs.

"Where is everyone this morning? Still asleep? I thought there would be a packed house after yesterday." Maryssa takes another bite.

"Jackson and Haddie got up with the rooster too. Jackson said something about looking at a property somewhere for one of his projects. He is always cooking up something, that one. Haddie found a good one." Mary takes a bite of her own toast while watching Maryssa.

"Esther went to check on Beau and Chloe. Your daddy and Victoria are driving to Stonewall Resort to meet a friend of hers from cooking school. I think Malik is more nervous than you. Victoria is trying to keep him out of your hair. They should be at Poppy's by lunchtime. That just leaves Mr. Bubbles and us."

Maryssa rolls her eyes at the mention of the rooster as Nunnie smiles.

"You came in late last night. I'm sure Beau appreciated the company."

"I hope. Beau does so much for Aunt E and Chloe. He gives so much to everyone else. I am amazed by his character." She stuffs another mouthful of egg and toast in and realizes Nunnie is watching her with an ornery look. She wipes her mouth. "What? Do I have egg on my face?"

"No, no. I was just admiring my lovely granddaughter. Your mother would be so proud of you. Regardless of what those fancy food judges say about Poppy's, you are still a gifted chef. You have already succeeded in my book."

"Thank you, Nunnie. That really means a lot. The sticky notes are much appreciated along with the breakfast."

Maryssa carries her empty plate to the sink and rinses it. The window above the sink showcases a beautiful morning. The sun bounces off the hills, illuminating the surrounding green scenery. Her chiming phone pulls her back into the present. She pulls it out and sees a new text alert.

Good Morning, Gorgeous! I'm in town. Riding with the judges to the resort then I'll drive out to see you. Can't wait to see your little project. XO J

Tension and nerves surge through Maryssa as she reads the text from Jacques. She breathes in deeply and rolls her shoulders backward. Her feet slightly and effortlessly open to first position as she steels herself for the task. She needs to stay focused today. It amazes her how her inner ballerina comes out when feeling pressure. Maryssa pulls up through her spine and lifts her chest, stretching.

"Maryssa, is everything okay, sweetie?"

"Everything is great, Nunnie!" Maryssa turns with a smile on her face. "God is working for my good, remember? Regardless of what happens today or with the judging, I will focus on that." She winks and grabs her hot pink travel mug, already filled with coffee. She walks over and kisses her grandmother on the cheek. "Thank you for this morning. I love you very much. I'll see you later?"

"I will be there with bells on and with an empty stomach!" Mary exclaims.

Maryssa opts for her car this morning instead of the golf cart. Typically, she heads to the restaurant in a ponytail, but this morning, she attempted to tame her thick curls. The early morning humidity is unusual, but Maryssa didn't let that stop her from trying to fix her hair. The bright sun is burning off the morning dew and illuminating the grassy hills of the property. She passes Sammy's truck along the side of the road. He walks the rows throughout the week to check on growth himself. Maryssa smiles, knowing how much more he loves the growing than the business side of his work. She understands, today more than ever.

Poppy's is quiet this morning. Maryssa loves this time of day. It reminds her of afternoons before a performance. The theatre was calm and peaceful in spite of people warming up and stretching. Musicians tuning their instruments. Dancers stretching and checking their costumes. Whispers and soft laughter between friends and coworkers. The anticipation of the show sparking in everyone. The air, electric and filled with promise. Maryssa inhales the energy around her as she heads into the kitchen. The room is bathed in stainless steel and Maryssa's favorite tools. Everything is organized and ready for the action.

Maryssa heads for her office in the back of the kitchen. As she turns on the light, she laughs aloud upon rounding her desk. Sticky notes cover her laptop and the calendar on her wall. One significant square piece of paper in the middle of the desk sticks out among the rest. "I couldn't tell Mary no. We're all cheering for you! Love you, Daddy" Her heart warms, and her eyes water. No matter what happens today, her blessings will outweigh anything else.

Maryssa goes about her work just as she does every day. She checks the menu and makes plans. She does a quick survey of the inventory before placing orders with her suppliers. Her favorite playlist lightly streams through the speakers in the restaurant and the kitchen. She assesses her arsenal of knives along the magnetic strip at her station. She pulls down her favorite utility knife. The six-inch carbon blade and wooden handle are perfectly balanced. The set was a gift from her father when she began school. The handle is well worn and fits perfectly in her hand. The familiarity and routine help to calm her nerves.

She takes this time to enjoy the preparation. The sound of chimes alerts her that someone has entered the kitchen, she assumes it's Frankie offering to help. The smooth, French voice of Jacques Boucher startles her. "Aw, tu m'as manqué ma douce."

Maryssa stills. She reverts to her ballet posture once again this morning. Feet in line with shoulders, toes slightly out, shoulders back, head high. She answers him with the perfect mix of sweet and sass, so he appreciates her affection, and more importantly, the boundaries. "Jacques. I am not your sweet, and I doubt you've missed me with your many adoring fans."

He glides across the kitchen and stealthily stands behind her, wrapping his arms around her waist. He leans down and smells her hair. "Always the feisty one ma plus chère. Look at you in your own little kitchen. Running the show as always."

Maryssa places her knife on the butcher block Beau cut for her. She leans back into the slim frame of Jacques, allowing her room to turn and face him while ducking away from his arms. "And you are always the condescending one, mon plus chère." She mocks his term of endearment.

Jacques props himself against her counter, crossing his arms and ankles as he leers at her. He scoffs, "My dearest, how, if ever am I condescending you? I'm here to applaud your adorable endeavors and tout your praises to a pretentious judging panel. What more must I do to win your affection?"

Maryssa laughs as she wipes her hands on a towel. "That is exactly my point, Jacques. 'Win me?' I'm not another trophy for you to win. 'Adorable, cute' are not words of high praise. Poppy's may seem like a pet project to you, but it means something to me. I've worked really hard for this."

"Ah, we are back to this same argument. I apologize. You have grown into a wonderful chef. What you have accomplished here is evidence of that. Why do you think I nominated you for the Geoffrey Barton Award? I just see more for you. I want you to come back to Washington with me. You deserve to be the center of attention. I fear you are wasting your talents here." He waves his arms in exaggeration.

"See? This is how you operate. Your compliments come with consequences. I will choose to believe your flattering words, you don't offer them freely, and ignore the rest." She shakes her head then lowers it.

Silence fills the room as Jacques begins inspecting the kitchen. He lifts a slightly dented pan from the stovetop. "You still have the same go-to pan, I see. This was always your favorite. It's like a lovie, a baby blanket for you in the kitchen."

He continues to look above and below counters, running his hand across the stainless steel surrounding him. His stroll brings him face to face with a stoic Maryssa. He lifts her chin with his finger and studies her face. "Truly, you have done a remarkable job. You have created something of beauty here in this place. No consequences, as you say, just my sincere compliments to the chef."

She tentatively hugs then quickly retracts from her mentor. "Thank you, Jacques. And thank you for the nomination, and for being here today."

Jacques, never accepting defeat, reaches for Maryssa's hands. He gently holds her tiny hands in his while rubbing his thumbs along her wrists. "I haven't seen that sparkle in your eyes before. You are happy here, no? Is there someone? Someone who gives you more than I did?"

"I have lived in Paris and New York and DC. I have traveled the world and lived a rich life, but this is home. There is a peace I haven't felt in years. This feels special. This is the land my family has worked for generations. This is where I'm supposed to be, it feels right."

Jacques examines the woman before him. "I think you are right. There is something special I haven't seen in you until now." He leans down and kisses her forehead as he releases her hands. He claps his own hands together and begins searching her kitchen. "I don't have to be back at the hotel for three hours, what shall we create?"

An hour and one large pot of chicken Basquaise later, Maryssa and Jacques begin scooping their work into large white bowls. The squeaking door diverts their attention to Beau, entering with a small gift bag. Maryssa beams as Beau walks into the kitchen.

"I'm sorry, I didn't mean to interrupt." Beau stammers as he rests the bag on the counter. "I just wanted to drop this off before it gets too crazy. It's for later. I noticed that Chloe demolished your candy drawer stash. I figured you would need a sugar fix later."

"You are so sweet. You are actually just in time. You have to come and taste this. It is ah-mazing! It's a braised chicken stew. It has peppers, onions, tomatoes, and just the right amount of spice to give it some heat. Your type of heat."

Maryssa, remembering her manners in all of the excitement makes introductions. "Oh my, I'm so sorry. Jacques, you remember Beau? Beau, Jacques. He came over early before the judges to make sure I hadn't lost my mojo." She laughs.

Realization and acceptance fill Jacques as he passes a bowl of French cuisine to the lumberjack looking man. "Beau, it is my pleasure. Maryssa has been filling me in on her life in West Virginia. I feel as if I already know you."

More commotion fills the room as Malik and Victoria walk in with Frankie. "What is that delicious smell?" Malik peers into Beau's bowl. "Chicken Basquaise? I hope you made enough." Maryssa's father holds out his hand to Jacques Boucher while the man is in mid-chew. "Jacques, so nice to see you."

Quickly wiping his mouth, he accepts the handshake. "Malik." The two men nod in acknowledgment.

"Oh, it smells absolutely amazing. Sign me up for a bowl." Victoria walks closer. Maryssa shouts introductions as she ladles the spicy and decadent meal into bowls.

"Can we please start making this? I'm dying." Frankie moans in delight.

As the kitchen begins to fill, Jacques takes the opportunity to make his exit. He walks to Maryssa and kisses her hand. "It was lovely spending time in the kitchen with you today. As it was lovely to see all of you. I shall take my leave to meet with the judges. Until tonight." He bows before leaving.

Malik leans into Beau and mutters quietly, but gruffly, "I have never liked that guy."

Chapter 37

Esther

Esther fiddles with the clasp on her white gold charm bracelet. She looks up as Haddie knocks on the opened door frame.

"Need some help, Mama?" Haddie sits on the edge of the bed beside her mother.

"Yes, please." Esther sighs in surrender. "Your father always did this for me. I never could get this on my own."

Haddie takes her mother's hand in her own as she twists the charm bracelet with her fingers. Once she fastens the hook, she tenderly lifts charms and warms at the memories. "I remember when Daddy got this for you. It was a birthday gift, wasn't it?"

Esther nods. "It was my fortieth birthday. I was completely shocked. I was expecting flowers and a nice dinner. I had no idea he had this planned." The corner of her mouth curves up into a grin.

"I remember. Aunt Ruth helped us decorate the restaurant for your surprise party. The whole West Virginia family drove down to celebrate, and you had no idea. Nunnie made all those Italian wedding cookies."

"That's right. I forgot about the cookies. Your father thought of everything." She chuckles. "I felt so bad, I only got him a card and a coffee mug for his fortieth. The party was present enough, but then he pulled out a wrapped box with this in it. He said he didn't want me to ever forget our memories." She wipes a stray tear.

"Lizzie and I used to sneak into your room and look at it. Lizzie would pretend to wear it. She would let me look but not touch. She was afraid I'd break it and get us caught." Haddie smiles up at her Esther. "My favorite charm is the ballet slipper for all the practices you drove me to. Lizzie's was her soccer ball. Lizzie was a brat." Haddie winked at her mother, attempting to lighten the mood.

"Ha! She said the same thing about you and Maryssa. You two cramped her style. She was used to being the only kid. She and Daddy would play soccer for hours in the back yard. That's probably what they're doing now; having a soccer match with angels." It is Haddie's turn to wipe her mother's straggling teardrop.

"God help those angels. Those two were competitive." Haddie laughs then looks back at her mother's hands. She touches the diamond wedding ring still on Esther's left ring finger. "I heard from Chloe that her friend Zachary from school is coming tonight with his grandpa. Could that be why you spent extra time in the bathroom with hot rollers today? And why your room smells of your favorite perfume?"

Esther playfully swats her daughter's arm as she stands to find her black strappy sandals. "Are you saying I smell bad normally? Can't a woman wear perfume without getting the third degree? My poor son-in-law. Do you harass him about his smells as well?"

"Stop it, Mama. You always smell nice. Jackson smells nice unless he's been at the gym." They both laugh as Esther finishes dressing. Haddie picks at a string on the quilted bedspread. "It's okay if you want to smell nice for Zachary's grandpa, you know."

Esther stops and looks directly at Haddie through the mirror. She turns to her and leans down and takes her daughter's face in both of her hands. She considers her words carefully. "I love your Daddy with every inch of my heart. He was an extraordinary man. A part of my heart died with him and with Lizzie. I might choose to give part of my heart away again, but not now. I'm learning that it's okay to look nice and smell nice for myself. I won't lie to you, it is nice to have an old friend to talk to, but I am still healing a broken heart." Esther pauses, studying Haddie's eyes, filled with love. "Thank you, my sweet."

"I just wanted to tell you that it's okay. Not that you need my blessing, but I want you to have it anyway when you are ready. You look stunning, by the way." Haddie brushes tears from her cheeks as she smiles at her Mama.

Esther gently squeezes Haddie's chin. "Thank you." She straightens then holds out her hand adorned with a lifetime of charms. "Now, let's go support Maryssa."

As the two women reach the bottom of the stairs, they run straight into Chloe and Jackson.

"You two look like you've been up to no good. What have you been doing?" Haddie crosses her arms to scrutinize the two scoundrels in front of her.

They share a conspiratorial look before Chloe breaks into a giggle. "Uncle Jackson pushed me really high on the tree swing. Then Travis ran over and yelled at Uncle Jackson. Then we snuck a cookie, but I gave one to Travis too so he won't be mad at Uncle Jackson anymore." The two hive five each other and giggle wildly.

"In my defense, who can say no to this face? If she asks to swing high, I'm swinging high. I take my role as the fun uncle very seriously. Right, Chloe?" More giggling and high fives.

"All right you two, we need to get moving." Esther takes Chloe's hand. "Have you seen Nunnie?" They walk down the hallway.

Haddie wipes a chocolate smudge off of her husband's face. "President Trouble Maker. Poor Travis. He deserves more than a cookie."

Haddie straightens his collar then turns to follow Esther. Jackson quickly gets in line with the others as he does a quick once over himself. "Hey Honey, do I smell okay?"

Esther and Haddie break into their own fits of laughter.

Chapter 38

Maryssa

Poppy's holds a steady buzz of joyful conversation, clanging silverware, and wine glasses clinking. The dinner rush finished hours ago, but there are still family and friends enjoying the specials prepared for the judges tonight.

The camera crew packs up their equipment in the corner. The judges left for the airport after an elaborate taste testing and grueling interview.

Maryssa relishes in her feelings of exhaustion and effort tonight. Still in her chef whites and Crocs, she walks into the dining room to a standing ovation. She blushes then bows. As she looks around the room, she is overwhelmed by the love and support. Poppy's is still packed with aunts, uncles, cousins, and her church family. They are clapping and cheering for her. She motions for them to sit and continue eating.

Jacques takes her hand as she escorts him to the front door. He kisses her on both cheeks while holding her hands in his. "Ma plus chère, you were wonderful tonight. I am positive that I am looking at the next Geoffrey Barton Award Winner for a rising star. You were magnificent."

"I'm just honored to be nominated," she pauses, "but I won't lie, I want it." She shrugs her shoulders, the honesty feels good. "Thank you again for nominating me and for coming today. You can be a nice guy when you want to be, Jacques." Maryssa winks and squeezes his hands.

"Hush. I can't let that rumor spread. It will ruin my reputation." He smiles while searching her face. "Maryssa, I am truly happy for you. As always, you have a place in any of my restaurants, but I can see that your heart is home."

Maryssa hugs Jacques Boucher tightly, taking them both by surprise. She whispers, "Thank you so much, for everything."

He pulls back and stares longingly at her. "There is something magnetic about you Maryssa Lavalier. I shall take my leave before I am bound to you forever." He places a kiss on the top of her head before leaving her.

Maryssa takes a long, soothing breath and exhales all the stress from the day. She turns slowly and walks back into the dining room. Malik and Victoria, Haddie and Jackson, and Esther and Mr. Anderson are laughing at some story Nunnie is telling. Tony is helping Frankie pass out pieces of cake. A table filled with kids coloring, sits back in the alcove. Sammy is filling glasses with Aunt Jo.

Tears fill Maryssa's eyes. Her clan all came tonight. Thick or thin, drought or high water, they were all here, for her. Maryssa understands and appreciates what a rare blessing it is to have a family like hers. They are a family built on the firm foundation of the Rock. Their lives are far from perfect. There have been deaths, sadness, joy, and triumphs, but their foundation has remained the same. At that moment, Maryssa praises the One from whom all blessings flow.

Every good and perfect gift comes from above.

The night continues with a celebratory feel. As the staff finishes their nightly rituals to close up the restaurant, the Marchios begin migrating out to Ruthie's Terrazza. Sammy has the fire pit roaring, and chairs are all pulled around it.

"This reminds me of harvest time." Mary rubs her arms to generate warmth. "We worked hard all day and ate all night. Trust me, I love the innovation Sam brought to the vineyard, but there was something special about family hand-picking grapes and berries together."

The stories begin pouring out about the talent shows and pranks pulled during harvest time. Even Wes Anderson has a few stories to share about helping with the harvest. Each tale brings new waves of laughter.

After thanking and walking out the last staff member, Maryssa heads to the terrace. She is equally tired and elated. As she walks through the glass doors, she hears joy being shared. She is filled with peace.

Maryssa scans the crowd to find Beau. As she was cleaning the kitchen, she realized that Beau is the person she debriefs with every night after work. Whether they were at the farmhouse, Poppy's, or his apartment with Chloe, Beau had become her confidant. As she searches for his face, she feels a hand gently touch the small of her back.

He whispers, "Hey, I need to show you something." Beau looks expectantly at her.

An electric current shoots up from her toes to her heart and butterflies settle in her stomach. Something she has never felt before now. She nods at Beau and attempts to steady her breathing. Shoulders back, neck straight. He takes her hand in his and leads her off the patio onto the grass. They come to the gazebo. Although it was uncovered for the judges, Maryssa hasn't seen it yet.

"I finished the gazebo last night." He pauses, watching her see it for the first time. "I've watched you for months fulfilling your dream. I've listened and seen how much joy you bring to everyone around you. You make everyone feel special, just like your mother, and your grandmother. I've watched you live out your faith every day, whether the days are good or bad, you have trusted in the Lord. You gave me a job, but more importantly, you gave me an inspiration that I thought was lost. This is my gift to you for all that you have given to me." Beau pulls her into the gazebo revealing an exquisite work of art.

Maryssa gasps in wonder at his workmanship. She walks and glides her hand along the wooden masterpiece. Walking in the gazebo is like walking into a tree tunnel. Twigs, vines, and branches intertwine with large posts to form a wall which surrounds the core of the structure. The pillars supporting the railing are large twisted logs. They mimic the branches of the old oak tree she climbed getting to Chloe. A circular bench surrounds the entire piece. The structure is large enough to cozily fit most of the family at once. Maryssa catches her breath when she notices the six posts. Her finger traces a pair of ballet slippers carved into one of the posts. Tears fill her eyes as she reads her mother's name scrolled into the wood by hand. Beau enters the gazebo but leaves space between them.

"Chloe and I have been collecting the twigs and branches on our walks. Nunnie told me about the logs on the hill on the other side of the property. I special ordered the posts. There are six. One for Nunnie and Poppy and one to represent each of their five children. I chose cedar because it is strong and durable yet soft and workable for carving. Did you know that cedars are mentioned over forty times in the Bible?"

Beau nervously pauses, gauging her expression. He speaks softly as he describes his work, humbled by the gift God has given him. "I tried to illustrate each family line in their post. Every piece of wood has ties to the vineyard, but Sam's family post contains the most detail. Jo's post highlights sports and blackberries since those are her favorite. On Ruth's post, I tried my best to show a celebration of food. Both you and Haddie have ballet slippers."

Beau watches Maryssa inspect the posts with her senses. Breathing in the sweet cedar, touching every carved line, looking intently at every detail. She makes her way around the circular tree house to stand directly in front of Beau Baker. Not her cousin's widow. Not her aunt's son-in-law, but a man she has come to depend on and know well.

Maryssa studies his face. His hair is a tussle of waves and curls. His hazel eyes are honest and kind. He has a spattering of pale freckles just across the bridge of his nose and across his cheeks. His broad shoulders are strong and sturdy like the logs he carried from the hillside. His countenance is soft and fragrant like the cedar he carved into a lifetime of memories. At that moment, she stills as realization fills her thoughts and heart. She takes both of his hands into hers.

"This is magical. You are beyond talented, you know that, right?" Beau bashfully smiles. "You thought of everything. Every detail, every dream, every personality. I have watched you work your tail off for months. You got here with Aunt E and Chloe and you just, hit the ground running. You worked with Tony, you worked here, you helped at the warehouse, you helped Nunnie at the farmhouse. Not once did you complain. Not once did you cut corners. You are like a machine. You did all of this while raising the most amazing five-year-old I know."

Beau lowers his gaze in humility. Maryssa continues talking while catching his attention by squeezing his hand. "Between the grand opening of Poppy's, my dad's wedding, and filming for the award, my life has been crazy and hectic, overwhelming at times. You were always there, knowing what I needed before I did. Always in the periphery, watching, supporting. You are the person I debrief with at the end of the day. Beau, you are my strong and sturdy cedar post. Am I crazy? Do you feel the same or is my exhaustion making me see things that aren't real?"

Beau's thumbs wipe the tears beginning to escape from Maryssa's eyes. He answers her without words, but with all the emotion he has to offer. Beau bends down and places a feathery kiss on Maryssa's lips. They melt into each other, both relieved and excited that their feelings are real and shared. Her hands hold tightly to the jacket at his waist. His hands gently holding her face. They smile as they both relax into their usual banter.

"I hope this doesn't mean Angelica is going to scratch my car too." She laughs as Beau drops his head, shaking it back and forth. "What? Too soon?" They both quietly laugh. He kisses the top of her head and pulls her close into his embrace.

She looks up at him, "Are they all watching us?"

"Yep, but they are doing their very best to pretend they aren't." He laughs.

"I'm surprised my dad isn't over here breaking this up yet, no offense, of course."

Beau feigns a hurt look before smiling down at her. "For the record, I talked to him first. You should also know that apparently Mary and Esther have been playing us both for a while now."

Maryssa looks over her shoulder, "I love how they all knew before we did." She shakes her head.

"I don't know about everyone, but Esther and Mary have been waiting for us to figure it out on our own. I think they got impatient." Beau shrugs with a grin.

Maryssa quickly backs away a little, realizing how this may look. Beau's worried expression has her quickly explaining. "We can't do this right now. There is someone I need to talk to first before anything happens between us." Maryssa quickly scans the crowd to make sure little eyes weren't watching them too.

<h1 style="text-align:center">Chapter 39</h1>

<h1 style="text-align:center">Maryssa</h1>

Early the next morning, Maryssa dresses in her favorite hot pink sweatshirt and jeans. Her hair is pulled back into a wavy ponytail. The restaurant won't open for a few hours so there is plenty of time for baking a pie. Maryssa feels so nervous on the drive over to Poppy's. She prays for the right words and an understanding heart. As Maryssa climbs the outside steps and knocks on the apartment door, a feeling of overwhelming peace quiets her mind and soul. She takes a deep breath in and lifts her face to the warmth of the sun.

Beau opens the door and winks at Maryssa. He looks much calmer than Maryssa feels. Chloe bounds to the door and pounces on Maryssa's leg. The little girl squeezes Maryssa tightly before taking her hand and dragging her inside their apartment.

"Daddy says we're going to go pick berries and that you are coming too," Chloe squeaks.

"I am. Wild berries grow on the other side of the field. Sammy saw a few ripened ones. I thought maybe we could bring them back to Poppy's and bake a pie or maybe a cobbler. We can try making berry ice cream too. Does that sound fun?"

"Mmm, I love ice cream! Let's go." Chloe pulls on Maryssa's hand, dragging her to the door. Maryssa risks a stiff neck by glancing over her shoulder to Beau, who is smiling and laughing. "I have an extra princess bucket for you, but not one for Daddy. He says he'll just put his berries in our buckets. Do you think we'll have enough buckets?"

Chloe fills every second with the chatter of a five-year-old girl. She talks about school and Nona's new friend Wes, and Haddie, and Jackson, and Travis, and her new friend Kelli Marie who also does not like Jen Z. Maryssa is conditioned to listening to Chloe after spending months after school with her, but Chloe seems even more animated today.

Beau's pickup truck drives slow over the dirt path that cuts through the property on the other side of the vineyard. Chloe pops up and jumps out the door as soon as the truck engine quiets. Beau reaches across the center console and squeezes Maryssa's hand. Chloe is already bouncing in the direction of the bushes with her pink princess bucket in hand.

Beau walks around the truck and whispers into Maryssa's ear, "That's the trouble with these newer pickups, no more bench seats, and close driving. I think I need to buy an older truck." Electricity shoots through Maryssa as he reaches around and tightens his arm around her waist.

They spend an hour picking berries and listening to Chloe talk about everything and anything that comes to her mind. They drive back to Poppy's and head straight to the kitchen. Chloe is already comfortable in the space thanks to her time with Maryssa after school. She pulls out a box from under the counter with her secret stash of measuring cups and an apron Maryssa bought her. A stool is hidden between a table and the stainless steel, prep refrigerator. Chloe carries it to the bar and climbs up just as Maryssa brings over the ingredients. Beau stands back and watches the two of them work together. His eyes moisten as he wonders how he missed seeing this unique relationship blossom under his nose.

"All right, Chef, are you ready?" Maryssa straightens Chloe's unicorn apron.

Chloe nods all seriousness now.

Beau excuses himself to give the girls time alone, but also to call Esther and ask her to babysit tonight. He also needs to make a phone call about a vintage pickup truck.

"Maryssa, do you miss your Mama?"

Straight to the heart. "I do miss her, but I know I'll see her in Heaven one day, so I try to think about how much fun she is having with Jesus instead of how much I miss her."

"I didn't really know my Mama, but she is in Heaven too with your Mama, and my Grandpa, and Jesus. I like hearing stories about her. I think she would want me to have a Mama here on earth. Like God sent Victoria to be your Mama. Do you think so too?"

Maryssa gulps down her emotions. She whispers a response, "I do."

How clearly and honestly little children see.

Maryssa helps Chole cut butter into the flour mixture. They giggle when flour gets in Chloe's hair.

"Did you cook with your Mama?"

"I did. In my house, my Mama and my Daddy cooked together every night. It was a family affair. Just like we do at Nunnie's house."

"My friend Kelli Marie bakes with her mommy. I like baking with you."

"I like baking with you too, Chloe." Maryssa taps the tip of Chloe's nose with a finger.

The pie is baking in the oven. The kitchen is clean. Maryssa helps Chloe put away the stool hidden in the kitchen just for her.

"Can we go upstairs while the pie bakes?"

"Sure, let me just start the timer on my phone. We can come down and check it in a little bit."

Beau finishes up a conversation as they enter the apartment. "That sounds great, thanks. I'll be by around three this afternoon to get her." He writes down some notes on the paper in front of him.

"How do you two feel about fixing up a 1969 Dodge pickup truck? It's in bad shape, but the bones are good."

Maryssa laughs, "What? You are joking, right?"

"Dead serious. Chloe and I have talked about fixing up a truck for a while, right, Chloe?"

"Yes, Daddy said we could paint it turcles, I mean turquoise." She giggles as she runs to her bedroom.

"My Paps drove one. I saw it at the junkyard a few weeks ago when I was with Tony. I called the guy, and he has been praying for someone to care for it." He winks at her, "It has bench seats, for riding right next to my girl."

Maryssa laughs and shakes her head, then drops it into her hands. "What have I gotten myself into with you?"

She hears Chloe giggling before she feels the little girl's arms around her waist. "Here, I made you something." Chloe hands Maryssa a folded piece of paper.

Beau walks over to them as Maryssa unfolds the drawing. In the middle of the page are three stick figures. Their fat bubble hands are touching, and they are all smiling. Two have triangle dresses and long, curly hair. The tallest one has blue stick legs and a red square for a shirt. They are standing next to a house. The top of the page is blue. In the right corner is a bright yellow sun. In the left, another stick figure with long curly hair, a white triangle dress, wings, and a big smile.

"That is Daddy. That is me, and that is you in the middle. And that is Mama in Heaven. She is happy because she sent you to us." Chloe beams at Maryssa. "Do you like it?"

Maryssa looks at Beau, who is smiling as widely as Chloe. He holds his hands up in denial. "I only helped with the windows and the front door."

"I love it, Chloe. It means more to me that you know. Are you okay if I spend more time with you and your Dad?" Maryssa watches her closely.

"Silly, I want you to spend all of your time with us." Chloe's giggles are full of life.

"Chloe, why don't you go change out of those clothes? You look like a mud and flour pie."

"Okay, Daddy." She bounces to her room.

Beau wraps his arms around Maryssa's waist as he draws her into himself. Maryssa's arms rest on his shoulders.

"She saw us kissing last night and came out with her crayons this morning. We talked, well she talked." They chuckle. "Apparently, she has been praying for God to send someone to us like He sent Victoria to you and Malik."

"Can that kid get any more amazing?" Maryssa stares at him in disbelief.

"Ornery, yes, so I'm hoping yes on the amazing part too." He grins back at her. "She is right about something, God sent you to us, I have no doubt about that. You are like a healing balm to my tired heart. For the record, I am also in favor of you spending all of your time with us."

"I'm all in Beau Baker. I'll take you, Chloe, Aunt E, a truck restoration, even your crazy ex-girlfriend."

He groans at the last comment before leaning down and kissing her gently, but passionately.

Epilogue

The farmhouse kitchen is full of life. Spaghetti sauce is simmering on the stove. Homemade pasta boils beside it. Uncle Sam and Uncle Dom are carving ham while Sammy and DJ are tasting faster than their fathers can cut. Aunts and cousins are setting the table and prepping last-minute dishes while the kids are counting the plastic Easter Eggs for the hunt later.

Victoria and Maryssa cut vegetables to roast on the sheet pan. Malik and Mary fill pasta shells with Mary's to-die-for ricotta filling. Esther and Jo argue over how much vinegar to mix with the olive oil for salad dressing. Frankie slices Easter Bread for dessert. That recipe is more coveted than the galettes from Christmas.

Jackson sits at one end of the long table, staking his claim, away from the middle. Beau walks up behind Maryssa and places a hand on her hip before kissing the top of her head. She raises a strip of red pepper above her head in his direction for him to eat. Victoria glances at Malik who is smiling peacefully at Maryssa and Beau's seamless familiarity with one another.

Mary announces that everyone should finish their dishes and get everything to the table. Platters and baskets are passed from the kitchen to the dining room. People dance around each other to find seats and fill cups. Haddie asks Jackson to scoot down a place so Wes can sit beside Esther. He scoots down another chair position so that Chloe can sit between him and Haddie. Uncle Sam makes him move again so that Tony is not sitting next to Frankie. The dust finally settles when Jackson looks down at his seat. He is sitting in front of three pounds of spaghetti with nothing in it but a serving fork. The table erupts with laughter as his face shows realization. He looks directly at Haddie, "Et tu, Brute?" She shrugs in response.

Mary pulls a large forked spaghetti spoon from behind her back and hands it to Jackson. "Here, you get a promotion since you came back for more after Christmas Eve." The laughter continues as everyone sits.

Quiet spreads across the table without a word as Mary bows her head and takes the hands of her sons sitting to her left and right into hers. "Oh, Father, You are so amazing. Thank you for Jesus. Today we celebrate the resurrection of Your Son, Jesus Christ. Because He rose, we can have a relationship with You. Because He rose, we know that we will be able to spend eternity with You. Because He rose, we know that all of our sins have been washed away. Because He rose, we know of a love so deep and pure that we are given mercy and grace that we don't deserve. Because He rose, we can cling to Him during our hardships and trials. Because He rose, we are given hope. So today, we remember why we are celebrating, the Savior of the World is alive! Please bless this feast before us to the nourishment of our bodies and us to Your service. He is risen indeed!"

A chorus of "Amen" rings around the Marchio family table.

Food is scooped, plates are passed. Jackson finally sits, feeling accomplished. Mary gives him the nod of approval and a wink. He relishes in her high praise. Conversation flows from everyone freely. The volume increases with each new story.

"Maryssa, how was your meeting in New York last week?" Uncle Sam asks from the other end of the table.

"It was packed with information." Maryssa takes a sip of water.

Beau rubs his hand across her shoulders. "Apparently, winning the Geoffrey Barton Rising Star Award comes with a lot of perks. She has offers coming from every direction."

His bragging provokes a shoulder to shoulder nudge followed by a humble smile to the table. "I definitely have a lot to think about as far as options. I met with a publishing team first. They are interested in a series of cookbooks. The first will feature recipes from Poppy's. The second, if Nunnie agrees, will be family recipes, but she gets to choose which are omitted." Chuckles resonate from everyone. "Jacques actually approached them about a joint cookbook featuring regional recipes from around Italy. He is gifting us a three week trip for Beau and me to tour the country and collect recipes."

"That is my favorite perk." Beau smiles.

"After meeting with the publisher, I was approached by a streaming service about doing some cooking specials. They want to call it *Italian Holidays*. Depending on the ratings, it could expand to my own show, *The Family Table*. They will even send a crew to Poppy's to film it."

"You? You will have your own television show?" Sammy bursts into laughter. "Personally, I think they should have filmed you, the three amigos, restoring that jalopy truck of yours outside. I mean, come on, half the time Maryssa was covered in grease from head to toe." Sammy falls back into his chair in hysterics.

"DJ, remember that time we drove up just when Chloe honked the horn, and it scared Beau so bad that he hit his head on the hood?" His face is red from laughing.

"That was epic! What about the time Maryssa slammed her own elbow in the car door, and Chloe caught her saying a 'potty' word?" DJ joins the fun. Both boys are crying now.

Maryssa lobs a roll at DJ's head, who is sitting next to her. "I don't know if I'm ready for television. It's a lot to process. I asked for a couple of weeks to think about it."

Haddie almost spits out her drink. "What? What is there to think about, Maryssa? You signed me up for a reality dating TV show without my knowledge, and now *you* have to think about being on television." She offers a mocking laugh.

"Uh oh, here we go, again." Malik shakes his head at the two girls.

Maryssa, laughing, points to Jackson. "Hads, you are welcome."

Haddie rolls her eyes. "That's not my point. I'm just saying, this is a no brainer. Take the deal. A show? From your own home? This is perfect."

"Says the person who complains non-stop about the spotlight," Sammy interjects with a smirk.

Haddie picks up a roll and tosses it at Sammy's head. "Brat."

"Girls, I'm the only one allowed to throw bread at the table." Nunnie cuts through the laughter erupting around the table. "Let's clean up and watch the wedding photo slideshow on Frankie's smart TV. Since she moved in after Christmas, we've been watching everything high def. She's teaching us to *binge*." Mary scoots back her chair from the table. "Come on, many hands make light the work."

The family works together like a well-oiled machine. All the parts doing different jobs, but working seamlessly together for the greater good. The dishes are cleared. Food is left out for those still picking. Dessert is being eaten while everyone settles into the family room. Maryssa snuggles tightly into the crook of Beau's arm. Chloe sits between Esther and Malik, smiling like a Cheshire cat. Frankie turns on the smart TV and finds the app where she helped Nunnie upload all of the family photos. She clicks on the folder *Beau and Maryssa's Wedding Album* and the slideshow begins for all to see.

Beau and Maryssa were married under the Oak Tree by the pond. The exact same spot where her parents were married. October painted the perfect canvas for the day. The hillside was alive with vibrant reds, yellows, oranges, and purples. The temperature was warm, and the sunshine beamed down on them all day. It was an intimate family affair. Not a dry eye could be found by the pond.

Jacques catered the reception, complete with gumbo. Frankie designed the most spectacular cake. The Italian buttercream icing, rich and decadent, covered dark chocolate and vanilla layers of moist cake. However, the best part was the topper. Esther found a friend from high school who was a sculptor. He designed a turquoise old pickup truck with three people inside the cab; a bride, a groom, and a six-year-old maid of honor.

Extending from the top of the cake, behind the truck was a tall picture hook with a four-by-four card colored by Chloe. The picture showed Lizzie, Ruth, and Jesus sitting on a cloud, smiling.

As the entire Marchio clan sits around oohing and ahhing over the slide show, Chloe unbuttons her pink and white sweater just in time for the last picture. A sonogram image with the caption, "Coming out of the oven in October!" Chloe begins squealing as she points to her newly revealed t-shirt, "I'm the Big Sister!"

The American Post

World Enlightening News

Scene & Heard

Baby News:

Maryssa Lavalier Baker, Geoffrey Barton Rising Star Award winner, host of the *Family Table* and author of two cookbooks, welcomed her first son on October 29th. John Boaz Baker, 7lbs and 11oz. Mom, Dad, big sister Chloe, and baby are all doing well.

The End

The Perfect Peanut Butter Cookie

Ingredients:

- 1 cup of softened butter

- 1 cup of peanut butter

- 1 cup of sugar

- 1 cup of brown sugar

- 2 eggs

- 2 ½ cups unbleached flour

- 1 tsp baking powder

- 1 tsp baking soda

- ½ tsp salt

- 1 tsp vanilla

- Optional: bowl of sugar for rolling, peanut butter cups, chocolate kisses or chocolate pieces)

Directions:

1. Cream butter and sugars. Add peanut butter, eggs, and vanilla.

2. Combine dry ingredients.

3. Combine dry ingredients with creamy mixture of yumminess.

4. Make 1 inch balls and roll them in sugar. Place on cookie sheet. (If using the peanut butter cups, we placed the dough in mini-muffins

pans)

5. Bake at 350 for 10-12 minutes (until they are golden brown).

6. Optional: Place chocolate in the middle of cookie while still warm.

Discussion Questions

1. What was your overall reaction to Ruthie's Daughter?

2. Do you think Ruthie's Daughter was plot-based or character-driven?

3. Could you relate to any of the characters? Which ones and why?

4. What were your impressions of the Stanley family?

5. How did you feel about Wes and Esther's relationship, then and now?

6. Do you think Governor Marchio's conversation with Jackson will impact Jackson's next move?

7. How does Ruthie's Daughter align with the book of Ruth?

8. Did you have a favorite quote or piece of advice from Nunnie Mary?

Acknowledgements

Book two has been two years in the making. Just like the characters in Ruthie's Daughter, I have weathered my own storms along the way.

The book of Ruth is alive with love, redemption, second chances, loyalty, grace, mercy, and healing. Ruth is a beautiful story that personifies beauty from ashes. I have learned so much from Naomi, Ruth, and Boaz. I have cried with Esther and Beau and laughed with Nunnie Mary. I hope you enjoyed the characters as much as I have while learning their stories.

I am beyond grateful for the characters in my life who have supported me through this writing journey. My husband, kids, and dog who waited patiently while I finished "just one more paragraph." My daughter, mother, niece, and sister have read, reread, listened, and shared their opinions on everything from character progression to font size. The entire crew is better than a marketing team. They are my biggest cheerleaders and the loves of my life.

I want to thank my team of prayer warriors and daily life battlers. Danielle, Heather, and Jessicup (not a typo-a nickname from my daughter), you grow me in ways I never imagined. I love you all more than words.

Thank you to my Wednesday morning Bible Study. You prayed for me when I had no words to pray myself. You are my mentors and my friends. I love you, dearly.

Thank you to Janel for always being a phone call away and for not letting me dye my hair grey. I would fly across the country if you needed me.

As characters introduced themselves to me, I learned about them and gave them words. Some spoke to me more than others. I have my own Nunnie and Mama, who taught me to love Jesus, go to church, trust God when the bottom falls out, and keep looking for rainbows. I am who I am because of the foundation they gave me.

Another character from Ruthie's Daughter was especially close to my heart. Victoria was inspired by one of my "second mothers." I grew up with three best friends and their mothers were like my own Mama. I spent as much time at their houses as I did my own. I went on family vacations with them and ate weekly meals in their kitchens. The character of Victoria is inspired by one of those women. Vicki was a force to be reckoned with in life. She was fiercely loyal and loved with everything in her. Her laugh was contagious and her heart was always open to others. She was an amazing cook and taught me to make pizza and how to check if spaghetti is ready by throwing it on the wall. I will never look at a full moon without thinking of her. I know she's breaking bread and dancing in Heaven, but she is sorely missed here on Earth.

Finally, and most importantly, thank you Jesus. Thank you for loving this hot mess. Thank you for pruning me and growing me. Thank you for making beauty from ashes. Thank you for filling the Bible with stories of broken people. Thank you for being the God of all creation and the God who knows my heart. Thank you for the storms and thank you for calming them. I love you most.

Also By Amy

Vineyard Seeds Series:

Future FLOTUS?

Ruthie's Daughter

Frankie's Confections

Thank you for reading!

If you enjoyed *Ruthie's Daughter*, please take a minute and write a review. As a new author, your recommendation means the most to me!

Check out www.amydensonbooks.com for other books and updates!

I am an Indie author. I am human. My beta readers and editors are human. If you catch a typo, please shoot me an email and let me know (amydensonbook s@gmail.com).

Thanks, friend!

About the Author

Amy Denson grew up in a big Italian family from West Virginia. She loves hearing and telling stories about her family history. Her Nunnie and mother taught her to love Jesus with all her heart. She loves cooking, reading, writing, and learning. In her spare time (obvious sarcasm), Amy is the mom to four kids, a lovely daughter-in-law, one scrappy dog, and another dog who thinks she's a cat. She is married to her college sweetheart. Together, they ride the unpredictable rollercoaster of life, hanging on by the seats of their pants. Amy loves spending time with her friends and family, usually around a table breaking bread and laughing a lot.